"[The] strong characterization of a complicated hero is one of the qualities that makes Green's series effective. With dark humor and psychological horror he rivals urban horror writers such as Jim Butcher and Christopher Golden; Laurell Hamilton fans should enjoy this series as well."
—*Romantic Times*

Agents of Light and Darkness

"I really enjoyed Green's first John Taylor novel and the second one is even better. The usual private eye stuff—with a bizarre kick."
—*Chronicle*

"The Nightside novels are a great blending of Lovecraft and Holmes . . . an action-packed thiller, a delightful private eye investigative fantasy tale." —*Midwest Book Review*

Something from the Nightside

"The book is a fast, fun little roller coaster of a story—and its track runs through neighborhoods that make the Twilight Zone look like Mayberry. Simon Green's Nightside is a macabre and thoroughly entertaining world that makes a bizarre and gleefully dangerous backdrop for a quickmoving tale. Fun stuff!"
—Jim Butcher, author of *Dead Beat* and *Furies of Calderon*

"A riveting start to what could be a long and extremely addictive series. No one delivers sharp, crackling dialogue better than Green. No one whisks readers away to more terrifying adventures or more bewildering locales. Sure, it's dangerous, but you're going to follow him unquestioningly into the Nightside."
—*Black Gate Magazine*

SHARPER THAN A SERPENT'S TOOTH

SIMON R. GREEN

ACE BOOKS, NEW YORK

THE BERKLEY PUBLISHING GROUP
Published by the Penguin Group
Penguin Group (USA) Inc.
375 Hudson Street, New York, New York 10014, USA

Penguin Group (Canada), 90 Eglinton Avenue East, Suite 700, Toronto, Ontario, M4P 2Y3, Canada
(a division of Pearson Penguin Canada Inc.)
Penguin Books Ltd., 80 Strand, London WC2R 0RL, England
Penguin Group Ireland, 25 St. Stephen's Green, Dublin 2, Ireland (a division of Penguin Books Ltd.)
Penguin Group (Australia), 250 Camberwell Road, Camberwell, Victoria 3124, Australia
(a division of Pearson Australia Group Pty. Ltd.)
Penguin Books India Pvt. Ltd., 11 Community Centre, Panchsheel Park, New Delhi—110 017, India
Penguin Group (NZ), Cnr. Airborne and Rosedale Roads, Albany, Auckland 1310, New Zealand
(a division of Pearson New Zealand Ltd.)
Penguin Books (South Africa) (Pty.) Ltd., 24 Sturdee Avenue, Rosebank, Johannesburg 2196,
South Africa

Penguin Books Ltd., Registered Offices: 80 Strand, London WC2R 0RL, England

This is a work of fiction. Names, characters, places, and incidents either are the product of the author's imagination or are used fictitiously, and any resemblance to actual persons, living or dead, business establishments, events, or locales is entirely coincidental. The publisher does not have any control over and does not assume any responsibility for author or third-party websites or their content.

SHARPER THAN A SERPENT'S TOOTH

An Ace Book / published by arrangement with the author

PRINTING HISTORY
Ace mass market edition / March 2006

ISBN: 978-0-441-01387-6

ACE
Ace Books are published by The Berkley Publishing Group,
a division of Penguin Group (USA) Inc.,
375 Hudson Street, New York, New York 10014.
ACE and the "A" design are trademarks belonging to Penguin Group (USA) Inc.

PRINTED IN THE UNITED STATES OF AMERICA

10   9   8   7   6   5

London holds an awful secret close to her heart, like a serpent to her bosom. The Nightside. A dark and corrupt place, a city within a city, where the sun has never shone and never will. In the Nightside you can find gods and monsters and spirits from the vasty deep, if they don't find you first. Pleasure and horror are always on sale, marked down and only slightly shop-soiled. I was born in the Nightside, some thirty years ago, and someone's been trying to kill me ever since.

My name is John Taylor, and I operate as a private investigator. I don't do divorce work, I don't solve mysteries, and I wouldn't know a clue if I fell over one. I find things, no matter how well hidden, though mostly what I seem to find is trouble. My father drank himself to death after discovering my missing mother wasn't human. The Authorities, those grey faceless men who run things in the Nightside, inasmuch as anyone does, see me as a dangerous rogue element. Mostly they're right. My clients see me as their last hope, while others see me as a King in waiting; and there are those who would risk anything to kill me because of a prophecy that one day I will destroy the Nightside, and the rest of the world with it.

Finally, after a trip through Time into past incarnations of the Nightside, I have discovered the truth. The Nightside had been created by my missing mother to be the one place on Earth free from the influence of Heaven or Hell. The only truly free place. Her own allies thrust her out of this reality and into Limbo, because they feared her so much. Now she's back, and threatening to remake the Nightside in her own terrible image. My mother, Lilith. Adam's first wife, thrown out of Eden for refusing to accept any authority. She descended into Hell and lay down with demons, and gave birth to all the monsters that have ever plagued this world. Or so they say.

Lilith. Mommie Dearest.

All I have to do now is figure out how to stop her, without destroying the Nightside and the whole damned world in the process . . .

ONE

Somewhere in the Night

Strangefellows is said by many and considered by most to be the oldest bar in the world, and therefore has seen pretty much everything in its time. So when Suzie Shooter and I appeared suddenly out of nowhere, looking half-dead in blood-stained and tattered clothing, most of the bar's patrons didn't so much as raise an eyebrow, cosmopolitan bastards and general scumbags that they are. Suzie and I leaned heavily on the long, polished wooden bar and spent some time just getting our breath back. We'd been through a lot during our trip through the Past, including being possessed by angels to fight demons from the Pit, so I felt very strongly that we were entitled to a little time out. Alex Morrisey, Strangefellows' owner, bartender, and general miserable pain in the arse, stood behind the bar putting a lot of effort into cleaning a glass that didn't need cleaning, while he fixed us both with his familiar unwavering scowl.

"Why can't you walk through the door like normal people, Taylor?" he said finally. "You always have to make an entrance, don't you? And look at the state of you. Don't either of you dare drip blood over my nice, new, and very expensively cleaned floor. I haven't seen the natural colour of that floor in more years than I care to remember, and I'm trying to memorise it before it inevitably disappears again. I have got to get some new clientele. When I inherited this place I was promised a nice upmarket bar with a select and discreet group of regular drinkers."

"Alex," I said, "you couldn't drive this bar upmarket with an electric cattle prod and a branding iron. Now bring me many drinks, all in the same glass, and a bottle of the old mother's ruin for Suzie."

"Two," said Suzie Shooter. "And don't bother with a glass."

Alex looked at Suzie, and his expression changed abruptly. During our brief stop-off in Arthurian times, Suzie had lost the left side of her face. The flesh had been ripped and torn away; then seared together with fire. Her left eye was gone, the eyelid sealed shut. Suzie glared at Alex with her one remaining cold blue eye, daring him to say anything. Alex's face tried to show several things at once, then went blank. He gave Suzie his best professional bartender's polite nod and went to get us our drinks. Suzie had no time for pity or compassion, even from those she considered her friends. Perhaps especially from them.

But I knew there was more to it than that. Alex and I had seen that face before, on a future incarnation of Suzie, who'd travelled back through Time from a potential future to kill me, right here in this bar. I might have killed that Suzie. I wasn't sure. Alex came back with a large glass of wormwood brandy for me, and two bottles of gin for Suzie. He scowled disapprovingly as I gulped down the expensive liquor, and tried not to see Suzie sucking gin straight from the bottle like it was mother's milk.

"How long have we been gone?" I said finally.

Alex raised an eyebrow. "About five hours, since you and Tommy Oblivion left here with Eamonn Mitchell, that new client of yours."

"Ah," I said. "It's been a lot longer for us. Suzie and I have been Time travelling. Back into the various Pasts of the Nightside."

"I've got no sympathy for you," said Alex. "Don't you have enough problems in the here and now, without upsetting people in the Past? Who did you piss off this time? You look like you've both been through a meat grinder."

"That's nothing," said Suzie. "You should see the meat grinder."

She belched and farted, then went back to sucking on her bottle.

"I don't suppose you thought to bring me back a present?" said Alex.

"Of course not," I said. "I told you; we were in the Past, not the Present."

"You're so sharp you'll cut yourself one of these days," said Alex.

I persuaded Suzie to put down her gin bottle long enough to make use of the rechargeable clothing spell Alex always keeps at hand behind the counter. A few Words of Power followed by a couple of quick passes with an aboriginal pointing-bone, and our clothes were immediately clean and repaired. Our bodies remained battered and bloody and exhausted, but it was a start. The spell was standard equipment in all Nightside bars and hostelries, where the general joie de vivre could be very hard on the appearance. Suzie and I admired ourselves in the long mirror behind the bar.

I looked like myself again, if just a little more world-weary around the eyes. Tall, dark, and handsome in the right kind of light, wrapped in a long white trench coat. I like to think I look like someone you could trust, if not take home to meet the parents. Suzie Shooter, also known as Shotgun Suzie, and *Oh Christ it's her, run!* looked as cold and dangerous and downright scary as she always did. A tall blonde in her late twenties, but with a lot of mileage on the clock, standing stiff-backed and arrogant in black motorcycle leathers, lavishly adorned with steel chains and studs, a pump-action shotgun holstered on her back, and two bandoliers of bullets criss-crossing her substantial chest. Knee-length black leather boots with steel-capped toes completed the distressing picture. She had a strong-boned face, a mouth that rarely smiled, and a gaze older than the world. She'd shot me in the back once, but it was only a cry for attention.

(Alex was dressed all in black, as usual, even down to the designer shades and snazzy black beret perched on the back of his head to hide a spreading bald patch. He was in his late twenties but looked ten years older. Running a bar in the Nightside will do that to you.)

"So," said Suzie, returning to her gin bottle, "what do we do now, Taylor?"

"We put together an army," I said, "Of every Power and Being and major player in the whole damned Nightside, and turn them into a force I can throw at Lilith's throat. I'll use my gift to track down wherever she's hiding herself, and then . . . we do whatever we have to, to destroy her. Because that's all there is left, now."

"Even though she's your mother?"

"She was never my mother," I said. "Not in any way that mattered."

Suzie considered me thoughtfully. "Even with an army to back us up, we could still lay waste to most of the Nightside, fighting to bring her down."

"She'll destroy it anyway, if we don't do something. I've Seen what will happen if we don't stop her, and anything would be better than that."

I didn't look at her scarred face. I didn't think of her half-dead, half-mad, come back through Time to kill me, with the awful Speaking Gun grafted where her right forearm should have been.

"What if the others don't want to get involved?"

"I'll make them want to."

"And end up just like your mother?"

I sighed, and looked into my empty glass. "I'm tired, Suzie. I want . . . I need for this to be over."

"It should be one hell of a battle." Shotgun Suzie ran one thumb caressingly over her bandoliers of bullets. "I can't wait."

I smiled at her fondly. "I'll bet you even take that shotgun to bed with you, don't you?"

She looked at me with her cold, calm expression. "Someday, you just might find out. My love."

She blew me a kiss, then returned all her attention to her bottle of gin. Alex looked at me with a mixture of awe, horror, and utter astonishment, and seized the opportunity for a quiet chat while Suzie was preoccupied. He pulled me aside and lowered his voice to a whisper.

"Did I just hear right, John? *My love?* Am I to take it you and the psycho bounty hunter from Hell are now an item?"

"Looks like it," I said. "I'm as shocked and surprised as you are. Maybe I should have checked the wording in my Personals Ad more carefully."

"But . . . *Suzie*? I mean, ten out of ten for courage, yes, but . . . she's crazy!"

I had to smile. "You think anyone sane would hook up with me?"

Alex considered the matter. "Well, there is that, yes. Good point. But John . . . her face . . ."

"I know," I said quietly. "It happened in the Past. There was nothing I could do."

"John, she's one step closer to becoming the future Suzie who tried to kill you. Shouldn't we tell her about that?"

"I already know," said Suzie. I hadn't heard her approach, and from the way Alex jumped, he hadn't either.

She was gracious enough not to smile. "I've known for some time. You can't keep secrets long in the Nightside, especially when they include bad news. You should know that, John. Don't worry about it. I never worry about the future. Mostly because I don't believe I'm going to live to see it. It's a very liberating attitude. Worry about the present me, John."

"Oh I do," I assured her. "I do."

I put my back against the bar and looked out over the place. Just another night in the oldest bar in the world. Alex's muscle-bound bouncers, Betty and Lucy Coltrane, were throwing out a bunch of burly masked Mexican wrestlers, and making them cry like little girls in the process. Never mess with the Coltranes. Especially when they're wearing their ROLLERBALL HELLCAT MUD-WRESTLING CHAMPIONS T-shirts. Not far away, a cyborg with glowing golden eyes ordered another bottle of neat ethanol from Alex, in a strange buzzing voice. He'd dropped in from a possible future via a Timeslip, and was currently trying to mend his left leg with a pair of pliers and a sonic screwdriver someone had left behind in the bar. I was actually pleased to see him. It was good to know that other futures, apart from the terrible devastated future I feared so much, were still possible.

Not far enough away, half a dozen flower fairies in drooping petal outfits were singing a raucous Victorian drinking song, buzzed up on pollen. Soon they'd start getting nasty, and go looking for a Water Baby to beat up. Coming down the metal stairs into the bar proper was Kid Psychoses, in his tatterdemalion rags, doing his rounds and peddling his appalling wares. The Kid sold brief interludes of mental illness, for people who wanted to go really out of their heads. He once told me he started out selling mental health, but there was no market for it in the Nightside. I could have told him that.

And the King and Queen of America were passing through, smiling and waving.

"So," said Alex, freshening my glass, "what was the Nightside like, in the Past?"

"Messy," said Suzie. "In every possible sense of the word."

"Kill anyone interesting?"

"You'd be surprised," I said. "But a gentleman doesn't kill and tell. Have you seen Tommy Oblivion recently?"

"Not since he left here with you earlier. Was I supposed to?"

Tommy Oblivion, the existential private eye, had gone back into the Past with Suzie and me, but we'd had a falling-out. He accused me of being cold and manipulative and more dangerous than the people I was trying to stop. I had to send him back to the Present. It was either that or kill him, and I'm trying to be one of the good guys, these days. But I had a feeling I might have missed the mark, just a bit. I could remember Tommy appearing in this bar quite suddenly, out of nowhere, some months back when I was working the Nightingale's Lament case. Back then, he'd threatened to hunt me down and kill me. I'd wondered why, but now I think I knew.

I sighed and shrugged mentally. Tommy Oblivion could take a number and get in line. There was never any shortage of people trying to kill me, in the Nightside. There was a loud creaking of heavy leathers as Suzie moved in beside me, her back to the bar, gin bottle in hand. It was already half-empty, and she had a cigarette in one corner of her mouth. Smoke curled up slowly past her sealed-shut eye.

"I'll find you a spell," I said. "To repair your face."

"I'm thinking of keeping it," Suzie said calmly. "It'll help my image as a desperate character and ruthless killer."

"Your image doesn't need any help."

"You always know the right things to say, Taylor. But I've never cared about being pretty. At least now my outside matches my inside."

"Suzie . . . I won't have you hurt, because of me."

She looked at me coldly. "You start getting protective, Taylor, and I will drop you like a hot elephant turd."

"Speaking of really big shits," said Alex, "Walker was in here a few hours ago, John. Looking for you."

I didn't like the sound of that. Walker, that perfect city gent in his smart city suit and bowler hat, represented the Authorities. His word was law in the Nightside, and peopled lived and died and worse at his whim. They say he once made a corpse sit up and answer his questions. He doesn't approve of me, but he's thrown some work my way from time to time, when he's needed a deniable and completely expendable agent. He was mad at me at the moment, but he'd get over it. Or he wouldn't, in which case one of us would almost certainly end up killing the other.

"He brought his people in here and had them search the place from top to bottom," said Alex, sounding distinctly aggrieved. "Hence my need for a thorough and very expensive cleanup crew, just before you dropped in."

"You let them search your bar?" I said.

Alex must have heard the surprise in my voice, because he had the grace to look a little ashamed. "Hey, he brought a *lot* of people with him, all right? Serious people with serious weaponry. Some of whom are still missing, presumed eaten. I warned them not to go down into the cellars."

I shook my head. Walker must be getting really desperate to lay hands on me if he was prepared to raid a bar protected by Merlin Satanspawn. Merlin had been buried in the cellars under the bar, after the fall of Camelot; but being dead doesn't necessarily keep you from being a major player in the Nightside. I wouldn't go down into those cellars with a gun at my back.

"I have to go take a piss," I announced. "I've been holding it in for over two thousand years, and my back teeth are floating."

"Thank you for sharing that with us," said Alex. "Try and keep some of it off the floor this time."

I headed for the toilets at the back of the bar. Without making a big thing of it, people moved slowly but deliberately out of my way. Partly because of my carefully maintained reputation, but mostly because bad things had a habit of happening to and around me, and wise people kept a safe distance. I pushed open the door with the stylised male genitals painted on it, and headed for the row of stalls. I've never been one for urinals. Far too easy to be ambushed. I took a quick glance around me, breathing through my mouth to avoid the worst of the smell, but it seemed I had the place to myself. The small, dimly lit stone chamber looked as disgusting as ever. I don't think Alex ever cleans the place; he just fumigates it now and again with a flamethrower. The bare stone walls dripped with condensation, and the floor was wet with a whole bunch of liquids that had nothing to do with condensation. The graffiti hadn't improved either. Someone had daubed the Yellow Sign on one wall, and beside it someone had painted *Gods do it in mysterious ways.* Next to the row of stalls, someone else had written *For a good time, knock on any door.*

I entered the first stall, and locked the door securely behind me. I then unzipped and attended to business, letting out a long sigh of relief. First rule of the private eye—always go when you can, because you never know when you might have to stand stakeout. On the wall above the toilet, someone had written *What are you looking up here for? Ashamed?* I smiled, shook off the last few drops and put it away, then stood very still. I hadn't heard or seen anything, but somehow I knew I wasn't alone in the stall any more. In the Nightside, you either develop survival instincts fast, or you don't develop past childhood. I started to reach for one of the little surprises I keep in my coat pockets for occasions like this, then stopped as something small and hard pressed into my back, directly above the kidney.

"There's something small and hard pressing into my back," I said. "And I'm really hoping it's a gun."

"Heh-heh-heh," said a soft breathy voice behind me. "I can always rely on you for a little quip, Mr. Taylor. Helps the business go down so much more smoothly. Yes, it is a gun, and quite a special gun, I'll have you know. An energy pistol from some cyborg's future that I acquired just for this occasion. Heh-heh. So don't even try your little trick of removing the bullets from my gun. Because it hasn't got any."

"Sneaky Pete," I said, grimacing. "Bounty hunter, sneak thief, and all-around scumbag. How did you get past that locked door?"

"I didn't, Mr. Taylor. I was already hiding in the next stall. Heh-heh. Sneaked over the partition while you were . . . occupied. Heh. You know no-one ever sees me coming, Mr. Taylor. I have trained with ninjas. I am a thing of mists and shadows."

"You're a sneaky little bastard," I said firmly. "And lower than a worm's tit. What do you want with me, Pete?"

"Why, you of course, Mr. Taylor. There is an awful lot of money being offered for your head, not necessarily attached to your body, and I mean to collect it. Oh yes. Now, we can either walk out of here together, nice and easy with not a word to your companions, to where I have transport waiting . . . or I can carry you out. Or at least, part of you. Heh-heh. Your choice, Mr. Taylor."

"You mind if I flush first?" I said.

"Always ready with a cheerful quip! I do so enjoy doing business with a fellow professional. Makes it all so much more civilised. Heh-heh. Be my guest, Mr. Taylor. But carefully, yes?"

I leaned forward slowly and flushed the toilet. And while Sneaky Pete's attention was fixed on what I was doing with my hands, I fired up the spell I normally use for taking bullets out of guns, took all of the water flushing through the toilet and dumped the lot of it in Sneaky Pete's lungs. The thing pressing into my back disappeared abruptly as he fell backwards, making horrible gurgling noises. I spun round, ready to grab the energy gun, but his hands were empty. There never had been a gun, just a finger poking me in the back. Sneaky Pete. He sat down on the floor abruptly, water spilling out of his mouth, scrabbling frantically with his empty hands. I considered him for a moment. Bounty hunter. Sneak thief. Peeping Tom and blackmailer. He might not have killed me himself, but he would have handed me over to be killed without a second thought . . . I sighed, placed my foot against his chest and pushed hard. Water gushed out of him, and after a series of really nasty choking noises, he started breathing again.

I let him live. I didn't like to think I was getting soft, but . . . maybe I needed to convince myself that I wasn't my mother's son.

I left the toilets and returned to the bar. I gave Alex Morrisey my best hard look. "I just had a run-in with Sneaky Pete in the toilet, and not in a good way. Is there perhaps something you haven't got around to telling me yet?"

"Ah," said Alex. "Yes, there's been a whole lot of bounty hunters in and out of here recently. Apparently the rich and very well connected families of the thirteen Reasonable Men you killed, for perfectly good reasons I'm sure, have got together and placed a truly impressive bounty on your head."

"How much?" said Suzie. I looked at her, and she shrugged. "Sorry. Force of habit."

I was about to say something sharp when fortunately my mobile phone rang. I answered it with my usual "What?"

"Taylor," said Walker, in his smooth and very civilised voice. "So glad you've returned safely from your little trip into the Past."

"Walker," I said. "Word does get around fast, doesn't it? I didn't think you knew my private number."

"I know everyone's number. Comes with the job."

"I am not going to come in and give myself up to you and the Authorities. I have important things to do."

"Oh, I think you will, Taylor."

There was something in his voice . . . "What have you done, Walker?"

"Only what you have forced me to do, to get your attention. I have reluctantly given the order for your delightful young secretary Cathy Barrett to be kidnapped. By now she will be in safe hands, being held somewhere very secure. Turn yourself in peacefully, and you have my word that she will be freed unharmed. But if you insist on making life difficult for me by continuing to defy me in this manner . . . Well, I'm afraid I can't answer for the young lady's continued well-being."

"You bastard."

"I only do what I have to, John. You know that."

"If anything happens to Cathy . . ."

"That's entirely up to you, isn't it? I regret to inform you that the people entrusted with this kidnapping bear you a considerable amount of ill will. The longer you take to come to a decision, the more likely it is they'll vent their spleen on her. And much as I might regret that . . . the situation is out of my hands. I have my orders, and my duty. Whatever happens . . ."

I hung up on him. He had nothing else to say worth listening to. He was only keeping the conversation going in the hope his people would be able to track my location through my phone. I explained the situation to Suzie and Alex.

"I can't turn myself in," I said. "I have to be free to operate if I'm going to stop Lilith. The whole Nightside's at risk, and maybe the world, too. But I won't, I can't, abandon Cathy."

"Of course not," said Suzie. "She's your secretary."

"Your friend," said Alex.

"My daughter," I said. "In every way that matters."

"Then we must go and get her," said Suzie. "We can't give in to threats like this. If people thought we could be pressured into doing things, they'd take advantage. So go on, Taylor. Do your thing."

I raised my gift, my single supernatural inheritance from my inhuman mother, and opened up my Sight. And through my third eye, my private eye, I looked out over the Nightside, searching for Cathy. I can find anyone, or anything, if I look hard enough. I don't like to use my gift too often, because when I do I blaze so brightly in the dark that I am easy to see. And then my Enemies send agents to kill me. But for the moment, I was too mad to care.

The Nightside spread out below me, naked to my Sight, and I looked down upon it like an angry god. Streets and squares and places within places, with people and things not at all people coming and going. Bars and clubs and more private establishments flashed past beneath my searching inner eye, houses and warehouses and lock-ups and dungeons, and no sign of Cathy anywhere. The Fae sparked briefly in the shadows, and the Awful Folk moved unhurriedly on their unguessable missions, invisible to the material world. I could feel Cathy's presence now, all alone somewhere in the night, but I couldn't seem to pin her down. I concentrated till my head ached, but finally I was forced to settle for a general location. Something or someone was blocking my gift, obscuring my Sight, and that was a new thing to me. I shut down my gift, and carefully re-established my mental shields. You can't have an open mind in the Nightside. You never know what might walk in.

"She's somewhere near the Necropolis," I said. "But I can't be more specific than that."

Suzie raised an eyebrow. "That's . . . unusual."

I nodded shortly. "Stands to reason Walker wouldn't chose just anybody to hide Cathy from me."

"But Walker knows about your gift," said Alex. "He must know you'll come looking for her. It has to be a trap."

"Of course it's a trap," I said. "But I've been walking

in and out of traps all my life. So, first Suzie and I will rescue Cathy, after making it clear to her kidnappers that getting involved in my business was a really bad idea, then . . . I will go walking up and down in the Nightside, and raise an army big enough to give even Walker nightmares."

"One thing first," said Suzie.

"Yes?" I said.

"Do up your flies, Taylor."

TWO

And Dead Men Rise Up Never

Getting out of Strangefellows wasn't going to be easy. Knowing Walker, it was a safe bet that all of the bar's known and suspected exits were being watched by his people, heavily armed with guns, bombs, and spells of mass destruction. It was what I would have done. I said as much to Alex Morrisey, and he scowled even more fiercely than usual.

"I know I'm going to regret this," he said heavily, "but there is one way out of this bar I can guarantee Walker doesn't know about. Because no-one does, except me. My family have run this place for generations, and given the weird shit and appalling trouble Strangefellows tends to attract, we've always appreciated the need for a swift, sudden, and surreptitious exit. So we've carefully maintained a centuries-old hidden exit, for use by us in the direst of emergencies, when it's all gone to Hell in a handcart. Understand me, Taylor—the only reason I'm prepared to reveal it to you now is because I don't want Walker's people crashing back in here looking for you, wrecking the place again. The quicker you're out of here, the sooner we can all breathe easily."

"Understood, Alex," I said. "This isn't about friendship. It's just business."

"Damn right," said Alex. He beckoned for Suzie and me to join him behind the bar. "I wouldn't want people to get the idea that I was going soft. That I could be taken advantage of."

"Perish the thought," I said.

"There is . . . one small drawback," said Alex.

"I knew it," Suzie said immediately. "I knew there had to be a catch. We don't have to go out through the sewers, do we? I'm really not in the mood to wrestle alligators again."

"Even worse," said Alex. "We have to go down into the cellars."

Suzie and I both stopped short and looked at each other. Strangefellows's cellars were infamous even in the Nightside; they were so dangerous and generally disturbing that most sane and sensible people wouldn't enter them voluntarily without the holy hand grenade of St. Antioch in one hand and a tactical nuke in the other. Merlin Satanspawn was buried in the cellars, and he really didn't care for visitors. Alex was the only one who went down there on a regular basis, and even he sometimes came back up pale and twitching.

"I've got a better idea," said Suzie. "Let's go out the front door and fight our way through Walker's people."

"He could have a whole army out there," I said.

"Somehow that doesn't bother me nearly as much as it did a few minutes ago," said Suzie. "I could handle an army."

"Well, yes, you probably could, in the right mood," I said. "But we can't rescue Cathy if Walker knows we're coming. We need to stay under the radar, keep him off-balance. Lead the way, Alex."

"Have I got time to go to confession first?" said Suzie.

"You leave that priest alone," I said firmly. "He still hasn't got over your last visit."

Alex produced an old-fashioned storm lantern from underneath the bar, lit the wick with a muttered Word, and then hauled open the trap-door set in the floor behind the bar. It came up easily, without the slightest creak from the old brass hinges, revealing smooth stone steps leading down into pitch-darkness. Suzie and I both leaned over and had a good look, but the light from the bar didn't penetrate past the first few steps. Suzie had her shotgun out and at the ready. Alex sniffed loudly.

"This is an ancient family secret I'm entrusting you with. Whatever you see down there, or think you see, it's private. And don't show me up in front of my ancestors, or I'll never live it down."

He led the way down the steps, holding the lantern out before him. Its pale amber light didn't travel far into the dark. Suzie and I followed him, sticking as close as possible. The steps continued down for rather longer than was comfortable, and the roar of voices from the bar was soon left behind. The air became increasingly close and clammy, and the surrounding darkness had a watchful feel.

"There's no electricity down here," said Alex, after a while. His voice sounded small and flat, without the faintest trace of an echo, even though I could all but feel a vast space opening up around us. "Something down here interferes with all the regular means of power supply."

"Don't you mean someone?" said Suzie.

"I try really hard not to think about things like that," said Alex.

The stone steps finally gave out onto a packed-dirt floor. The bare earth was hard and dry and utterly unyielding under my feet. A blue-white glow began to manifest around us, unconnected to the storm lantern or any other obvious source. It rapidly became clear we were

standing at the beginnings of a great stone cavern, a vast
open space with roughly worked bare stone walls and an
uncomfortably low ceiling. I felt like crouching, even
though there was plenty of headroom. And there before
us, stretching out into the gloomy distance, hundreds of
graves set in neat rows, low mounds of earth in the floor,
with simple, unadorned headstones. There were no
crosses anywhere.

"My ancestors," said Alex, in a soft, reflective, quietly
bitter voice. "We all end up here, under the bar we give
our lives to. Whether we want to or not. Merlin's inden-
tured servants, bound to Strangefellows by his will, down
all the many centuries. And yes, I know everyone else
who dies in the Nightside is supposed to have their fu-
nerals handled by the Necropolis, by order of the Authorities, but Merlin's never given a damn for any authority
other than his own. Besides, I think we all feel safer here,
under his protection, than any earthly authority's. One
day I'll be laid to rest here. No flowers by request, and if
anyone tries to sing a hymn, you have my permission to
defenestrate the bastard."

"How many graves are there?" I said.

"Not as many as you'd think," said Alex. He put his
lantern down on the bottom step and glowered around
him. "We all tend to be long-lived. If we don't get killed
horribly somewhere along the way. Only useful thing we
inherited from our appalling ancestor."

He started out across the cavern floor. Despite the limited lighting, he was still wearing his sunglasses. Style
had never been a sometime thing with Alex Morrisey.
Suzie and I followed, trying to look in all directions at
once. We passed by great barrels of beer and casks of
wine, and bottles of rare and vicious vintage, laid out re-
spectfully in a wine rack that looked even older than its
contents. There were no cobwebs, and not even a speck
of dust anywhere. And somehow I knew it wasn't because
Alex was handy with a feather duster.

"It occurs to me," I said carefully, "that there's no sign

anywhere of the people Walker insisted on sending down here. Not any bodies. Not even any bits of bodies."

"I know," said Alex. "Worrying, isn't it?"

We stopped again, to consider a grave set some distance away from the others. Just another low mound of earth, but with no headstone or marker. Instead, there was a massive silver crucifix, pressing down the length of the earth mound. The silver was pitted and corroded.

"Presumably put there in the hope it would hold him in his grave and keep him from straying," said Alex. "They should have known better. You couldn't keep Merlin Satanspawn down if you put St. Paul's Cathedral on top of his grave."

"You have to wonder exactly what's in there," I said. "After all these centuries."

"You wonder," said Suzie. "I like to sleep soundly at night."

"Just bones?" I said. "No different from anyone else's?"

"No," said Alex. "I think, if you dragged away the crucifix and dug him up . . . he'd look exactly like he did the day he was buried. Untouched by time or the grave. And he'd open his eyes and smile at you, and tell you to cover him up again. He was the Devil's son after all, the Antichrist in person, even if he did refuse the honour to make his own path. You really think the world is finished with him yet? Or vice versa? No . . . the bastard's still hoping some poor damned fool will find his missing heart and return it to him. Then he'll rise out of that grave and go forth to do awful things in the Nightside . . . and no-one will be able to stop him."

"God, you're fun to be around, Alex," I said.

We moved on, giving the grave plenty of room. The blue-white light moved with us, cold and intense, and our shadows seemed far too big to be ours. The darkness and the silence pressed in around us. Finally, we came to a bare and undistinguished-looking door, set flush into the stone wall. A gleaming copper latch, inscribed with

blocky Druidic symbols, held it shut. I reached out a hand
to the latch, then snatched it quickly back again. Some
inner voice was shouting loudly that it would be a very
bad idea for anyone but Alex to touch it. He smiled at me
tiredly.

"This door will open out onto anywhere you want,
within a one-mile radius of the bar," he said. "Announce
your destination out loud, and I'll send you on your way.
But be really sure of where you want to go, because once
you're through the door, that's it. It's a one-way door."

"Who put it here?" said Suzie.

"Who do you think?" said Alex.

"You mean this door's been here for fifteen hundred
years?" I said.

Alex shrugged. "Maybe longer. This is the oldest bar
in the world, after all. Now get the hell out of here. I've
got customers waiting upstairs with my money burning a
hole in their pockets."

"Thank you, Alex," I said. "You didn't have to do
this."

"What the hell," said Alex. "You're family. In every
way that matters."

We smiled briefly at each other, then looked away.
We've never been very good at saying the things that matter.

"Where do we want to go to?" said Suzie, probably
not even noticing the undercurrents. She'd never been
very good at emotions, even hers. "You can bet Walker's
people will be guarding all the approaches to the Necropolis."

"Not if we go directly there," I said.

"Not possible," Alex said immediately. "I told you,
nothing over a mile radius."

I grinned. "I was thinking of paying the Doormouse a
visit."

Suzie winced visibly. "Do we have to? I mean, he's so
damned . . . cute. I don't do cute."

"Brace yourself," I said kindly. "It'll be over before you know it."

I announced our destination in a loud, clear voice, and Alex hit the latch and pulled the door open, revealing a typical Nightside street. People and other things bustled briskly back and forth, and the gaudy Technicolor neon pushed back the gloom of the cellar. I strode forward into the welcoming night, with Suzie right behind me, and Alex slammed the door shut.

To the crowds in the street, we must have seemed to appear suddenly out of nowhere, but that was nothing new in the Nightside, so no-one noticed, or if they did, no-one gave a damn. They were all intent on pursuing their own pleasures and damnations. The twilight daughters cat-called to prospective customers from the street corners, sticking out their breasts and batting kohl-stained eyes. Club barkers cried their wares to the more unsuspecting tourists, and the traffic on the road roared past without ever, ever stopping.

I hurried down the rain-slick pavement, noting without surprise that some people were already muttering my name and Suzie's into mobile phones. Must be a really good price on my head. And there was the Doormouse's shop, right ahead. It was set between a new establishment called the Bazaar of the Bizarre and a music emporium that specialised in rare vinyl LPs from alternate dimensions. I paused despite myself to check out the latest specials in the window. There was a Rolling Stones album with Marianne Faithfull as the lead singer, a Pink Floyd debut LP where they were fronted by Arthur Brown, and a live double album of Janis Joplin, from her gigs as an overweight, middle-aged lounge singer in Las Vegas. I wasn't tempted. Not at those prices.

The frosted-glass doors hissed open as I entered the Doormouse's excellent establishment. Then I had to go back out again and drag Suzie Shooter in. Inside, it was all very high-tech, with rows of computers and towering stacks of futuristic technology, most of which I couldn't even identify, let alone hope to understand. The Doormouse had very good contacts and an uncanny eye for a bargain. But what he did best . . . was doors. He came bustling forward to meet us, a cheerful six-foot-tall roughly humanoid mouse, with dark chocolate fur under a pristine white lab coat, complete with pocket protector. He had a long muzzle with twitching whiskers, but his kind eyes were entirely human. He lurched to a halt before us, clapped his paws together, and chattered pleasantly in a high-pitched but perfectly clear voice.

"Welcome, welcome, sir and lady, to my humble establishment! Am I correct in thinking I am in the presence of two of the Nightside's most noted celebrities? John Taylor and Shotgun Suzie, no less! My, my, what a day! I know, I know, you weren't expecting all this technology, were you? No-one ever does. You hear the name Doormouse, and immediately your thoughts go all rustic, but I, sir and lady, am a Town Mouse! And proud of it! Now, what can I do for you? I have doors for everyone, to everywhere, and all points between. And all at very reasonable prices! So, just state your travelling needs, and I shall rush to satisfy them! Why is she growling at me?"

"Don't mind her," I said. "She's being herself. Are you the only mouse in the Nightside? That is . . ."

"I quite grasp your meaning, sir. There were others, once, but they all moved away to a small town in the countryside. Wimps. I am the only one of my kind currently residing here."

"Good," said Suzie. "I was beginning to think I'd have to start putting bigger traps down."

"I need a door," I said, loudly. "One that will take us directly to the Necropolis. Is that going to be a problem?"

"Oh no, sir, not at all," said the Doormouse, edging just a little further away from Suzie. "I always keep a number of the more common destination doors in stock, ready for sale. Both inside and outside the Nightside. This way if you please, sir and . . . lady . . ."

He scurried away deeper into his shop, with Suzie and me in close pursuit, to a showroom full of doors standing upright on end, apparently entirely unsupported. Neat handwritten labels announced the destination they opened onto. *Shadows Fall, Hy Breasil, Hyperborea, Carcosa.* Together with a whole series of doors that would take you practically anywhere inside the Nightside. But it was two other doors that caught my attention, standing a little off to one side. They were labelled simply *Heaven* and *Hell.* They looked no different than any of the others—simple waxed and polished wood, each with a gleaming brass handle.

"Ah yes," said the Doormouse, easing chummily in beside me. "Everyone notices those."

"Can they really take you where it says they go?" I said.

"That is a matter of some debate," the Doormouse admitted, crinkling his muzzle. "The theory's sound, and the mathematics quite clear. Certainly no-one who's gone through has ever come back to complain . . ."

"Let us talk of other things," I said.

"Yes, let's," said the Doormouse.

He led us past other doors, some labelled in languages and ideographs even I couldn't identify. And I've been around. We finally came to a door labelled *Necropolis.* The Doormouse patted it affectionately with one padded paw.

"I always keep this one charged up and at the ready for people who need to visit the Necropolis for a sad occasion. Much more dignified than fighting the traffic in a black Rolls Royce. This door will deliver you and the . . . lady, to right outside the main entrance."

"Not inside?" I said sharply.

"She's started growling again," said the Doormouse. "No, no, sir. Never inside! My doors lead only to exterior locations. If word got out that I was willing to provide access to the interiors of buildings, thus circumventing all usual security measures, you can be sure the Authorities would send Walker to shut me down. With prejudice. Now, sir, let us talk of the price."

We haggled for a while, and he drove a really hard bargain for a mouse. We finally settled for an only moderately painful extortionate sum, which I paid with gold from the traveller's pouch Old Father Time had given me, when I travelled back in Time. The pouch was seemingly bottomless, and I'm pretty sure Time meant for me to give it back to him when I returned, but I fully intended to hang on to it until it was wrestled from my grasp. The Doormouse opened the door with a flourish, and Suzie and I stepped through into another part of the Nightside.

The Necropolis looked just as I remembered it; big, dark, and supernaturally ugly. I'd been here not long ago, with Dead Boy, to clean up an incursion by Primal demons. Which meant that technically speaking the Necropolis staff still owed me a favour. How much weight that had, when set against Walker's publicly stated disapproval, remained to be seen.

The Necropolis itself was a huge towering edifice of old brick and stone, with no windows anywhere and a long, gabled roof. The various owners had been adding exteriors to it for years, in a clashing variety of styles, and yet the building maintained a traditional aspect of gloom and depression. The one and only front door was a massive slab of solid steel, rimmed with silver, covered with deeply etched runes and sigils and a whole bunch of nasty words in dead languages. Two huge chimneys at the back pumped out thick black smoke from the on-site crematorium.

The Necropolis serves all the Nightside's funereal needs. Any religion, any ritual, any requests, no matter how odd or distressing. Cash up front and no questions asked. People paid serious money to ensure that their dearly departed could rest peacefully in their graves, undisturbed and unmolested by any of the many magicians, necromancers, and creatures of the night who might profess an unhealthy interest in the helpless dead. And, of course, to ensure that the dead stayed dead and didn't turn up unexpectedly to contest the will. In the Nightside, you learn to cover all the bases. I considered the ugly, sprawling building before me. Cathy was being held there somewhere, very much against her will, and if she'd been harmed in any way, someone was going to pay for it in blood and horror.

"Enough travelling," said Suzie Shooter. "I feel the need to kill someone."

"Questions first," I said. "But if anyone doesn't feel like talking, feel free to encourage them in violent and distressing ways."

"You know how to show a girl a good time, Taylor."

"Except, your secretary isn't in there," said a calm, quiet, and very familiar voice.

We both looked round sharply and there he was, Razor Eddie, the Punk God of the Straight Razor, standing unnaturally still in the pool of light from a nearby streetlamp. Even though he very definitely hadn't been there a moment before. Razor Eddie, a painfully thin presence wrapped up in an oversized grey coat held together by accumulated filth and grime. His hollowed face was deathly pale and streaked with grime, dominated by fever-bright eyes and a smile that had absolutely no humour in it. We walked over to him, and the smell hit us. Razor Eddie lived on the streets, slept in doorways, and existed on hand-outs, and he always smelled bad enough to make a sewer rat's eyes water. I half expected the street-lights to start wilting.

"All right," said Suzie. "How did you know we'd be here, Eddie?"

"I'm a god," said Razor Eddie, in his quiet ghostly voice. "I always know what I need to know. Which is how I know exactly where your secretary is being held, John."

I regarded him thoughtfully. Eddie and I were friends, sort of, but given the kind of pressure Walker was capable of bringing to bear . . . Eddie nodded slightly, following my thoughts.

"Cautious as ever, John, and quite right, too. But I'm here to help."

"Why?" I said bluntly.

"Because Walker was foolish enough to try and order me to do his dirty work for him. Like I give a damn what the Authorities want. I go where I will, and do what I must, and no-one gets to stand in my way. No-one tells me what to do. So, your secretary isn't being held inside the Necropolis building, but rather in their private graveyard. Which is so big they keep it in a private dimension that they sub-let."

"Who from?" said Suzie.

"Best not to ask," said Razor Eddie.

I nodded. It made sense. I'd heard that the Necropolis's extensive private graveyard was kept in a pocket dimension, for security reasons, protected by really heavy-duty magics. Getting in wouldn't be easy.

"You can't just crash into the Necropolis and intimidate the staff into giving you access," said Eddie.

"Want to bet?" said Suzie.

"They know you're here," Eddie said patiently. "And they're already on the phone to Walker, screaming for reinforcements. By the time you've smashed your way through that building's defences, you'll be hip deep in Walker's people. And your only real hope for rescuing Cathy is a surprise attack. Fortunately, I can offer an alternative way in."

His right hand, thin and grey, came out of his pocket, holding a pearl-handled straight razor. He flipped the blade open, and the steel shone supernaturally bright. I could feel Suzie tensing beside me, but she had enough sense not to go for any of her weapons. Eddie flashed her a meaningless smile, turned away, and cut savagely at the empty air. The whole night seemed to shudder as the air split apart, widening and opening up like a wound in the world. And through the opening Razor Eddie had made, I could see another world, another dimension. It was a darker night than ours, and bitter cold air rushed out into our world. I shuddered, and so did Suzie, but I don't think it was from the cold. Razor Eddie, unaffected, stared calmly through the gap he'd made.

"I didn't know you could do that," I said.

"I went back to the Street of the Gods," said Eddie, putting away his razor. "Got an upgrade. Did you know, John, there's a new church there, worshipping your image. Unauthorised, I take it? Good. I took care of it for you. Knew you'd want me to. Follow me."

Poor bastards, I thought, as the Punk God of the Straight Razor stepped through the wide opening, and Suzie and I followed him through, into another world.

The terrible cold hit me like a fist and cut me like a knife, burning in my lungs as I struggled with the thin air. Suzie blew harshly on her cupped hands, flexing her fingers so they'd be free and ready if she had to kill someone in a hurry. Before us, the graveyard seemed to stretch away forever. Row upon row and rank upon rank of massed graves, for as far as the eye could see in any direction, from horizon to horizon. A world of nothing but graves. The Necropolis's private cemetery lay silently under an entirely different kind of night from the Nightside. It was darker, with an almost palpable gloom, apart from a glowing pearlescent ground mist that curled around our ankles and swirled slowly over the rows of tombstones. There was no moon in the jet-black sky, only vivid streaks of multi-coloured stars, bright and gaudy as a whore's jewels.

"We're not in the Nightside any more," said Eddie. "This is a whole different kind of place. Dark and dangerous and dead. I like it."

"You would," said Suzie. "Damn, but it's cold. I mean,

serious cold. I don't think anything human could survive here for long."

"Cathy's here, somewhere," I said. "Whoever has her had better be taking really good care of her. Or I will make them scream before they die."

"Hard-core, John," said Suzie. "And not really you. Leave the rough stuff to me. I'm more experienced." She looked around her and sniffed loudly to show how unimpressed she was. "The Necropolis could have chosen a more cheerful resting place for the Nightside dead."

"Perhaps all the alternatives were worse," I said. "Or more expensive."

"We didn't come here to admire the scenery," said Razor Eddie.

"Damn right," said Suzie. "Find me someone I can shoot."

I looked around. There was only the dark, and the graves and the mist. Nothing moved, not a breath of wind anywhere, and the place was utterly silent. The only sounds in the cemetery were those we made ourselves. Razor Eddie's rasping breathing, the creaking of Suzie's leathers.

"I don't see anyone," I said.

Eddie shrugged slightly. "Nothing lives here. That's the point. Even the flowers left on the graves are plastic."

There were headstones of all shapes and sizes, catafalques and mausoleums, statues of weeping angels and penitent cherubs and crouching gargoyles. All kinds of religious symbols, large and small, simple and complex, and a few even I didn't recognise. All the objects of death, and not one of life.

"I thought there might be at least a few mourners," said Suzie.

"Not many come here to visit," said Eddie. "I mean, would you? Now follow me and walk carefully. There are concealed traps here, for the uninvited and the unwary."

Suzie brightened up a bit. "You mean some of those

stone gargoyles might come to life? I could use some target practice."

"Possibly," said Razor Eddie. "But mostly I was thinking about bear traps and land mines. The Necropolis takes security very seriously. Stick to the gravel path, and we should be safe enough."

"I never get to go anywhere nice," I said, wistfully.

I fired up my gift, hoping that since I was closer to Cathy, it would at least be able to provide me with a direction. My Sight was limited, in this new dimension. There was no hidden world here, no secret lives for me to See; just the dead, lying at peace in their graves and mausoleums, like so many silent strangers at the feast. And yet there was a feeling . . . of being watched, by unseen eyes. I tried to focus in on Cathy, but a strangely familiar shadow still hid her exact position from me. At least I had a direction.

I set off down the gravel path, with Suzie Shooter and Razor Eddie on either side of me. Suzie had her shotgun in her hands, alert for any opportunity to show off what she did best. Eddie strolled along, his hands in his pockets, his unblinking eyes missing nothing, nothing at all. The sound of our feet crunching the gravel was uncomfortably loud, announcing our coming. I watched the shadows between the stone mausoleums, ready for any sudden attack from behind the larger tombstones; but I wasn't at all ready for what lay in wait for us around an abrupt corner.

They were sitting at a picnic around a pristine white cloth, laid out on a long earth barrow. There was a food hamper, with plates of cucumber sandwiches and sausage rolls and nibbles on sticks, and a bottle of quite decent champagne chilling in an ice bucket. And smiling calmly back at us—Tommy Oblivion, the existential detective, and Sandra Chance, the consulting necromancer. Tommy's usual New Romantic silks were mostly concealed under a heavy fur coat, but he still managed a certain dated style. He smiled easily at us, showing off a broad, toothy grin in his long, horsey face, and toasted me with a brimming glass of bubbly. Sandra just glared coldly, pale of face and red of hair, wearing nothing but apparently random splashes of dark crimson liquid latex from chin to toe. She looked like a vampire after a really messy meal, and not by accident. Sandra went out of her way to make an impression on people. Supposedly, the liquid latex also contained holy water and other useful protections. The tattoo on her back could make angels vomit and demons hyperventilate. Interestingly enough, she'd had all of the steel piercings in her face and body removed, recently enough that some of the holes were still closing. A simple leather belt, carrying a series of tanned pouches holding the tools of her unpleasant trade, surrounded her waist. She didn't feel the cold because she thrived in graveyards. Sandra Chance loved the dead—and sometimes even more, if that was what it took to get them to talk.

We'd worked together on a few cases, successfully, if not entirely happily. Sandra only cared about getting results, and to hell with whoever got caught in the crossfire. I liked to think that wasn't true of me, any more.

"Hello, old thing," said Tommy Oblivion. "So glad you could join us. And you've brought company! How sweet. Do sit down and have a little something with us, and a splash of champers. I think it's terribly important we all remain civilised in situations like this, don't you?"

"Want me to shoot him?" said Suzie.

"I'm thinking about it," I said. "Hello, Tommy. I should have known it was you, with your existential gift, hiding Cathy. Still sticking with the effete image, I see."

He flapped his long, bony fingers in an affable sort of way. "Stay with what works, that's what I say."

"How's your brother?"

"Still dead. But he says he's starting to get used to it. And he's a better private eye now than he ever was while he was alive."

"I think that's enough civilities," I said. "Tell me

where Cathy is, or I'll have Suzie shoot you somewhere really unfortunate."

"Any violence and you'll never see her again," said Sandra. Her voice was deep and vibrant and bitter as cyanide. "You'll never find Cathy Barrett without our help."

"Where is she?" I said, and my voice was colder than the night. Tommy and Sandra sat up a little straighter.

"She's sleeping peacefully," said Sandra. "In one of these graves. I put a spell on her, then Tommy and I opened up a grave, put her in it, and covered her over again. She's quite safe, for the time being. All you have to do is turn yourself in to Walker, and Tommy and I will dig her up and return her safely to the Nightside. Of course, the longer she stays underground, the more difficult it will be to wake her from the spell . . ."

"Of course," I said. "You're never happy with a spell unless it's got a sting in the tail." I looked at Tommy. "Why are you doing this? Sandra I can understand. I've never known her to balk at anything if the price was right. But you . . . what happened to those principles you used to trumpet so loudly? Cathy's the only innocent in this whole business."

His cheeks flushed a little, but he held my gaze steadily. "Needs must when the devil drives, old sport. You're just too dangerous to be allowed to run loose any more. I saw what you did with Merlin and Nimue, remember? You don't care about anyone or anything, except getting your own way."

"No," said Razor Eddie. "That's not true."

We all glanced at him, a little startled. He was so quiet and still it was easy to forget he was there.

"You have to be stopped," said Tommy, a little more loudly than was necessary. "You're cold and ruthless and . . ."

"You got back from the Past months ago," I said, talking right over him. "Why didn't you do something before this? Why wait till now?"

"I was keeping my head down, out of sight, while I thought things through," said Tommy. He was trying hard not to sound defensive. "I put a lot of thought into how best to stop you. It took me a while to admit I couldn't hope to do it alone. So I came up with this plan, and went to Walker with it, and he put me together with Sandra. Not at all a nice plan, I agree, but you brought it on yourself. Fight fire with fire, and all that. You might say . . . this was my last test for you, John. One last chance to see what you're really made of, to see if you care for anyone other than yourself. Prove me wrong about you. Prove to me and to Walker that you're not the evil we think you are by turning yourself in. And I give you my word that Cathy will be released, entirely unharmed."

"I can't," I said, trying hard to make him hear the need and urgency and honesty in my voice. "My mother Lilith is back, and she's worse than I'll ever be. I'm the only one who can stop her from destroying the Nightside."

"Such arrogance," said Sandra. "We'll stop her, after we've dealt with you."

"I could blow your head right off your shoulders," Suzie Shooter said casually.

"You could try," said Sandra Chance. The two women smiled at each other easily. Sandra leaned forward to put down her champagne glass, and Suzie moved her shotgun slightly to keep her covered. "I am a necromancer," said Sandra. "And this is my place of power. With this much death to draw on, even the Punk God of the Straight Razor can't hope to stand against me. Your presence here was not expected or required, little god. This is nothing to do with you."

"Yes it is," said Eddie. "I know what you found in the future, John. I know who you found. I've always known."

I looked at him sharply. I saw him die, in the Timeslip future. I helped him to die. But I never told anyone.

He shrugged easily. "I'm a god, remember?"

"This doesn't have to end in violence," Tommy said

urgently, sensing the undercurrents. "You know I'm an honourable man, John."

"You might be," I said. "But Sandra works for Walker. And Walker . . . has his own very personal take on honour, when it comes to the Nightside. He'd sacrifice any number of innocents to preserve the Nightside for the Authorities."

"He was supposed to be here," said Tommy, frowning slightly. "To reassure you of his good intentions. But unfortunately he was called away. It seems something really unpleasant is happening on the Street of the Gods."

We all looked at Razor Eddie, who met our gaze a little reproachfully. "Nothing to do with me," he said.

"Hell with this," said Sandra Chance, rising to her feet in one smooth feline movement. "It's time to take care of business."

"No!" said Tommy, scrambling untidily to his feet. "He has to be given a chance to surrender! You agreed!"

"I lied," said Sandra. "His existence offends me. He killed the Lamentation."

"Ah yes," I said. "Your . . . what was the term, exactly, I wonder? You never did have much taste in lovers, Sandra. The Lamentation was just a nasty little Power with delusions of godhood, and the world smells better now that it's gone."

"It was the Saint of Suffering, and it served a purpose!" Sandra said loudly. "It weeded out the weak and punished the foolish, and I was proud to serve it!"

"Exactly what was your relationship with the Lamentation?" said Tommy Oblivion. His voice was thoughtful and not at all threatening, as his gift manifested subtly on the still air. Tommy could be very persuasive when he chose to be. I don't know whether Sandra could feel what was happening, but she answered anyway, her cold green eyes locked on mine.

"I used to investigate insurance fraud," she said. "And a cluster of unexplained suicides brought me to the Church of the Lamentation. We talked, and we . . . connected. I don't think it had ever met anyone like me, with my fetish for death."

"Kindred spirits, who found each other in Hell," I said softly. "What did you do for the Lamentation, Sandra? What deal did you make with your devil?"

"Your devil, my god," said Sandra Chance. "I became its Judas Goat, leading the suffering to their Saint, and it taught me the ways of the necromancer. It gave me what I'd always wanted. To lie down with death and rise up wreathed in power."

"Of course," said Tommy, "such knowledge usually drives people insane. But you were functionally crazy to begin with."

"Takes one to know one," said Sandra. "Now shut up, Tommy, or I'll do something amusing to you. You're only here on sufferance."

"It was my plan!"

"No," said Sandra. "This was always Walker's plan."

"And you never gave a damn, for all the poor bastards you delivered to your nasty lover?" I said. "To die in despair, then linger in horror, bound even after death to the service of the Lamentation?"

"They were weak," said Sandra. "They gave up. I never broke under the strain, never gave up. I save my help for those who deserve it."

"Of course you didn't care," said Suzie Shooter. "You're even more heartless than I am. I'm going to enjoy killing you."

"Enough talk," said Sandra. "It's time to dance the dance of life and death, little people. I shall raise all those who lie here because of you—John Taylor, Shotgun Suzie, Razor Eddie. All your victims gathered together in one place, with hate and vengeance burning in their cold, cold hearts. And they will drag you down into the cold wet earth and hold you there in their bony arms until finally . . . you stop screaming. Don't say I never did anything for you."

She raised her arms high in the stance of summoning,

and chanted ancient Words of Power. Energies crackled fiercely around her extended fingers . . . and nothing happened. The energies dissipated harmlessly on the freezing air, unable to come together. Sandra stood there awkwardly for a long moment, then slowly lowered her arms and looked about her, confused.

"The Necropolis graveyard is protected by seriously heavy-duty magics," said Eddie, in his calm, ghostly voice. "I thought everyone knew that."

"But the magics were supposed to have been suppressed!" said Sandra. "Walker promised me!"

"That wasn't the deal!" said Tommy. "I wasn't told about any of this!"

"You didn't need to know."

There was a pleasant chiming sound, a brief shimmering on the air, and there was Walker, standing before us in his neat city suit and old-school tie. He smiled vaguely about him. "This . . . is a recording. I'm afraid I can't be here with you, on the grounds it might prove injurious to my health. By now you should have realised that the magics of this place have not been shut down, as promised, Sandra Chance. My apologies for the deception; but it was necessary. You see, this isn't just a trap for John Taylor; it's a trap for all of you. Taylor, Shooter, Oblivion, and Chance. I'm afraid you've all become far more trouble than you're worth. And I need to be free to concentrate on the Really Bad Thing that all my best precogs insist is coming. So the decision has been made to dispense with all of you. I have at least extracted a promise from the Authorities that after you've all killed each other, or the cemetery has killed you, your bodies will be buried here, free of charge. It's the least I could do. Good-bye, John. I am sorry it had to come to this. I protected you for as long as I could . . . but I've always known my duty."

The image of Walker raised his bowler hat in our general direction, then snapped off. There was a long moment of silence.

"We are so screwed," said Suzie.

I looked at Eddie. "He didn't know you'd be here. You're our wild card in this situation."

"It's what I do best," said Eddie.

"Walker, you supercilious son of a bitch!" said Sandra Chance, actually stamping one bare foot in her outrage.

"I wouldn't argue with that," I said. "Ladies and gentlemen, it would appear we have all been declared redundant. Might I suggest it would be in all our best interests to work together, putting aside old quarrels until we're all safely out of here?"

"Agreed," said Sandra, two bright red spots burning on her pale cheeks. "But Walker is mine to kill."

"First things first," I said. "Where is Cathy?"

"Oh, we put her in the mausoleum right behind us," said Tommy. "Sleeping peacefully. You didn't really think I'd stand for her being buried alive, did you? What kind of a person do you think I am?"

"I ought to shoot you both right now, on general principles," said Suzie.

"Later," I said firmly.

The mausoleum was a huge stone Victorian edifice, with all the usual Gothic trimmings, plus a whole bunch of decidedly portly cherubs in mourning. The Victorians could get really sentimental about death. Tommy heaved open the door, and when I looked in there was Cathy, lying curled up on the bare stone floor like a sleeping child. She was wearing something fashionable, under a thick fur coat someone had wrapped around her like a blanket. She was actually snoring slightly. Tommy edged nervously past me, leaned over Cathy, and muttered a few Words under his breath. Cathy came awake immediately and sat up, yawning and knuckling at her sleepy eyes. I moved forward into the mausoleum, and Cathy jumped up and ran forward into my arms. I held her very tightly.

"I knew you'd come and find me," she said, into my shoulder.

"Of course," I said. "How would I ever run my office without you?"

She finally let go, and I did, too. We went out of the mausoleum and into the night, where Tommy Oblivion and Sandra Chance were standing stiffly a little to one side. Cathy stepped briskly forward, got a good hold on Sandra's breasts with both hands, then head-butted her in the face. Sandra fell backwards onto her bare arse, blood spurting from her broken nose. Tommy opened his mouth, either to object or explain, and Cathy kicked him square in the nuts. He went down on his knees, tears streaming past his squeezed-shut eyes, with both hands wedged between his thighs. Perhaps to reassure himself that his testicles were actually still attached.

"Messing with the wrong secretary," said Cathy.

"Nicely done," I said, and Cathy grinned at me.

"You are a bad influence on the child," Suzie said solemnly.

Sometime later we all assembled around the earth barrow. Tommy moved around slowly and carefully, packing up the picnic things, while Sandra stood with her back to all of us, sniffing gingerly through the nose she'd reset herself. Suzie glared suspiciously about her, shotgun at the ready. She was convinced Walker wouldn't have abandoned us here unless he knew there was Something in the cemetery strong and nasty enough to see us all off. She had a point. I turned to Razor Eddie.

"Walker didn't know you'd be here. And I'm reasonably sure he doesn't know about your new ability to cut doors into dimensions with that nasty little blade of yours. Take us home, Eddie, so we can express our extreme displeasure to him in person."

He nodded slightly, and the pearl-handled straight razor gleamed viciously in the starlight as he cut at the air before him, in a movement so fast none of us could follow it. We all braced ourselves, but nothing happened. Eddie frowned and tried again, still to no effect. He slowly lowered his blade and considered the air before him.

"Ah," he said finally.

"Ah?" I said. "What do you mean, *ah*? Is there something wrong with your razor, Eddie?"

"No, there's something wrong with the dimensional barriers."

"I don't like the sound of that, Eddie."

"I'm not too keen on it myself. Someone has strengthened the dimensional barriers, from the outside. No prizes for guessing who."

Cathy hugged my arm tightly. "How does he know things like that?"

"I find it better not to ask," I said. "Eddie, I . . . Eddie, why are you frowning? I really don't like it when you frown."

"Something's . . . changed," he said, his voice stark and flat. He looked around him, and we all did the same. The night seemed no different, cold and still and quiet, the graves unmoving and undisturbed under the gaudy starlight. But Eddie was right. Something had changed. We could all feel it, like the tension that precedes the breaking storm.

"You achieved something, with that spell of yours," Eddie said to Sandra. "It's still trying to work, undischarged in the cemetery atmosphere. It's not enough to affect the dead, but . . ."

"What do you mean, 'but'?" I said. "You can't stop there!"

"She's disturbed Something," said Razor Eddie. "It's been asleep a long time, but now it's waking . . . and it's waking angry."

We moved closer together, staring about us and straining our ears against the silence. The atmosphere in the graveyard was changing. There was a sense of potential on the air, of something about to happen, in this place where nothing was ever supposed to happen. Suzie turned her shotgun this way and that, searching in vain for a target.

"What am I looking for, Eddie?" she said calmly. "What lives in this dimension?"

"I told you. Nothing lives here. That's the point."

"Could the dead be rising up after all?" said Tommy.

"It's not the dead," Sandra said immediately. "I'd know if it was that."

"It's coming," whispered Razor Eddie.

The ground rose sharply beneath our feet, toppling us this way and that. Headstones collapsed or lurched to one side, and the great mausoleums trembled. My first thought was an earthquake, but all around us the graveyard earth was rising and falling, lifting like an ocean swell. We all scrambled onto our feet again, finding things to cling to for support.

"There were rumours," said Sandra Chance, "of a Caretaker, set to guard the graves."

"I never heard of any Caretaker," said Razor Eddie.

"Yes, well, just because you're a god doesn't mean you know everything," said Sandra.

And that was when the graveyard dirt burst up into the air from between the rows of graves, great fountains of dark wet earth shooting up, high into the chilly air. It rained down all around us, forming itself into rough shapes. Dark, earthy human shapes, with rough arms and legs, and blunt heads with no faces. Golems fashioned out of graveyard dirt. They started towards us, slow and clumsy with the power of earth, closing in on us from every direction at once. The ground grew still again, save for the heavy thudding of legs with no feet.

Suzie opened up with her pump-action shotgun. She hit everything she aimed at, blowing ragged chunks of earth out of the heavy lumbering figures, but it didn't slow them down. Not even when she blew their heads off. Sandra chanted Words of Power and stabbed at the advancing earth golems with an aboriginal pointing-bone, and none of it did any good at all. Razor Eddie darted for-

ward, moving supernaturally quickly. Several of the earth
figures just fell apart, sliced through again and again. But
for every golem that fell, a dozen more rose out of the
graveyard earth and headed our way with silent, implacable intent.

I heard muttering beside me. Tommy Oblivion was
using his gift to try to convince himself he was somewhere else, but it seemed Walker's dimensional barriers
were too strong even for him. Cathy pulled a Kandarian
punch dagger from the top of her knee-length boot, and
moved to watch my back. She knew her limitations. Sandra was reduced to throwing things from her belt pouches
at the approaching golems. None of them did any good.

"I'll have Walker's balls for this!" she screamed.

"Join the queue," I said.

I took out my Club Membership Card. Alex Morrisey
gave it to me some time back, when he was in an unusually expansive mood. When properly activated, the magic
stored in the Card could transport you right into Strangefellows, from wherever you happened to be at the time. I
had perhaps used it more often than Alex had intended,
because he was always nagging at me to return it, and yet
somehow I kept forgetting on purpose to do so. But once
again, the magic in the Card was no match for whatever
Walker had done to the dimensional barriers. I turned to
Suzie.

"Do you have any grenades?"

"Silly question," she said. "You think I'd go out half-
dressed?"

"Spread some confusion," I said. "I need some time to
concentrate, to raise my gift."

"You got it," said Suzie. "Blessed or cursed grenades,
do you think?"

"I'd try both."

"Excellent notion."

She started lobbing grenades in all directions, and
everyone else ducked and put their hands over their ears.
The explosions dug great craters out of the ground, and

bits of golem, coffin wood, and even body parts rained down all around us. Stone fragments from headstones and mausoleums flew on the air like shrapnel. The golems were shredded and rent, flattened and torn apart. And still more rose, forming themselves out of the torn earth.

I closed my eyes and studied the cemetery through my third eye, my private eye. Without Tommy's gift interfering, I could See clearly again. And it only took me a moment to find the source of the consciousness animating the earth golems. It was a diffused, widely spread thing, scattered throughout the whole of the cemetery, and beyond. This was the great secret of the Necropolis graveyard. The last line of defence for the helpless dead. This whole world, the earth and the soil of it, was alive and aware, and set to guard. The Caretaker. A living world, to protect a world's dead.

The Caretaker decided the golems weren't working, or perhaps it sensed my probings into its nature. All the earth in the cemetery rose before us, in a great tidal wave, and thundered forward like a horizontal avalanche. Enough earth to pulverise and drown and bury us all. There was nowhere to run, nowhere to hide, no way to defend ourselves. But I had finally found the weak spot in Walker's plan. He'd strengthened the spells containing the cemetery dimension, made very sure that nothing could get out. But it had never occurred to him to stop anything from getting in . . . I reached out with my gift, and found a place in the Nightside where it was raining really heavily. And then all I had to do was bring the rain to me and let it pour down. The driving rain hit the tidal wave of earth and washed it away. Thick mud swirled around our feet, but its strength and power were gone. The rain kept hammering down, and the Caretaker couldn't get its earth to hang together long enough to form anything. And while the Caretaker was preoccupied with that, I reached out with my gift again and located the weakest spot in the dimensional barriers containing us. I showed Eddie where it was, and he cut it open with one stroke of his godly razor.

We all ran through the opening, while Eddie strained to keep it open. Then we were all back in the Nightside, and the opening slammed shut behind us. We stood together, soaking wet and smeared with mud, breathing hard. I looked around me. I'd been half-expecting a crowd of Walker's people, set to stand and watch in case we found a way out, but there was no-one. Either Walker hadn't expected any of us to get out . . . or his people were needed somewhere else. Sandra said he'd been called away, to deal with trouble on the Street of the Gods . . . Could Lilith be making her move at last?

Sandra stomped wetly towards me, and I raised an eyebrow. "Relax, Taylor," she said curtly. "You saved my life, and I always pay my debts. Walker has to be shown the error of his ways. I can help. Of course, once that's over . . ."

Cathy fixed Sandra with a thoughtful eye, and the consulting necromancer winced despite herself. Cathy smiled sweetly. "Leave my boss alone, bitch."

"Play nicely, children," I said. "We have to go to the Street of the Gods. I think the shit is finally hitting the fan. Tommy, escort Cathy back to Strangefellows, and stay there with her. And don't argue. Neither of you has the firepower for what we're going to be facing. Lock and load, people; we have a Biblical myth to take down."

THREE

Playtime's Over, Children

I wasn't there at the time, but the survivors told me what happened.

It was just another day on the Street of the Gods. That magical, mercurial, and entirely separate place where you can worship whatever you want, or whatever wants you. There are Beings and Powers and Forces, things unknown and things unknowable, and it's all strictly buyer beware. Religion is big business in the Nightside, and on the Street of the Gods you can find something to fit anyone's taste, no matter how bizarre or extreme. Of course, the most popular faiths have the biggest churches and the most magnificent temples, and the best positions on the Street, while everyone else fights it out in a Darwinian struggle for cash, congregations, and more commanding positions. Some gods are very old, some are very rich, and some don't even last long enough to pass around the collection plate.

Gods come and go, faiths rise and fall, but the Street of the Gods goes on forever.

Gargoyles crouched high up on cathedral walls, studying the worshippers below with sardonic eyes, chatting and gossiping and passing round a thick hand-rolled. Strange forms walked openly up and down the Street, going about their unguessable business. Wisps and phantoms floated here and there, troubled by every passing breeze—old gods worn so thin they weren't even memories any more. There were paper lanterns and human candles, burning braziers and bright gaudy neon. Living lightning bolts chased each other up and down the Street. Rival gangs chanted dogma at each other from the safety of their church vestries, and here and there mad-eyed zealots practised curses and damnations on hated enemies. Some of the more fashionable gods strolled up and down the Street in their most dazzling aspects, out and about to see and be seen. And Harlequin danced, in his stark chequered outfit and black domino mask, spinning and pirouetting as he always had, for as long as anyone could remember, on and on, dance without end. Under candlelight, corpselight, and flashing neon, Harlequin danced.

It had to be said—the Street of the Gods had known better days. Just recently, Razor Eddie had lost his temper in the Street and done something extremely distressing, as a result of which some gods had been observed running out of the Street screaming and crying their eyes out. Walker's people were still coaxing them out of bars and gutters and cardboard boxes. On the Street, people were clearing up the wreckage and taking estimates for rebuilding. Churches were surrounded by scaffolding, or held together by glowing bands of pure faith, while those beyond saving were bulldozed flat by remote-controlled juggernauts. The barkers were out in force, drumming up new business, and there were more tourists about than ever. (They do so love a disaster, especially when it's somewhere picturesque.) Some worshippers were still wandering around in a daze, wondering whether their deities would ever return.

Just another day on the Street of the Gods, then—until dead angels began dropping out of the night sky. They fell gracelessly and landed hard, with broken wings and stupid, startled faces, like birds who have flown into the windows of high-rise buildings. They lay on the ground, not moving, creatures of light and darkness, like a child's discarded toys. Everyone regarded the dead angels with awe and some timidity. And then they looked up, the worshippers and the worshipped, to see a greater dark miracle in the starry night sky.

A moonbeam extended lazily down into the Street of the Gods, shimmering silver starstuff, splendid and coldly beautiful, just like the great and awful personage who sailed slowly down it like an ethereal moving stairway, smiling and waving to the crowds below. Lilith had been planning her return for some time, and she did so love to make an entrance.

Inhumanly tall, perfectly formed, and supernaturally feminine, with a skin so pale it was the very antithesis of colour, and hair and eyes and lips blacker than the night, she looked like some screen goddess from the days of silent film. Her face was sharp and pointed, with a prominent bone structure and a hawk nose. Her mouth was thin-lipped and far too wide, and her eyes held a fire that could burn through anything. She was not pretty, but she was beautiful almost beyond bearing. She was naked, but there was nothing vulnerable about her.

Her presence filled the air, like the roar of massed cannon announcing the start of war, or a choir singing obscenities in a cathedral, like the first scream of being born or the last scream of the dying. No-one could look away. And many a lesser god or goddess knelt and bowed, recognising the real thing when they saw it, come at last to the Street of the Gods. There was a halo round Lilith's head, though it was more a presence than a light. Lilith could be very traditional, when she chose. She stepped down off the moonbeam into the Street of the Gods, and smiled about her.

"Hello, everyone," she said, in a voice rich and sweet as poisoned honey. "I'm Lilith, and I'm back. Did you miss me?"

She walked openly in glory through the night, and everyone fell back before her. The great and small alike bowed their heads, unable to meet her gaze. The ground shook and cracked apart beneath the thunder of her tread. Even the biggest and most ornate cathedral seemed suddenly shabby, next to her. She kicked dead angels out of her way with a perfect pale foot, not even looking down, and her dark mouth made a small moue of annoyance.

"Such simple, stupid things," she said. "Neither Heaven nor Hell can stand against me here, in the place I made to be free of both."

Some tourists made the mistake of pressing forward, with their cameras and camcorders. Lilith just looked at them, and they died screaming, with nothing left to mark their presence save agonised shadows, blasted into the brickwork of the buildings behind them.

Lilith stopped abruptly and looked about her, then called in a commanding voice for all the gods to leave their churches and present themselves before her. She called for them by name and by nature, in a language no-one spoke any more. A language so old it couldn't even be recognised as words, only sounds, concepts from an ur-language so ancient as to be beyond civilised comprehension.

And out of the churches and temples and dark hidden places they came, the Beings and Power and Forces who had called themselves gods for so long. Out came Bloody Blades and Soror Marium, the Carrion in Tears and the Devil's Bride, Molly Widdershins, Abomination Inc, the Incarnate and the Engineer. And more and more, the human and the humanoid and the abhuman, the monsters and the magical, the scared and the profane. And some who hadn't left the dark and secret places under their churches for centuries, unseen by generations of their worshippers, who, having finally seen the awful things they'd prayed to for so long, would never do so again. And last of all, Harlequin stopped dancing and came forward to kneel before Lilith.

"My masters and my mistresses," he said, in a calm, cold, and utterly hopeless voice. "The revels now are ended."

The watching crowd grew loudly agitated, crying out in awe and shock and wonder at the unexpected sights before them. They argued amongst themselves as to what it all meant, and zealots struck out at those nearest with fists and harsh words. No-one likes to admit they may have backed a losing horse. The quicker-thinking in the crowd were already kneeling and crying out praises to Lilith. The prophesiers of doom, those persistent grey creatures with their hand-made signs saying THE END IS NIGH seemed most put out. They hadn't seen this coming. Lilith smiled at them.

"You are all redundant now. I am the End you have been waiting for."

More shadows, blasted into crumbling brickwork, more fading echoes of startled screams.

Lilith looked unhurriedly about her, considering the various divine forms gathered before her, in all their shapes and incarnations, and they all flinched a little under that thoughtful gaze, even if they didn't remember why. She made them feel nervous, unworthy, on some deep and primal level. As though she knew something they had tried very hard to forget, or, if never known, had somehow always suspected.

"I am Lilith," she said finally. "First wife to Adam, thrown out of Eden for refusing to acknowledge any authority but mine own. I descended into Hell and lay down with demons, and gave birth to monsters. All my marvellous children—the first to be invited to dwell in my

Nightside. You are all my children, or descendants of my children. You are not gods, and never were. It takes more than worship to make you divine. I made you to be splendid and free, but you have grown small and limited down the many years, seduced by worship and acclaim, allowed yourselves to be shaped and enslaved by the imaginations of humanity. Well, playtime is over now, children. I am back, in the place I made for us, and it's time to go to work. I've been away too long, and there is much to be put right.

"I have been here for some time, watching and learning. I walked among you, and you knew me not. You've been playing at being gods for so long you've forgotten you were ever anything else. But you owe your existence and loyalty to me. Your lives are mine, to do with as I please."

The Beings and Forces and Powers looked at each other, stirring uneasily. It was all happening so fast. One minute they were being worshipped as divine, and the next . . . Some of them were beginning to remember. Some shook their heads in hopeless denial, even as tears ran down their faces. Some didn't take at all kindly to being reminded of their true origins and obligations, and shouted defiance. And quite a large number were distinctly resentful at finding out they weren't gods at all and never had been. The watching worshippers retreated to what they hoped was a safe distance, and let the gods argue it out amongst themselves. The argument was getting quite noisy, if not actually raucous, when Lilith silenced them all with a single sharp gesture.

"You," she said, pointing to a single figure at the front of the pack. "I don't know you. You're not one of mine. What are you?"

The Engineer stared calmly back at her, while everyone else edged away from him. He was squat and broad and only vaguely humanoid, with blue steel shapes piercing blue flesh, and long strips of bare muscle tissue held together with bolts and springs. Steam hissed from his naked joints, his eyes glowed like coals, and if you got close enough you could hear his heart ticking. He was surrounded and protected by a group of gangling metal constructions, of intricate design and baroque sensibilities, though whether they were the engineer's worshippers or his creations was unclear.

"I am a Transient Being," said the Engineer, in a voice like metal scraping against metal. "A physical incarnation of an abstract idea. I am immortal because I am a concept, not because I have your unnatural blood in my ancestry. The world has become so much more complex since your time, Lilith. All of this . . . is none of my business. So I'll leave you to get on with it."

He turned and walked sideways from the world, disappearing down a direction most of those present couldn't even comprehend, let alone identify, and in a moment he was gone. The steel-and-brass constructions he left behind collapsed emptily, so much scrap metal littering the ground. Lilith stood silent for a moment, nonplussed. That hadn't been in the script. Emboldened by the Engineer's defiance, some of the Beings stepped forward to confront Lilith.

"We heard you were banished," drawled the Splendid, leaving a shimmering trail behind him as he moved. "Forced out of the world you made, by those you trusted and empowered."

"Thrust into Limbo," said La Belle Dame du Rocher, in her watery voice. "Until some damned fool let you out, let you back into the Nightside to trouble us again with bad dreams of our beginnings."

"Some say you've been here for years," said Molly Widdershins, showing her stained and blocky teeth in something that was only nominally a smile. "So where have you been hiding, all this time?"

"Not hiding," said Lilith, and the chill in her voice made them all fall back a pace. "I've been . . . preparing. So much to do, and so many to do it to. And then, of course, I had to produce a new child, and see to his edu-

cation. He is mine, body and soul, even if he doesn't realise it yet. My dearest darling John Taylor."

The name rumbled through the crowd, from worshippers and worshipped alike, and not in a good way. Many
shifted uneasily, and aspects flickered on and off in the
crowd like heat lightning. The Splendid opened his perfect mouth to protest further, and Lilith reached out and
touched him lightly on the forehead. He cried out in
shock and horror as his life energy was ripped right out
of him, to feed Lilith's endless hunger. She sucked him
dry in a moment, watching calmly as he crumpled and
shrivelled up before her, all his power nothing more to
her than a drop in her ocean. The Splendid blinked out
and was gone, as though he had never been. Lilith smiled
about her.

"Just a little illustration of my mood, so everyone
knows where they stand. I may be your mother, but I
won't abide over-familiarity. Now, where are those who
banded together to betray me, so very long ago? To ban-
ish me from my own creation? Step forward, that I might
look upon your faces once again."

There was a long, uncomfortable pause, then the
Devil's Bride stepped forward reluctantly, the conjoined
twin in the hump on her back peering over her shoulder.
"They're all gone, mistress," said the little twin, in a
sweet seductive voice. "Long and long ago. They killed
each other, or were brought down, or grew irrelevant to
the modern world and just faded away. There's only one
left that we know of. Its original name is lost to us. We
call it the Carrion in Tears, and it is quite insane."

She darted back into the safety of the crowd, while
others pushed forward the Carrion in Tears, a huge body
of rotting flesh, red and black and purple, with jagged
ends of bones protruding from suppurating flesh. Forever
decaying, never dying, quite mad. It snapped at the world
with broken teeth, dull grey in muddy scarlet flesh, and
its cloudy eyes were fixed and staring.

"It incorporates dead things into itself," volunteered Molly Widdershins. "They keep it going. Make it strong."

"And this . . . has followers?" said Lilith.

"Of a kind," said Molly.

"Proof, if proof were needed, that some people will worship absolutely anything," said Lilith. "As long as it has the stink of immortality about it."

Some of the Carrion in Tears' worshippers were thrust forward through the crowd, to face Lilith. They dressed in soiled rags and torn plastic, with grime artfully smeared across their faces. The oldest among them raised his head proudly and stood defiantly before Lilith.

"We worship it because it shows us the truth. The real world is filth and rot, pollution and corruption. Our god shows us the dirty truth behind the pretty face. When all else is fallen into ruin, our god will remain, and we will be with him."

"No you won't," said Lilith. "You offend me even more than he does." And she killed them all, with a glance.

The Carrion in Tears didn't notice. It was too busy digesting a dead angel it had noticed lying by its foot. Inch by inch, the dead angel was sucked into the Being's corrupt flesh and absorbed. The smell was awful, and even other Beings looked away. The Carrion in Tears straightened up abruptly, as the last lingering traces of the angel's divine energies surged through it, and shocked the slumbering mind awake. It cried out, a thick choking sound of horrid awareness, and fixed Lilith with its staring eyes.

"You! This is all your fault! See what has become of me! Look at what driving you out did to me!"

"I see it," Lilith said calmly. "Fair punishment, I'd have said, for a traitor and a fool."

"It was necessary," said the Carrion in Tears, but it sounded tired, as though repeating an old, worn-out argument. "And now you're back, and it was all for nothing. I told them, but they wouldn't listen . . . Kill me if you want. I don't care. I was beautiful once, and adored . . . I don't recognise this Nightside. You won't either. It's all changed. It's moved on and left us behind."

"Killing you would be a mercy, in your current state," said Lilith. "But what the hell. Don't say I never did anything for you."

She absorbed all its living energies in a moment, then made a moue of distaste with her night-dark mouth as the Carrion in Tears vanished into her. "Nasty," she said to the silent crowd. "But I promised myself that I'd kill all of my old enemies who survived, and I always keep my word. Now, step forward, my children. The original productions of my young and lusty flesh."

She called for them by their original names, and again there was a long pause. Finally, a mere handful of Beings made their way to the front of the crowd to face their long-forgotten mother. First was the Harlequin, who knelt before her in his chequered finery and bowed his masked head to her.

"I am here, mother dear, though much-changed by time and circumstance. I allowed myself to be shaped by fashion and fad, but still I survive, and still I dance. I would like to think that you could still see something in me that you would recognise."

"I change, too, when I must," said the Incarnate, bowing elegantly to Lilith. He was young and pretty, dressed in an immaculate white suit of impeccable cut, his noble face attractively androgynous under a white panama hat. "The details change, but I go on, worshipped and adored. At present I am a pop sensation, singing for my supper, and teenage girls worship my image on their bedroom walls. I am the Thin White Prince, and they love my music and they love me. Don't you, my little doves?"

A pack of fierce young girls surrounded him, dressed just like him, their overly made-up faces sullen and aggressive. You could see in their faces that he was more than life itself to them, and they would die for him in a moment. Some actually spat and hissed at Lilith, sensing a threat to their beloved idol. The oldest of them couldn't have been more than fifteen.

"I know," said the Thin White Prince. "But one takes one's adoration where one can find it."

And finally, there was Bloody Blades. He crouched uncertainly before Lilith, snorting and quivering, held in place by ancient instinct. He was huge and hairy, with hooves and horns and terrible clawed hands. He stank of sweat and musk and uncontrolled appetites. He glowered at Lilith with stupid, crafty eyes, attracted by her femininity but cowed by the sheer power he sensed in her.

"There's not much left of Bloody Bones," said Harlequin. "He's been reduced to a purely animal nature, a god of wild actions and transgression without conscience. There are always men and women ready to worship the beast within. There are those who say he did this to himself, quite deliberately, to free his needs and appetites from the tyranny of reason."

"How very depressing," said Lilith. "From all the thousands who spilled from my fecund loins, only three remain? And all of you so much less than I made you to be."

She killed them all, contemptuously, sucking in their life energies, then murdered all of the Incarnate's child followers with a casual wave of her hand, just to be thorough. Her power beat on the air like a storm that sweeps all before it, and the assembled crowd quailed under her cold gaze.

"It's time," said Lilith, and all those present shuddered at the power in her voice. "Time for you to choose which side you're on. I'm back, ready to remake the Nightside in my own image, to restore it to what I originally intended it to be. It was never meant to be this . . . small, shabby thing. I will make the Nightside glorious again, and you with it. Unless you choose to stand against me, in which case no-one will even remember your names."

Beings and Forces and Powers glanced at each other uneasily, and there was much muttered conversation. The main gist of it was that they liked things the way they were. They liked being gods, being worshipped and feared and adored. They liked being rich and famous and revered. (And if these were all very human things for a god to value, no-one said so.) Give all this up, to see their world and their very selves remade according to Lilith's whim? Unthinkable. And yet . . . she was Lilith. No-one doubted that. Greater than the Nightside and destroyer of those who only thought themselves to be gods. In the name of survival, it might be wise to go along . . . for a while . . . and hope some opportunity might arise where they could rid themselves again of this unwanted matriarch. And so the argument went this way and that, while Lilith waited patiently, amusing herself by killing people at random if they didn't look respectful enough. And in the end, it was left to one of the more modern manifestations, Abomination Inc, to step forward and speak first.

Ever since the law decided that corporations were, technically speaking, both persons and immortal, it was inevitable that one would grow large and powerful enough to be worshipped as a god. Abomination Inc manifested itself through a crowd of faceless worker drones, all dressed exactly the same. Grey men in grey suits, they spoke in chorus.

"We are a god of this time. It suits us, and we are suited to it. Why should we give up all that we are, and that we intend to be? We have no reason to believe that you have our best interests at heart."

Next up were the Little Sisters of the Immaculate Chain-saw. Terrifying figures in stark black and white, these nuns were dogmatists first and foremost, and modern dogmatists at that. They cursed and abused Lilith in rich, vibrant voices and defied her with awful threats.

Others stepped forward, representing the modern religions of a modern world, but already other voices were rising in the crowd to shout them down. Older voices, remembering old ways, and lesser voices seeing hope in a changed future. And so, just like that, the god war started.

Beings and Forces and Powers went head to head, aspects clashing like mighty engines in the night, while strange energies boiled on the still air. And as above, so below, with whole armies of the faithful going for each other's throats. Hot and vicious murder ran up and down the Street of the Gods, sucking everyone in, and bodies piled up as blood flowed thickly in the gutters.

Lilith rose gracefully into the starry sky, looking down upon what she had brought about, and laughed aloud to see such slaughter done in her name. She encouraged those of her children who followed her to kill their brothers and sisters who didn't, and encouraged their followers to fight and riot and delight in the death of their enemies. She wanted them to get a taste for it. There would be much more of this, when they went out into the Nightside. But for now, murdering their fellows would help to bind the survivors more closely to her.

She walked in glory down the Street of the Gods, treading the air high above the conflict that surged back and forth, while lesser beings raged beneath her. Wherever she passed, churches and temples and cathedrals juddered and shook themselves to pieces, and were swallowed up by the ground breaking apart beneath them. Lilith was sending them all to Hell, by the direct route. Gods and followers caught within these sanctuaries, too scared to come out and face Lilith, died screaming.

"There shall be no other gods but me," said Lilith, her voice rising effortlessly above the roars and screams and howls of the violence below. "All who live in the Nightside shall worship only me. This is my place, and I am all you need to know."

And that was when Walker showed up. He came strolling casually down the Street of the Gods, in his smart city suit, and everything slowed to a halt as word of his progress went ahead of him. People and Beings stopped fighting, backing away from each other and from him. They withdrew to the sidewalks and watched silently as he passed by, not even acknowledging their presence. Beings and Forces and Powers stopped doing distressing things to each other and stood still, waiting to see what would happen. A slow sullen silence fell across the bloody Street, and the god war stopped. All of this, simply because Walker had come to the Street of the Gods.

He brought no backup with him, no bodyguards, specialised operatives, or armed forces. His presence was enough to calm and intimidate all those around him. Gods and their followers looked sheepishly at the destruction they'd wrought, like children caught in the act of doing something naughty. Because this was Walker, the Voice of the Authorities, whose word was law. The single most implacable force in the Nightside. He finally came to a halt, looking up at Lilith standing on the air. They considered each other for a while, then Walker smiled and tipped his bowler hat to her. Walker had style. Lilith dropped elegantly down to stand on the bloody Street before him, and if he was aware of her nakedness or the sexuality that burned in her like a furnace, he gave no sign of it. He looked around at the scattered bodies, the burning churches, then at the watching gods and their followers, none of whom could meet his gaze.

"That's quite enough of that," he said crisply, not looking at anyone in particular, though everyone just knew he was talking to them. "Never seen such a mess. You will stop this nonsense immediately and start clearing up. You wouldn't want me to get upset, would you?"

Some of the gods and their congregations were already backing away, muttering excuses and apologies, and in some cases actually trying to hide behind each other. They all knew the names and legends of those poor unfortunates who'd upset Walker in the past, and the terrible things that had happened to them. But all that stopped as Lilith addressed Walker in a loud and carrying voice that had not the slightest trace of fear or unease in it. If anything, she seemed . . . amused.

"Dear Henry, so good to see you again. You've come such a long way, since we last met."

Walker raised an elegant eyebrow. "You have the advantage of me, madam. I seem to recognise the voice, but . . ."

"Oh Henry, have you forgotten your dear little Fennella Davis so soon?" said Lilith, and Walker actually caught his breath, as though he'd been hit.

"So . . ." he said finally. "Lilith. This is what you really look like."

Lilith laughed, shaking her head a little coquettishly. "This . . . is as much of me as human senses can stand. You must remember that the whole Eden thing is just a parable. Really, this body is something I use to walk around in, in your limited world. Once I have refashioned the Nightside into something more suited to my needs and nature, I will bring all of myself here, and I will be glorious indeed."

"What are you?" said Walker. "I mean, what are you, really?"

"I am of the first creation," said Lilith. "I am what came first, long before this world was. I am also Charles Taylor's wife and John Taylor's mother. I am what three foolish boys summoned into the world, unknowingly. Oh dear Henry, am I everything you thought I'd be?"

"Stand where you are," said Walker, and his words thundered on the air. He was using the Voice the Authorities had given him, that could not be denied by the living or the dead. *"Surrender yourself to me, Lilith, and do no more harm."*

Lilith laughed at him, and the Voice's power shattered on the air like cheap glass. "Don't be silly, Henry. Your Voice was only ever designed to work on the things of this world, and I am so much more than that. Run away, dear Henry, and hide until I come for you. I have a special reward in mind for you. You will worship me, and love me, and I will make you immortal in some more pleasing shape, so that you can sing my praises for all eternity. Won't that be fun?"

"I'd rather die," said Walker.

Lilith slapped him aside contemptuously, and her slender pale arm hit him like a battering ram. His bones broke under the force of the blow, and blood flew on the air as he flew backwards, crashing into the wall of a half-buried church. He fell to the ground like a broken doll, and the church wall collapsed on top of him. The gods and their worshippers watched the rubble settle, then watched some more, but Walker, who could have called down armies from both Church and State with but a word, did not emerge.

The god war was over. Everyone had seen the Authorities' Voice crushed and broken in a moment, his power brushed aside like an annoying insect, and that was enough for them. They knelt and bowed their heads to Lilith, then joined up behind her as she led her army in triumph down the Street of the Gods and out into the Nightside.

Not long after that, I finally turned up, with Shotgun Suzie, Razor Eddie, and Sandra Chance. The Street was a mess, with ruined buildings to every side, unattended fires sending up thick black smoke that stank of incense, and the dead and the dying lying ignored. The survivors and the walking wounded stumbled this way and that, deep in shock, only left behind because they were too damaged to be of use. It said something for Razor Eddie's reputation that broken, dazed, and defeated as they were, many of them took one look at Eddie and started running. Rather more unsettlingly, a whole lot more took one look at me and came forward to kneel before me, praising me as Lilith's son and calling on me for mercy and deliverance.

"All right," said Suzie, curling her upper lip. "This is seriously freaking me out."

"You're not alone," I said. "You! Let go of my leg, right now."

"No-one ever kneels to me," said Suzie. "You there! Yes, you, stop shaking and tell us what the hell happened here."

It took a while, but we finally got the story out of them. Lilith had made her triumphant return to the Nightside, and I'd missed it. The shivering wrecks before us made it very clear that Mommie Dearest was looking for me. And not necessarily in a good way. It seemed she had some special purpose in mind for her only begotten child.

"Tough," I said. "I don't happen to feel like obliging her. At least, not yet. When we finally do meet, I want it to be on my terms, on my home ground."

By now, word of my arrival had spread up and down the Street of the Gods, and a mob of ragged people formed around us, half out of their minds with fear and anger, crying out *Blasphemer!* and *Drag him down!* and *Take him to Lilith!* Suzie and Eddie and Sandra moved in close beside me, but the mob didn't even see them. There were hundreds of them now, with more coming, faces twisted with hate and loathing, reaching out for me with clawed hands. They surged forward from all sides, and before I could say anything, Suzie opened up with her pump-action shotgun, blowing great holes in the advancing ranks. They kept coming. Razor Eddie cut a bloody path through them, moving too fast for the human eye to follow. Then Sandra Chance raised the bodies of the fallen dead to attack the living, and that was too much for the mob. The crowd broke apart and quickly dispersed, scattering in all directions, leaving the dead and dying behind. I couldn't feel angry at them. None of this was their fault, really. It was just that my mother made such a powerful impression on people. Suzie lowered her shotgun and reloaded. Eddie reappeared at my side, his razor dripping blood. Sandra let the dead lie down again. A shivering acolyte in an Aztec feathered headdress approached her timidly.

"If you can raise the dead, could you perhaps . . . ?"

"Sorry, no," said Sandra Chance. "Raising dead gods is beyond me. Besides, if he stays dead, he probably wasn't much of a god to begin with, was he?"

The acolyte burst into tears, and we left him sitting there on the shattered steps of what had once been his temple.

"Ms. Tact," said Suzie, to Sandra.

"You'd know," said Sandra.

"Where's Walker?" said Eddie. "I don't see a body anywhere, and you know what they say in the Nightside—if you don't see a body, they're almost certainly not dead."

"I think I can help you there," said a sad-eyed priest. "You'll find him over there, under what's left of my church."

We thanked him and approached the remains of what might once have been a pretty impressive edifice. Half of it was still on fire, burning sullenly in the still night air. In the end, we had to dig through a pile of rubble, hauling it away brick by brick, to uncover Walker. His suit was tattered and torn and soaked with blood, but he still opened his eyes the moment I leaned over him. He even managed a small smile.

"John," he said faintly. "Late, as usual. I've been having a few words with your mother."

"So I see," I said. "You can't get on with anyone, can you?"

We dug him out, and sat him up with his back against a wall. He never made a sound the whole time. Suzie checked him over with brisk efficiency. Suzie knows a lot about wounds, from both ends. Eventually she stood back and nodded to me.

"He's damaged, but he'll live."

"Oh good," said Walker. "For a while there, I was almost worried."

"You should be," said Sandra Chance. "You trapped us all in the cemetery dimension and left us there to die. We had an agreement, and you broke it. No-one does that to me and lives."

"You can't kill him now," I said.

"Why not?" said Sandra, turning the full force of her cold, angry gaze upon me. I looked back at her steadily.

"Because he was my father's friend. Because I don't kill in cold blood. And because I have a use for him."

"Practical as ever, John," said Walker.

Sandra frowned. "This plan. Will he like it?"

"Almost definitely not."

"Then I'll wait," said Sandra Chance.

I crouched down before Walker so I could look right into his face. "She's back," I said. "Lilith. My mother. Back to tear down the Nightside and replace it with something that will have no room in it for Humanity. And if I try to stop her, just maybe she'll bring down the whole world. I can't do this alone, Walker. I need your help."

He smiled briefly. "We're finally on the same wavelength. Pity it took such dire straits to bring us together."

"Don't kid yourself," I said. "All we have in common is a mutual enemy."

"Yes. Someone who's worse than either of us."

"You should know," I said. "You brought her here, through the Babalon Working. You, and the Collector, and my father."

"Ah," said Walker. "So you worked it out, finally. I was beginning to think you were a bit slow. You'll have all the support I can raise from the Authorities, but it'll take more than an army of warm bodies and everyday magics to stop Lilith."

"I have a few old friends and allies in mind," I said. "And a plan I can practically guarantee no-one's going to like." I turned to Suzie. "Take Sandra and Eddie and get Walker back to Strangefellows. Alex can fix him up, but make sure he doesn't try to put it on my tab. Then you wait there, till I get back."

"Hell with that," Suzie said immediately. "Wherever you're going, you'll need me to watch your back."

"Not this time," I said gently. "I need you with the others. You're the only one I can trust. And besides . . . I don't want you to see some of the things I might have to do."

She smiled briefly. "You pick the damnedest times to worry about my feelings, John."

"Somebody has to," I said.

FOUR

Not Fade Away

How do you take down an army of ex-gods? Well, when the living can't help you, start with the dead. I left the Street of the Gods by one of the less-travelled exits and made my way through the crowded streets of the Nightside, heading for Uptown, where they keep all the really weird clubs. I was looking for Dead Boy, and I didn't have a lot of time. Given the sheer size and scope of the Nightside, it would take even Lilith and her army quite a while to make any real impression, but the news would start to spread soon enough. Bad news always does.

The night air was crisp and clear, the pavements were slick from a recent rain, and the scene was jumping, like always. There might be rumours of riot and mayhem and imminent apocalypse, but that was simply business as usual in the Nightside. Especially at weekends. And yet . . . I sensed a growing jittery feeling among people I passed, a sense of nervous anticipation, even if no-one seemed too sure about what. I fought down an urge to hurry, not wanting to attract attention to myself. I had time. Even with Walker taken out of the picture, the Authorities would still be able to throw whole armies into Lilith's path, armed with guns and blades and magics and all the usual nasty surprises. They'd slow her down. For a while.

People around me kept glancing up at the night sky, as though half-expecting the stars to have changed position, or the oversized full moon to have turned bloodred. Something new and dangerous had come into the Nightside, and they could all sense it, like cattle approaching a slaughterhouse. Everyone seemed sharper and almost spookily alert, and the intensity of the night moved up another notch.

Striding back and forth outside the ever-welcoming doors of disreputable clubs, the barkers hawked their wares with a new urgency, while on every street corner the come-ons from the scarlet lips of the twilight daughters was a little bit more aggressive. Tides of people surged this way and that, the casual stroll giving way to the determined march, as though the punters were afraid that what they were looking for might not be there when they got there. A new Special Edition of the Nightside's only daily paper, the *Night Times*, was just hitting the streets, and people crowded round the news vendors, almost snatching the papers out of their hands, then chattering animatedly over the heavy black headlines. I had no doubt that Lilith had made the front page, and probably most of the other pages, too. I needed to get my plan up and running before everything started falling apart. And for that, I needed Dead Boy.

It wasn't hard to find the lap-dancing club where he was working as a bouncer. Bit of a come-down, for the Nightside's most eminent vigilante, dark avenger, and first line of defence against the legions of the dead, but presumably there were fringe benefits. I stopped before the club and studied it carefully from what I hoped was a safe distance. The flashing neon sign over the gaping door spelled out the club's name, NOT FADE AWAY, in colours so bright and garish they practically stabbed into my eyes. To either side were neon figures of dancing girls, jiggling eternally from one uncomfortable-looking position to another, back and forth, back and forth. A grubby window held photographs of the glamorous girls one could hope to find inside the club, though experience led me to believe the girls actually on display would look nothing like the photos.

The barker lounging by the door inhabited a brightly coloured check coat, with a revolving bow tie and a grin so fixed it bordered on the unnatural. He'd started out life as a ventriloquist's dummy, and never really got over it. Seeing my interest he fixed me with his brightly shining eyes and launched into his spiel.

"They're dead, they're naked, and they dance!"

I fixed him with my best cold stare. "Do I look like a tourist?"

He sneered and moved away from the door, waving me in. I passed him by with as much dignity as was possible under the circumstances. Inside the lap-dancing club, someone tried to take my coat, and I punched him out. Start as you mean to go on . . . The transition from chilly night to sweltering lounge was abrupt, and I stopped inside the main area to get my bearings. The management kept the lights down to a comforting gloom, partly to give the punters a sense of privacy, but mostly so you wouldn't get too good a look at the rest of the clientele. The air was thick with all kinds of smoke, and rank with the stink of sweat and desire and desperation. There were ratty-looking tables and chairs for the scattered audience, and cheap plywood booths at the back for more private encounters. The customers were mostly men, mostly human, their eyes fixed hungrily on the four separate spotlighted stages where the dancers swayed back and forth to the over-amplified music.

There were girls, up on the stages and in and among

the audience, showing off what they'd got and what they could do, all of them naked, all of them dead. The spirits of departed women, condemned to wander the Earth for this reason or that, lap-dancing for the living. Some seemed completely real and solid, while others were only wisps of smoke or mist, tinted all of the colours of the rainbow by the coloured gels rotating in front of the stage lights. Most of the girls drifted from one state to the other and back again, as they stamped and spun and shook their breasts, pumping their hips and curling around the steel poles on the stages, all the time favouring the nearest customers with wide smiles that meant nothing, nothing at all. Ghostly girls, the dancing dead—the ultimate look but don't touch.

There was a tacky-looking bar set to one side, and leaning up against it, the legendary Dead Boy himself. Technically speaking, he wasn't old enough to be in a club like this. Dead Boy was seventeen, and had been for some thirty years, ever since he was murdered—clubbed down in the street for his credit cards and mobile phone. He came back from the dead, after making a deal with someone he still preferred not to name, and took a terrible vengeance on his killers, only to find that his deal made it impossible for him to go to his rest afterwards. And so he walks the Nightside, forever young, forever damned, his spirit possessing his own dead body, doing good deeds in the hope that eventually he'll accumulate enough goodwill in Heaven to break the terms of the deal he made.

He was tall and adolescent thin, wrapped in a dark purple greatcoat, over black leather trousers and tall calf-skin boots. He wore a black rose on one lapel and a large floppy black hat perched on the back of his head. His coat hung open, revealing a corpse-pale torso held together with stitches and staples and duct tape. He doesn't feel pain any more, but he can still take damage. If I looked closely I could see the bullet hole in his forehead that he'd filled in with builder's putty.

His long white face had a weary, debauched look, with burning fever-bright eyes and a pouting sulky mouth with no colour in it. He had experimented with makeup, but mostly he just couldn't be bothered. Long dark hair fell to his shoulders in oiled ringlets. He looked calm, casual, even bored. He was drinking whiskey straight from the bottle and eating Neapolitan ice cream straight from the tub. He nodded easily as I came over to join him.

"Hello, Taylor," he said indistinctly, around a mouthful of ice cream. "Pardon my indulgence, but when you're dead you have to take your pleasures where you can find them. I'd offer you a drink, but I've only got the one bottle. And don't order anything from the bar—their prices are appalling, and the drinks are worse."

I nodded. I already knew that. I'd been here once before, working a case, and had allowed myself to be persuaded to order what passed for champagne. It tasted like cherry cola. Nothing was what it seemed here. Even the waitress had an Adam's apple.

"So you're the bouncer?" I said, leaning easily back against the bar beside him.

"I run security here," he corrected me. "I keep an eye on things. Most of the punters take one look at me, and know better than to start anything."

"I thought you had a steady gig, body-guarding that singer, Rossignol?"

He shrugged. "She's off touring Europe. And I . . . prefer not to leave the Nightside. This job's just temporary, until I can scare something else up. Even the dead have to earn a living. Hence the girls here."

I nodded. The Nightside accumulates more than its fair share of ghosts and revenants, one way and another, and they all have to go somewhere.

"Where do the girls go, when they're not working?" I asked.

Dead Boy gave me a pitying look. "They're *always* working. That's the point. It's not like they ever get tired . . ."

"What do the girls get out of this? The money can't be that good."

"It isn't. But a clever girl can make a lot from tips, and the management guarantees to keep the girls safe from necromancers, plus all the other unsavoury types who use the energies of the departed to fuel their magics. And of course all the girls hope to hook an appreciative customer, turn him into a regular, and milk him for all he's worth."

I looked out over the widely spread audience. "Anyone interesting in tonight?"

"A few names, a few faces, no-one you'd know and no-one worth noting. Though we do have several diminutive professors, who claim they're here researching modern slang. They loved it when I told them this club was licensed to dispense *spirits* . . ."

I smiled dutifully. Dead Boy shrugged and took a good slug from his bottle. It was nearly empty.

I watched the ghost girls dance. Putting off the moment when I'd have to tell Dead Boy why I was there. They were currently spinning and gyrating to an old Duran Duran number, "Girls on Film," and being ghosts they were all supernaturally beautiful, impossible lithe, and utterly glamorous. They danced with implacable grace, stamping their bare feet and jiggling their oversized breasts, rising from the stages to slide and sweep through the smoky air. Those in and among the audience drifted around and sometimes even through the customers, giving them a thrill they wouldn't find anywhere else. And why not? The steel poles were the only truly solid things on those stages.

"Don't get tempted," said Dead Boy, putting down his empty bottle and scraped-clean ice cream tub. "It's all just a glamour. You wouldn't want to see what they really look like when they drop their illusions between sets. Unfortunately, being dead I always see them as they really are, which takes a lot of the fun out of this job."

One girl swayed deliciously down from her stage,

seemingly completely solid, until she extended one finger to a chosen customer, and he breathed it in, inhaling it like cigar smoke. The girl's hand unravelled, disappearing into his mouth and nostrils, until he couldn't take any more, and let it all back out again in coughs and snorts. The girl giggled as her hand reassembled. Up on one of the stages, a girl suddenly caught fire but kept dancing, unconsumed.

"An old flame of mine," Dead Boy said solemnly.

There are quite a few clubs in Uptown that cater to the various forms of death fetish, from mummification to premature burial, and some places that would freak out even hard-core Goths; clubs like Peaceful Repose, where you can try out being dead for a while to see what it feels like. Or the brothel where you can pay to have sex with female vampires, ghouls, and zombies. There are always those who like their meat cold, with the taste of formaldehyde on their lips . . .

I said as much to Dead Boy, who only showed any interest when I got to the brothel. He actually got out a notebook and pencil for the address.

"Trust me," I said firmly. "You really don't want to go there. You'll end up with worms."

And then one of the ghost dancers caught my attention, as she beckoned coyly to a customer and led him, half-walking and half-swaying, across the gloomy club to one of the private booths at the rear. The customer was tall and skinny, with a furtive air about him. The two of them disappeared into a booth and shut the door firmly behind them. I turned to Dead Boy.

"All right, what's the point of that? I mean, if she's not solid enough to touch . . ."

"Love always finds a way," said Dead Boy. "Instead of an exchange of fluids, an exchange of energies. All purely consensual, of course. The ghost girl absorbs a little of the customer's life energy, which I'm told feels very nice, and she becomes a little more solid, so she can . . . take care of him. A benefit to both sides. The more life energies a girl collects, the more solid and real she can become. Theoretically, she could even become alive again . . . Sometimes the girls go too far and drain the customer dry. Then we end up with a really pissed off customer ghost haunting the place and acting up dead cranky. Management keeps an exorcism service on speed dial for just such occurrences . . ."

The door to the private booth opened, and the customer came out again. He hadn't been in there long. And when he'd gone in he'd been skinny as a whip, but now he was noticeably overweight, with an extensive bulging belly. Dead Boy cursed briefly and pushed himself away from the bar.

"What is it?" I said.

"The bastard's a soul thief," Dead Boy said curtly. "He's *inhaled* the ghost girl, every last smoky bit of her, and now he's containing her inside himself, hoping to smuggle her out. Let's go."

We headed purposefully across the floor, and the punters hurried to get out of our way. The fat man saw Dead Boy coming, pulled an intricate glass charm out of his pocket, and threw it on the floor. The glass shattered, releasing the pre-prepared spell, and Dead Boy stopped as though he'd run into an invisible wall, his colourless face twisted in a pained grimace.

"It's an antipossession spell," he grunted. "Trying to force me out of my body. Stop the bastard, John. Don't let him get away with the girl."

I hurried forward to block the fat man's way. He stopped, studied me cautiously, and reached into his pocket again. I fired up my gift just long enough to locate the spell he was using to contain the ghost within him and ripped it away. I shut down my gift as the fat man convulsed, staggering back and forth as his imposing stomach bulged and rippled like a sheet in the wind. I got behind him, grabbed him in a bear hug, and squeezed with all my strength. Thick streams of smoke came pouring out of his mouth and nostrils, quickly forming into the ghost girl. The bulging stomach flattened under my grip, and the ghost girl stood fuming before us. She solidified one leg just long enough to kick the soul thief really hard in the nuts, then she stalked away. I let go of the soul thief, and he collapsed to the floor, looking very much as though he wished he was dead.

I left him there and went back to Dead Boy, who was looking much better.

"Cheap piece of rubbish spell," he said cheerfully. "Almost an insult, expecting something like that to take me out. My soul was put back by an expert. Leave the soul thief to me, John. I'll arrange for something suitably humiliating and nasty to happen to him."

We strolled back to the bar, where the barmaid had a fresh bottle of whiskey waiting for Dead Boy. He reached for it, then hesitated, and gave me a long, considering look.

"You didn't come here just to inquire after my non-existent health, Taylor. What do you want with me?"

"I need your help. My mother is finally back, and the shit is hitting the fan in no uncertain manner."

"Why is it people only ever come to me when they want something?" Dead Boy said wistfully. "And usually only after everything's already gone to Hell and worse?"

"I think you just answered your own question," I said. "That's what you get, for being such a great back-stop."

"Give me the details," said Dead Boy.

I gave him the edited version, but even so he winced several times, and by the end he was shaking his head firmly.

" No. No way. I do not get involved with Old Testament forces. They are too hard-core, even for me."

"I need your help."

"Tough."

"You have to help me, Dead Boy."

"No I bloody don't. I don't have to do anything I don't want to. Being dead is very liberating that way."

"My mother is leading an army of Beings from the Street of the Gods. She has to be stopped."

"Good luck with that, John. Do send me a postcard as to how you got on. I'll be in the Arctic. Hiding under a polar bear."

"I have a plan . . ."

"You always do! The answer's still no. I do not go up against gods. I know my limitations."

I fixed him with my best cold stare. "If you're not with us, you're against us. Against me."

"You'd really threaten an old friend, John?"

"If you were really a friend, I wouldn't have to threaten you."

"Dammit, John," he said quietly. "Don't do this to me. I can't afford to have my body destroyed, and lose my grip on this world. Not with what's waiting for me . . ."

"If Lilith isn't stopped, the Hell she'll make of the Nightside will be just as bad."

"You're a real piece of work, Taylor, you know that? All right, I'm in. But I know I'm going to regret this."

"That's the spirit," I said.

"You're not even safe being dead, these days," Dead Boy said mournfully.

FIVE

Down in Dingley Dell

"So," said Dead Boy, "you've definitely got a plan?"

"Oh yes."

"But you're not going to tell me what it is?"

"It would only upset you."

"Can you at least tell me where we're going?"

"If you like, but . . ."

"I won't like that either?"

"Probably not."

"If I wasn't already dead, I think I'd probably be very depressed."

I had to laugh. It felt good to have something to laugh about. We were walking through one of the less salubrious areas of the Nightside, where the neon signs fell away like uninvited guests at the feast, and even working street-lamps were few and far between. We had come to Rotten Row, and the people who lived there liked it dark. We'd been walking for a while, and even though Dead

Boy couldn't get tired, he could get bored, and downright cranky about it. He'd wanted to use his famous futuristic car, the gleaming silver sensation that drove itself out of a Timeslip from some possible future, and adopted Dead Boy as its driver. But I had to work on the assumption that Lilith had agents everywhere now, and they'd be bound to recognise such a distinctive car. And they might well have orders to attack it on sight, just in case Dead Boy was giving his old friend a lift. Nothing like having a Biblical myth for a mother to make you really paranoid. I wasn't ready for a direct confrontation with Lilith's people. Not yet. So Dead Boy and I walked together through increasingly dark and dingy back streets, in search of that great Victorian Adventurer, Julien Advent.

I'd already phoned the main offices of the *Night Times*, and the deputy editor had reluctantly confirmed that Julien wasn't there. He might be the paper's editor and owner now, but Julien still remembered the days when he'd been the Nightside's leading investigative journalist. So every now and again he'd disappear for a few days on a personal assignment, without telling anyone where he was going. No-one could say anything because he always came back with one hell of a story. Julien did like to keep his hand in, and assure himself he was still an Adventurer at heart.

The deputy editor actually asked me if I knew where Julien was, because the whole paper was going crazy without him, trying to cover the huge story breaking on the Street of the Gods. Did I happen to know anything about what happened on the Street of the Gods? I admitted that I might know a thing or two, but that I would only talk to Julien. The deputy editor tried threats, insults, and bursting into tears before finally giving up on me and admitting that while Julien had turned off his mobile phone and pager, so he couldn't be traced, he had been heard asking questions about some of the nastier sweatshops still operating in the Nightside.

And so Dead Boy and I had walked to the extremely

low-rent district that was Rotten Row. There were fewer and fewer people around, and those on view had a distinctly furtive air about them. There were the homeless and beggars, ragged men in ragged clothes, with outstretched grimy hands and ripped paper cups for small change. There were things that stayed in the shadows so you couldn't get a good look at them—possessed animals with glowing eyes and cancerous faces, and half-breed demons offering to sell you their bodies or blood or urine. Plus any number of hard-faced working girls with dead eyes, rent boys with scarlet lips, and speed freaks in alleyways ready to sell you any drug you had ever heard of. And darker things still, offering darker services.

Rotten Row, where dreams go to die, hope is a curse, and death is sometimes the kindest thing that can happen to you.

Long rows of dilapidated tenement buildings crouched sullenly on either side of a rubbish-strewn street. Half the street-lamps had been smashed, and sulphurous steam drifted up out of rusted metal grilles in the pavement. The tenement walls were stained black with soot and pollution and accumulated grime. Graffiti in a dozen languages, not all of them human, sometimes daubed in dried blood. Windows boarded up or covered over with brittle paper. Doors with hidden protections that would only open to the right muttered words. And inside every dark and overcrowded room in those ancient tenements, sweatshop businesses where really low-paid piece work was performed by people who couldn't find work anywhere else. Or had good reason to stay hidden, off the books. The sweatshop owners took advantage of these desperate people, in return for "protecting" them. The sad part was that there was never any shortage of desperate people, ready and willing to be "protected." The Nightside can be very dark, when it chooses.

Grim-faced enforcers sauntered casually out of alleyways and side streets to make their presence known to us. Dressed up as dandified gangsters, they wore guns and knives openly, and a few even had ideograms tattooed on their faces, marking them as low-rank combat magicians. Some had dogs with them, on reinforced steel chains. Seriously big dogs, with bad attitudes. Dead Boy and I strolled openly down the middle of the street, letting the enforcers get a good look at us. The dogs were the first to realise. They got one whiff of Dead Boy, and backed away whining and cringing. Their owners took one look at me and started backing away themselves. The enforcers huddled together in tight little groups, muttering urgently, then pushed one of their number forward to meet us.

He affected a nonchalant swagger that fooled no-one, least of all him, and finally came to a halt a more-than-respectable distance away. Dead Boy and I stopped and considered him thoughtfully. He was wearing a smart pin-striped suit, white spats, and a grey fedora. He had twin pearl-handled revolvers on his hips, and a pencil moustache on his scarred face. He gave us each a hard look, which he might have pulled off if he hadn't been sweating so profusely.

And on a cold night, too.

"You here to cause trouble?" he said, in a voice so deep he must have had a third testicle tucked away somewhere.

"Almost certainly," I said.

"Right, lads!" said the enforcer, glancing back over his shoulder to address the rest of the street. "Pick up your feet, we are out of here. This is Dead Boy *and* John bloody Taylor, and we are not being paid nearly enough to take on the likes of them. Everybody round to Greasy Joan's café, where we will wait out whatever appalling things are about to happen."

"You've heard of us," said Dead Boy, sounding just a little disappointed.

"Too bloody right, squire. I signed on for security work and a little light brutality. Nothing was ever said about having to face living legends and death on two legs."

Behind him, the rest of the enforcers were rapidly melting away and disappearing into the distance at something only a little less than a dead run. I looked thoughtfully at the man standing before us, and his left eye developed a distinct twitch.

"You seem to have a lot of influence over your fellow thugs," I said. "Who are you, exactly?"

"Union representative, squire. I look out for my boys, make sure they've all got health insurance, and I'd really like to run away after them, if that's all right with you."

I'd barely finished nodding before he'd turned and hurried away. There's a lot to be said for a good, or more properly bad, reputation. One young enforcer was still standing in the middle of the street, looking a bit bewildered. He yelled after his union rep, who didn't even look back.

"Hell with this shit," snarled the young punk, sounding actually outraged. "We're supposed to be hard men! Spreading fear with a glance and crushing all opposition! We don't turn and run when a couple of serious faces turn up!"

"He's young," said a voice from the shadows of a very dark alley. "Doesn't know anything. Please don't kill him. His mother would give me hell."

The young enforcer went for the gun on his hip, but Dead Boy was already moving. Being dead, his body wasn't limited to normal human reaction times. He darted forward impossibly quickly, closing the distance between himself and the young enforcer in a moment. The punk actually got off two shots, and Dead Boy dodged both of them. He crashed into the young enforcer, ripped the gun out of his hand, and head-butted him in the face. He then examined the gun while the young man crumpled to the floor, before finally throwing it aside.

"I take it there won't be any more opposition?" I said, to the general surroundings.

"Not from us," said the voice from the shadows. "You do whatever you feel like doing, sir."

"Thank you," I said. "We will."

I gathered up Dead Boy, and we continued down the street. There wasn't a single soul to be seen anywhere, but I had no doubt we were still being surreptitiously observed. I raised my gift, opening up the inner eye in my mind, my private eye, to locate exactly where Julien Advent was hiding himself in all this hostile territory. I kept my Sight narrowed down to just the task at hand. I really didn't want to See the kind of dark forces that moved unseen in a place like Rotten Row. I was also concerned that I'd recently been using my gift too much. My Enemies were always looking, to send their horror troops after me. I found Julien almost immediately, observing a firm called Dingley Dell from a place of concealment in a tenement building only a little further down the street. I shut down my gift, checked that all my mental barriers and safeguards were securely in place, and told Dead Boy what I'd learned.

"You are seriously spooky sometimes, you know that, John?" he said. "The way you *know* things. Still, I wouldn't worry too much about these Enemies of yours. They probably won't be able to locate you at all, what with Lilith and her pals on the rampage, jamming the mental aether."

We walked on a while in silence. *"Jamming the mental aether?"* I said finally. "What the hell does that mean?"

"I don't know," said Dead Boy. "But you have to admit, it sounded really good there for a moment. Now then, Dingley Dell . . . Sounds almost unbearably twee. Probably makes lace doilies, or something . . ."

We came to a halt before the right building and studied the small cards tacked to the doorframe, beside the row of buzzers. The cards looked decidedly temporary, as though they had a tendency to change on a regular basis. The current occupiers of the three-storey building were Alf's Button Emporium, Matchstick Girls, Miss

Snavely's Fashion House, Shrike Shoes, the Stuffed Fish Company, and Dingley Dell.

"Top floor," Dead Boy said disgustedly. "Why do they always have to be on the top floor? And how are we supposed to get all the way up there, past all the other businesses, without anyone noticing us?"

"Firstly, it's only three floors we're talking about," I said. "Undoubtedly because this entire shit heap would have collapsed if anyone had added a fourth floor. And secondly, while I doubt very much that a dump like this has a fire escape, you can bet good money that there's a concealed exit round the back so company executives can make a swift departure unobserved if their creditors turn up unexpectedly. So, round the back."

We made our way down a narrow side alley almost choked with garbage and general filth, and a couple of sleeping forms who didn't even stir when we stepped over them. I found the back door without having to raise my gift again because it was exactly where I would have put it. (Having had occasion to dodge a few creditors myself, in my time.) Dead Boy checked the door out for magical alarms and booby-traps, which didn't take long. He only had to look at them, and they malfunctioned.

"My being dead and alive at the same time confuses them," he said happily.

"It's always confused me," I agreed.

Dead Boy went to smash the door in, but I restrained him. There could still be purely mechanical alarms in place that we hadn't spotted, and I didn't want to risk attracting attention and perhaps blowing Julien Advent's stakeout. So I raised my gift for a moment, located the right spot on the door, directly above the lock, and hit it once with the heel of my hand. The lock disengaged, and the door swung open. Dead Boy averted his gaze so he wouldn't have to see me looking smug, and we entered the tenement, quietly closing the door behind us.

There was hardly any light, and the place stank of poverty and misery and blocked drains. Every expense had been spared in the construction of this building, and everything about it screamed *fire trap*. We moved quietly down the gloomy corridor, alert for any sign that we'd been noticed, but the whole building seemed silent as a tomb. The stairway was so narrow we had to go up in single file, so I let Dead Boy go first, on the grounds that he could take a lot more damage than I. There were any number of magical alarms and booby-traps, but they all blew up in silent puffs of fluorescent smoke, rather than try to deal with Dead Boy's presence. On the second-floor landing a monstrous face formed itself abruptly out of the cracks in the plaster wall, looked at us, mouthed the words *Oh bugger*, and disappeared again.

The next stairway was wide enough for us to walk side by side. I was starting to relax when a wooden step sank just a little too far under Dead Boy's weight, followed by a slight but definite click, and I threw myself flat. A metal shaft shot out of a concealed hole in the wall, passed right over me, and speared Dead Boy through the left arm. He looked down at the spike transfixing his arm, sighed heavily, and carefully pulled his arm free. I got to my feet again, and we studied the metal spike.

"Why did this work when the others didn't?" said Dead Boy.

"Purely mechanical," I said. "Least there's no harm done."

"No harm? This is my good coat! Look at these two holes in the sleeve. Going to cost a small fortune to put those right. I've got this little fellow in Greek Street who does all my repairs (you'd be surprised how many outfits I go through), but they're never the same afterwards. He calls it invisible mending, but I can always see it . . ."

"Do you think you could perhaps lower your voice a tad?" I said, quietly but urgently. "We are supposed to be sneaking in, remember?"

He sniffed sulkily a few times, and we continued up the rickety stairway to the third floor, and along the shadowy passage at the top of the building. Every room we passed was a different business, sub-let presumably, and we caught glimpses of shabby people slaving away, working silently in appalling conditions for nothing remotely like minimum wage. Whole families packed so tightly round rough wooden tables there was hardly any room to move. Fathers and mothers and children, all working intently in dim light in rooms with windows that wouldn't open, making goods for pennies that would sell for pounds to their betters. None of them ever said anything, bent quietly over their work. The overseers might not be visible, but that didn't mean they weren't there. Trouble-makers didn't tend to last long in sweatshops.

I'd never seen such blatant misery before. Capitalism, red in tooth and claw. It was one thing to know that such things still went on and another to see it with your own eyes. I felt like tearing the building down with my bare hands . . . but the sweatshop workers wouldn't thank me for it. They needed the work, needed the lousy money and the protection that went with it, from whoever was looking for them . . . And I couldn't risk blowing Julien Advent's stakeout and getting him angry at me. I was going to need Julien.

Dead Boy really didn't like sneaking around. It wasn't his style. "When am I going to get to hit someone?" he kept asking.

"You'll get your chance," I said. "God, you're like a big kid. You'll be asking if we're nearly there, next."

We finally came to a closed door with a card tacked to it, saying *Dingley Dell*. I tried the door handle, slowly and very carefully, but it was locked. Dead Boy raised a boot to kick it in, and I pulled him away, shaking my head firmly. I listened, one ear pressed against the wood of the door, but I couldn't hear anything. I straightened up, wincing as my back creaked, and looked around. And there at the end of the corridor was a spiral stairway, leading even higher. I led the way up the curving steps, Dead Boy pressing close behind like an impatient dog, and we ended up in a disused gallery, looking down onto the

open room that was Dingley Dell. And there, at the end
of the gallery, was the Timeslipped Victorian Adventurer
himself, Julien Advent.

He was actually wearing his old opera cloak, the
heavy dark material blending him smoothly into the
gallery shadows. Dead Boy and I padded forward as
silently as we could, but he still heard us coming. He
spun round, ready to fight, and only relaxed a little as he
recognised us. He gestured sharply for us to crouch beside him. He was tall, and still lithely muscular despite
his years, with jet-black hair and eyes, and a face handsome as any movie star's; only slightly undermined by
his unswervingly serious gaze and grim smile.

Julien Advent was a hero, the real deal, and it showed.
We'd worked together, on occasion. Sometimes he ap-
proved of me, and sometimes he didn't. It made for an interesting relationship.

"What the hell are you two doing here?" he said, his
voice little more than a murmur. "I put a lot of effort into
getting silently into place here, and remaining unobserved, and now you two clowns . . . How do you know
you haven't tripped off every alarm in the place?"

"Because I saw them all," said Dead Boy. "There's not
much you can hide from the dead."

I looked at the two ragged holes in his coat sleeve, and
sniffed. "You don't half fancy yourself sometimes."

Julien shook his head despairingly, then we all looked
down into the open room of Dingley Dell, while Julien
filled us in as to what was happening, in a voice I had to
strain to hear.

It seemed Dingley Dell was a sweatshop for manufac-
turing magical items. Wishing rings, cloaks of invisibil-
ity, talking mirrors, magic swords, and so on. The usual.
I always wondered where they came from . . . Gathered
around a long trestle table were dozens of small shivering
forms like undernourished children, with big eyes and
pointed ears. Wee faeries no bigger than two-year-olds,
with bitter faces and crumpled wings, all of them looking

half-starved and beaten down. They would pick up some everyday object with their tiny hands and stare at it with fierce concentration until the sweat ran down their pointed faces. They were pouring their own natural magic into the items, making them magical through sheer force of will. As the faeries gave up some of their magic, they became visibly duller and less special. Dying by inches.

Every single one of them was held in place by heavy leg irons, and chains led from the irons to steel rings embedded in the bare floor-boards.

The faeries were refugees from a war in some other dimension, said Julien, fleeing and hiding from something awful: the Hordes of the Adversary. They were desperate not to be found, by anyone. Looking more closely, I could see they all had old scars, and more recent cuts and bruises. They wore rough clothing made from old sacking, with slits cut in the back for their crumpled wings to poke through. Now and again, in a brief look or a movement, I could see a glimpse of how wild and beautiful and charming they had once been.

And even as we watched, one small winged figure gave up the last of its magic and just faded away to nothing. His clothing slowly collapsed in on itself, and the empty leg iron clanked dully against the floor.

I couldn't remember when I'd last been so angry. It burned within me, knotting my stomach and making it hard for me to breathe. "This is sick!" I said fiercely. I actually glared at Julien Advent. "Why are you just sitting here, watching? Why haven't you done something before this?"

"Because I've been considering how best to deal with *that*," said Julien. "That is their overseer—the Beadle."

Dead Boy and I were already looking where he pointed. Emerging from an adjoining kitchen was a huge, hulking figure. He was easily eight feet tall—his head brushing against the ceiling—and his shoulders were broader and more muscular than any human's had a right to be. He was a construct, a patchwork figure of stitched-together human pieces. His only clothing was a collection of broad leather straps, perhaps to help hold him together, or maybe just to give him a feeling of security. He carried a large empty sack in one hand and a roast chicken in the other. He took a great bite out of the chicken breast, and waved the greasy carcass at the faeries, tauntingly.

Two feral children prowled beside him, one to each side, their naked bodies caked in old dried blood and filth. A boy and a girl, they were only ten or eleven years old, but still big enough to scare and intimidate the wee faeries.

"That is one big Beadle," said Dead Boy.

"Quite," said Julien. "I could probably take him, but I didn't want to start something I wasn't sure I could finish. For the sake of the faeries."

The Beadle approached the table, and the faeries all tensed visibly. Some started crying, quietly, hopelessly.

"Now then, have Santa's little helpers been busy, making nice little presents, like they were told to?" said the Beadle, in a harsh, growling voice. "Ho-ho-ho! I see another of you has escaped . . . but not to worry, my little cherubs; there's always fresh meat to replace the old."

He grabbed a handful of the completed magical items piled up in the middle of the table, and started stuffing them carelessly into his sack. One of the faeries wept a little too loudly, and the Beadle turned on it savagely.

"You! What are you snivelling for, you little work-shy?"

"Please sir," said the faerie, in a small, chiming voice. "I'm thirsty, sir."

The Beadle cuffed the faerie lightly across the back of the head, but it was still hard enough to slam the small face onto the table.

"No water for anyone until you've *all* made your quotas! And no food till the end of your shift. You know the rules." He broke off abruptly to examine a glowing dagger he'd just picked up. He sniffed dismissively and broke the blade in two with his bare hands, throwing the no-longer-glowing pieces aside. "Useless! Spoiled! All because *someone* wasn't concentrating! Don't think you can pass off inferior work on me! You all need to buck yourselves up, because the next one of you that doesn't measure up . . . gets fed to my little pets here!"

The feral children grunted and snarled, stamping their bare feet on the bare floor and making playful little darts at the nearest faeries, who cried out and cringed away as far as their leg irons and chains would let them. The feral children laughed soundlessly, like dogs.

"That's it," said Julien Advent, in a calm, quiet and very dangerous voice. "I have seen enough."

He dropped gracefully down from the high gallery, his open cloak spreading out like the dark wings of an avenging angel. He landed lightly before the astonished Beadle, who reared back. The feral children retreated, snarling. Dead Boy jumped down and landed heavily, the floor-boards cracking under the impact. He smiled easily at the Beadle, who threw aside his bag and his roast chicken so he could close his great hands into massive fists. I climbed down from the gallery, taking it one foot hold at a time. I knew my limitations. Julien Advent advanced on the scowling Beadle, and the giant construct actually backed away from the much smaller man, driven back by the incandescent rage in Julien's voice and eyes.

"I thought I'd left the evil of sweatshops behind me, in Victoria's reign. To see such cruelty still thriving in this modern age is an affront to all honourable men. To persecute such innocents, such helpless creatures, in the name of profit is an abomination! It stops now!"

The Beadle stopped backing away, and sneered down at Julien, his deep set eyes suddenly crafty as well as cruel. "I know you, Adamant. Crusading editor, bleeding heart, gentleman adventurer. Moves in all the best circles. But if I were to tell you the names of those who own this little business, and others just like them, I daresay you'd know them. Probably members in good standing of your precious gentlemen's clubs. They know the truth of the

Nightside—that at the end of the day it's all about wealth and power. And what you can get away with."

"I'll deal with them, too, in time," said Julien.

"But you're here now," said the Beadle. "Far away from home, in my territory. And no-one plays by gentlemen's rules here. I am authorised to deal with any and all intruders in whatever way I see fit. So . . . let's see what I can get away with . . ."

He spoke a Word of Power, and the two feral children suddenly changed. Thick fur sprouted out of their bare skins, and their bones creaked loudly as they lengthened. Muzzles full of sharp teeth thrust out of their dirty faces, and in moments the two children were two wolves. The Beadle laughed and urged his pets forward. The faeries cried out hopelessly, cringing away from the slavering wolves, tugging piteously at the steel chains that held them in place. The wolves stalked slowly forward, and Dead Boy went to meet them, drawing two long silver daggers from the tops of his calfskin boots.

"No," I said sharply. "Don't kill them. I think they're as much victims here as the faeries."

Dead Boy glanced back at Julien, then shrugged and stepped back again. He didn't put the silver knives away. I confronted the two wolves, hoping I was right in my assumption. The Beadle had brought about their change with a Word of Power, which suggested the boy and girl weren't natural werewolves, that the change had been enforced upon them. So I fired up my gift and found the spell that controlled the change. Then it was the easiest thing in the world for me to rip the spell away, and just like that two wolves shrank back into two dazed children. Only a boy and a girl again, at last. They could feel they were free, and their feral instincts told them who was responsible. They charged towards me, and I made myself stand my ground. The boy and the girl pressed affectionately against my legs, nuzzling me with their heads and faces, pathetically grateful. The Beadle shouted orders at them, trying his Word again, and they turned and snarled defiantly back at him. I patted them comfortingly on their matted heads, and they settled down again.

Dead Boy and Julien Advent and I turned our full attention to the Beadle. He eyed the only door, but could tell it was too far away. He flexed his great muscles, showing off his size and strength. His fists were bigger than our heads. He sneered at us.

"This changes nothing! You're not big enough to bring me down. Not even together. I will eat your flesh, and crack your bones for the marrow, then I'll stick your severed heads on the railings outside, to show everyone what happens when you mess with the Beadle. And don't think your magics will help you against me. The owners made me proof against all magical attacks."

"Good thing I'm not magic then," said Dead Boy. "Just dead."

He went to meet the Beadle, daggers in hand, and the Beadle turned to run. He'd barely made two steps before Dead Boy was upon him, plunging both his daggers deep into the Beadle's kidneys. The giant cried out horribly and fell to his knees. And Dead Boy cut the Beadle up into his respective original pieces, undoing the work that had first put the huge construct together. The Beadle kicked and screamed for a long time. John and I watched in silence, while the two feral children grinned and stamped their feet approvingly, and the wee winged faeries clapped their tiny hands together in joy and relief.

Dead Boy went about his business as methodically as any butcher, until nothing was left of the Beadle but blood and gore and piles of separated pieces, some of them still twitching. When it was over, and the Beadle's eyes had stopped rolling in his severed head, Julien took the ring of keys from the discarded leather belt and set about freeing the faeries from their leg irons. I helped as best I could. The faeries thanked us tearfully, in voices like the singing of birds. The iron shackles had burned the faeries' skin where they had touched, and even after they were freed the faeries stayed on their wooden benches, huddling together for comfort. One of them looked at Julien and raised an uncertain tiny hand.

"Please, sir, we're hungry."

"No problem!" Dead Boy said cheerfully. He gathered up an armful of body parts and assorted offal, and marched off into the adjoining kitchen. "I know a great recipe for chunky soup!"

Julien looked at me. "Is he serious?"

"Almost certainly," I said. "Fortunately, I've already eaten."

We moved a little away, so we could talk privately. The faeries and the two feral children looked at each other, equally uncertain, but finally the boy moved towards them, one step at a time, and crouched before the nearest faerie. The boy put forward his head to be petted, and after a long moment the faerie reached out a small hand and gently tousled the matted hair. The boy grinned happily, just like a dog, and the girl padded forward to join him. I allowed myself a small breath of relief and gave my full attention to Julien.

"What are we going to do with them?" I said quietly. "All right, we rescued them. Great. But they've still got to live. They can't go back to their own dimension, but they don't have anywhere else to go. And there are things out there in the Nightside that would eat them alive."

"Well," Julien said thoughtfully, "they've got a really good business going here, so why shouldn't they take it over and run it for themselves? Someone has to make all the magic artifacts . . . They could make a comfortable living for themselves. I'm pretty sure the boy and the girl could be retrained as bodyguards. And I'll underwrite the business to begin with and provide the faeries with someone suitable to act as a front, so no-one will know about them."

"That's very kind of you," I said, and I meant it, "but what about all the other sweatshops in this building? What about all the other people slaving away for pennies, in buildings just like this all over the Nightside?"

Julien met my gaze steadily. "I know. There are hundreds of places as bad as this, if not thousands. But one of the first things you learn in the Nightside is that you can't save everyone. You just . . . do what you can, save whom you can, and try to be content with that."

"And what about this business's original owners?" I said. "Won't they kick up a stink about being frozen out of their own business?"

"Not after the piece I'm going to write for the *Times*," said Julien. "I'll change some of the details to protect the faeries, but it will still be fine, loud, incendiary stuff. The owners won't want to be identified with the stink I'm going to generate. May I mention you and Dead Boy by name in my story?"

"I don't mind," Dead Boy said cheerfully, from the kitchen. Something was cooking, and it smelled really good.

"If you think it'll help," I said.

Julien Advent considered me for a long moment. "Maybe I won't mention you, John."

"I quite understand," I said. "Lot of people feel that way about me."

"Why did you come here looking for me?" said Julien.

"Ah," I said. "Now, you're probably not going to like this, Julien, but . . ."

SIX

Guardian Angel

When you're about to do something really risky, or really dumb, or both, it's nearly always a good idea to do it in company. That way, at least you've got someone to hide behind when it all starts going horribly wrong. So, while the freed faeries gathered happily around a huge cauldron brimming over with chunky soup, and the feral boy and girl gnawed meat off oversized bones and cracked them open to get at the marrow, I took Julien Advent to one side, for a quiet word.

"I need to talk with you and Dead Boy, somewhere private."

"Does this concern your cunning plan, the one I'm really not going to like?"

"Got it in one."

"I know just the place."

It turned out that Julien had stumbled across the Beadle's private living quarters while he was exploring the building. He led Dead Boy and me back up onto the gallery, to a concealed door at its end, and through that into a loft conversion. The bare-raftered room turned out to be a lot bigger on the inside than it appeared on the outside, but that's a common spell in the Nightside, where living space is at a premium. The Beadle's living quarters were all hanging drapes and throw cushions, in assorted eye-dazzling colours, along with fresh flowers in tall vases, Andy Warhol prints on the walls, and delicate little china statuettes of wide-eyed kittens.

Dead Boy headed immediately for the rack of wine bottles at the far end of the room, sampled several of them in an experimental sort of way, before finally settling for a thick blue liquor that seethed heavily against the containing glass. Personally, I wouldn't have used it for cleaning combs. Dead Boy took a long drink straight from the bottle, shuddered slightly, then grinned widely.

"It takes a lot to affect you, when you're dead," he said cheerfully. "But this stuff's got a kick like one hundred and twenty per cent embalming fluid."

I wrestled the bottle away from him and put it to one side. "Trust me," I said. "You really don't want to do what I've got in mind while you're drunk."

"I hate it already," said Dead Boy.

We arranged ourselves as comfortably as we could on the embroidered throw cushions, and I explained slowly and carefully just what it was I had in mind. First, I described in some detail the devastated future Nightside I'd seen in the Timeslip. The ruined buildings and the terrible silence, in which the only things moving were swarming mutated insects. Humanity was gone, and all the world was dead and cold. A future that was my fault, somehow. Julien and Dead Boy listened intently, drinking in the details. They'd heard rumours of what I'd seen, most of the Nightside had, but I'd never told anyone the whole story. And even now, I kept a few things to myself. They didn't need to know about the Razor Eddie I found there, the last living man in the world. They didn't need to know I killed him, with his own razor, as a mercy.

Of course, when I finished my story they had to argue with me. They were far too sophisticated to believe in a single, unavoidable future. In Fate, or Destiny.

"There are any number of potential time-lines, possible futures," said Julien, a little condescendingly. "None of them more certain than any other."

"Right," said Dead Boy. "My own car comes from an alternate future that clearly has nothing to do with the one you described."

"Once, that might have been true," I said. "But our future, the future our time-line is heading towards, is getting more certain all the time. I've . . . seen things. Signs, portents, details coming true despite everything I could do to avoid them. According to Old Father Time, the number of possibilities for our time-line is narrowing down, steadily decreasing to only one inevitable future."

"Because of your mother," said Julien.

"Yes," I said. "Because of Lilith. She's such a powerful Being that her mere presence here is enough to overturn the whole apple-cart and rewrite the rules of reality itself."

I let them consider that for a while, then pressed on. They had to understand the background of my thinking, in order to appreciate what I intended to do.

"I have become increasingly convinced," I said slowly, "that the War I'm supposed to start with Lilith and her followers could be the very thing that will bring about the destruction of the Nightside. That we'll tear the world apart, fighting over it. So I've decided I can't go any further, in good conscience, without better information. And the only people who can offer me that . . . are my Enemies. The people who've been sending their agents to kill me for as long as I can remember."

Julien leaned forward eagerly. "You finally found out who they are?"

"Yes," I said. "They're the last surviving major players

of the devastated future, hiding out in the final stages of the War, sometime before my visit in the Timeslip. The few remaining heroes and villains, desperately sending their agents back into the Past, to kill me before I do . . . whatever it is I do, to damn everyone."

Julien and Dead Boy looked at me, silenced by shock, by the staggering implications of what I'd just said.

"Who . . . ?" said Julien.

"Familiar names, familiar faces," I said. "You'd know them."

(I didn't tell Julien Advent that he would become one of my Enemies, in that terrible future. Or that he would die trying to kill me, and his dead body would be made over into one of the awful agents they sent back after me. He didn't need to know that.)

"Why have you never told me any of this before?" Julien said, finally.

"Because you would have told everyone," I said. "That's what you do. And I wasn't ready to trust . . . everyone."

"This is sounding more and more like a closed circle," said Dead Boy. "How can you . . . talk with your Enemies?"

"By travelling forward through Time into their future," I said steadily. "And confronting them. Because they're the only ones who *know* what happened, to bring about their future. They can tell me . . . what I mustn't do."

What can I do? I'd asked the future Razor Eddie, moments before I killed him. *What can I do to prevent this happening?*

Kill yourself, he said.

"But . . . they're your Enemies!" said Dead Boy. "They'll kill you on sight!"

"Then I'll have to be very persuasive," I said. "And talk really quickly."

"And if they kill you anyway?" said Julien.

"Well, that might solve the problem," I said. "But trust me, this is not a suicide run. I have every intention of coming back alive, with the information I need to put Lilith back in her box and avoid the end of the world."

"It's a good thing I'm already dead," said Dead Boy, "or I think I'd be very worried about this."

"Travel through Time takes a hell of a lot of power," said Julien, frowning heavily. "There's not many who can do it. Or would do it for you, John. I suppose I could talk to Old Father Time, on your behalf. Put in a good word for you."

"Oh, I think he's got a very good word for me," I said. "He's already arranged one trip through Time for me, and after the way that turned out, I don't think he'll be doing that again, anytime soon." Julien looked at me sharply, scenting a story, and I shook my head. "Trust me on this, Julien, you really don't want to know."

"All right," said Dead Boy, "if Old Father Time is out of the picture, who does that leave?"

"I've been thinking about that," I said. "The Collector is supposed to have a whole bunch of really weird Time travel mechanisms; but he's still mad at me. For a whole bunch of reasons."

Dead Boy sniffed loudly. "The Collector's mad at everyone. And vice versa. I wouldn't piss down his throat if his heart was on fire."

"Then there's the Chronovore," I said loudly. "Who eats up all the little lost moments of your life, the ones that you can never account for. But he works strictly for cash these days. Serious cash. There's always the Travelling Doctor, but you can never rely on him being around when you need him."

"That's everyone I know of," said Julien. "Who else is left?"

"This is where it all starts getting a bit risky," I said carefully. "I think I know someone On High who might owe me a favour. So . . . I plan to summon an angel down from Heaven."

I don't think I've ever seen two such appalled faces in my life. Dead Boy's eyes actually bulged in their sockets, and Julien Advent's face went as pale as Dead Boy's. They both tried to say something, but couldn't get the words out for spluttering.

"It's really not all that different from calling up a demon," I said quickly, trying hard to sound confident. "The principle is the same, only in reverse. That's why I needed both of you, for my plan to work. Dead Boy, to help me send my message beyond the planes of the living, and Julien, to help me contact the Courts of the Holy. You have a singular nature, Dead Boy, being both dead and alive at the same time, and I can use that ambiguity to punch my way through a lot of the usual barriers. Julien, you created a drug to split apart the best and worst elements in man. You embraced the best elements, of course, and became a hero, a pure soul. Or at least, as close to one as I'm going to find in the Nightside. Your purity of spirit will help my message get where it needs to go. Theoretically."

"And that's it?" said Dead Boy, when he finally got his voice back. "That's your marvellous plan? You were right, I don't like it. In fact, I think I would go so far as to say I hate it! *Have you lost your mind, John?* I can't even count all the ways this could go horribly wrong. You and Julien could get killed, I could . . . well, I'm not entirely sure what could happen to me, but I am ready to bet good money that it would be really, really bad! I think I'm going to have one of my turns . . . Look, you can't just go banging on Saint Peter's Gates and demand he send down an angel to talk to you! We're all going to end up as pillars of salt, I know it . . ."

"For once I find myself in complete agreement with Dead Boy," said Julien, glaring at me sternly. "If we summon an angel, and please note the emphasis I am placing on the word *if*, what we'll get will be the real thing. A messenger of God, complete in all its power and glory. Not the weakened, limited things that are normally all that can manifest in the Nightside. And you of all people should remember how much damage and loss of life those weakened presences brought about during the angel war last year. They're still rebuilding parts of the city. If we call down the real thing, what's to stop it wiping us all out on a whim?"

"First," I said, "the angel will be contained within a protective circle, just like a demon. Second, your presence and Dead Boy's will add to the protections considerably. That's why I waited to connect with you two, before I tried anything. It is . . . possible, for things to go wrong, yes. Summonings are a bit like fishing—you can never be sure whether you'll hook a sprat or a killer shark. The last time I tried this . . ."

"Hold everything," said Julien. "You actually tried this before?"

"Once, when I was a lot younger," I said defensively. "When I was really desperate for information about who and what my missing mother was. I thought, if anybody would know . . ."

"What happened?" said Dead Boy.

"Well," I said, "you know that really big crater, where the Hotel Splendide used to be?"

"That was you?" said Julien. "It's still radioactive!"

"I really don't want to talk about it," I said, with great dignity.

"Give me back my bottle," said Dead Boy. "There is no way in Hell I'm doing this sober."

"I have yet to be convinced we should do it at all," said Julien. "In fact, I'm still rather hoping this is all some terrible dream I'm going to wake up from soon."

"God, you're a pair of wimps! Everything's going to be all right." I leaned forward, doing my best to project certainty and trustworthiness. "I'm going after a specific angel this time, and I'm sure having you two along will make all the difference."

"Don't worry," Dead Boy said to Julien. "It's not that bad, being dead. It's actually quite restful, sometimes."

Julien helped me clear away the throw cushions and the rugs to reveal the bare floor-boards beneath, while Dead

Boy went downstairs, and came back with a bucket full of the Beadle's blood. He handed it over sulkily, muttering something about how he'd been saving that blood, to make blood pudding and stock later. I ignored him and had Julien prick his thumb and add a few drops of his own blood to the bucket, to purify it. (Working on the principle that some trace of the drug that brought out his best elements was still in his system.) I then used the blood to draw a really big restraining circle, surrounded by every protective symbol I knew. It took a long time and used up most of the bucket of blood.

"I don't even recognise some of the languages you're using," said Julien.

"Think yourself lucky," said Dead Boy, and I had to agree.

Finally, it was done. It looked pretty impressive, even if it did smell really rank. The three of us sat down together, inside a second smaller protective circle, holding hands; and that was it. No chanting, incense, dead chickens, or waving your hands around. In the end, most magic is really primarily a matter of will and intent. The signs I'd so carefully daubed were the spell's address, along with a few extra things to get the recipient's attention, and a few safeguards so the recipient couldn't simply wipe us all out for interrupting them at a particularly inconvenient moment. You'd be surprised how many demons screen their calls these days. Everything else was down to me, Julien Advent, and Dead Boy, and our combined will and determination.

"Something's happening," said Dead Boy, after a while. "I can feel energies forming all around us. I can See . . . I can See avenues opening up, levels of reality unfolding like the petals of a flower, more levels, more and more . . . I can See further than I ever could before . . . and I don't like it. It scares me. It's too big . . ."

"Look away," I said sharply. "Shut down your Sight and reinforce your mental barriers. Concentrate on the summoning."

"I can feel something," said Julien.

"Don't," I said.

Dead Boy and Julien both had their eyes squeezed shut now, beads of sweat standing out on their strained faces. I kept my eyes open. One of us had to, and I was more used to Seeing the unseen realms. I still kept my mental barriers firmly in place. There were things none of us could afford to see, if we wished to remain in the mortal world. The glory of the shimmering plains is not for mortals. By now we could all feel Something approaching, from a direction we all instinctively recognised but couldn't identify. It felt like *above,* in all senses of the word. Something was coming into our world, Something impossibly large and powerful, downloading itself into a mortal frame that wouldn't blow all the fuses in our merely human minds.

Brilliant light exploded within the main circle, and we all cried out and turned our heads away as an angel manifested; a blazing light far too fierce to look at directly. We could only catch brief glimpses of it, out of the corners of our watering eyes. It was vaguely human in shape, pure light, pure energy, pure magic, with just an impression of wide wings. Simply being close to it made me feel small and insignificant, simple and undeveloped, like a chalk drawing next to the Mona Lisa. The angel regarded us, and its attention embraced us all, like a judgement only barely tempered with mercy and compassion.

"Hi," I made myself say. "Glad you could drop in. Is that you, Pretty Poison?"

I don't use that name any more, said a Voice like thunder in my head. All three of us groaned out loud, as the angel's words filled our minds. *I have my old name back now. Thanks, in part, to you, John Taylor. I know what you want. We know everything. It's part of the job description. And yes, I will help you, just this once. Because of what you did, for me and my beloved. But understand this, John Taylor; although I can send you into the future, getting back again will be your own problem.*

"Can you help us against Lilith and her followers?" said Julien Advent. He was actually able to look at the angel for more than a few seconds at a time. Maybe he really did have a pure soul, after all. "You must know what she's done, what she plans to do."

Yes. We know. But all of Heaven and all of Hell are forbidden to intervene directly in the Nightside. Some of the lesser ranks from Above and Below volunteered to try to intercede, and were destroyed for their trouble. Lilith designed the Nightside specifically to diminish all spiritual messengers who entered it. So all future interventions have been forbidden, in the place where all the decisions that matter are made. In the Courts of the Holy. It's up to the Nightside to save itself, if it can. I am bending the rules to help you, John Taylor, and I will not do so again. Good luck. And don't call this number again.

I knew a hint when I heard it. She was telling me to get on with it, before Someone else called her back. So I raised my gift and focused my Sight on all the various time-lines radiating out from this place, this moment, this decision. I could only see the most immediate timetracks, but even so the sheer number of images almost overwhelmed me. I narrowed my regard still further, searching through the time-lines for the single path that led to my Enemies. Near futures flashed on and off all around me. I saw my friends die, fighting Lilith and her people. I saw different versions of myself, and them, and we all died fighting Lilith, over and over again. I saw my friends support Lilith, while I led a coalition of those who had once been my foes against her, and we all died again. I saw myself, wearing an expression I didn't recognise, sitting at my mother's feet as she contemplated a mountain of skulls and smiled, while monsters danced in the flickering light of burning buildings.

Other versions of the future pressed in from all sides—other, stranger, alien Nightsides. I saw inhuman structures that might have been buildings, with unnatural lights burning in them, while impossible forms lurched and mewled through the shifting streets. I saw huge cavernous shapes, rounded structures with an organic sheen, great insects crawling all over them. I even glimpsed a version of the carnivorous jungle I'd visited briefly in the Past, with its trees made of meat and lianas like hanging intestines, where hissing roses rioted in the ruins of long-abandoned cities. I fought hard to focus my gift, forcing aside all the irrelevant futures, until I found what I was looking for: the dark and devastated future that was home to my Enemies.

And once I was locked on to that terrible place, the angel tore me loose from the Present, and sent me rocketing forward through Time. The world speeded up around me, Time flashing by impossibly fast. Days became months became years, piling up behind me. I saw the Nightside fall, its great buildings crashing down, crumbling like sand castles in the path of an oncoming tide. I saw the great oversized moon in the night sky explode, its pieces raining down like fiery meteors. And I saw the stars start to go out, one by one by one.

There were Voices all around me, growling and muttering and howling, outside of Time. Strange Presences, all speaking at once in no human tongue, yet still I could understand the gist of it. Slowly they became aware of me, then the Voices began to cajole, to warn, and to threaten. I think they were frightened of me. I refused to listen, making myself concentrate only on my destination, until finally Time slammed to a halt again, and I was spilled out into the dark future I'd visited before. The dead end of the Nightside, and maybe all of history.

And all of it my fault.

SEVEN

The Night, So Dark

It was even worse than I remembered. A night dark as despair, cold as a lover's rejection, silent as the grave. Everywhere I looked, there were buildings fallen into ruin and rubble, whole areas stamped flat or burned down. As though a mighty storm had passed through the Nightside, levelling everything it touched. Only this storm had a name. I looked up into the night sky, and there was no moon and only a sprinkling of scattered stars. The end of the world, the end of life, the end of hope. And all because of me.

It was bitter cold, the harsh air burning in my lungs, so cold it even numbed my thoughts. All around me for as far as I could see, there were only the stumps and shells of what had once been proud, tall buildings. Shattered brickwork, cracked and broken stone stained from the smoke of old fires, windows with no glass and empty doorways like gaping mouths or wounds. The streets held only abandoned, crushed and burned-out cars, along with piled-up rubbish and refuse. And shadows, shadows everywhere. I'd never known the Nightside so dark, without its bright neon, its gaudy glare of bustle and commerce. What light there was had a deep purple hue, as though the night itself was bruised.

And yet I wasn't alone. I could hear something, vague sounds off in the distance. Something large, crashing through an empty street. I thrust my hands deep into my coat pockets, hunched my shoulders against the cold, and went to investigate. That's what I do. Curiosity killed the cat, but satisfaction brought it back. I made my way cautiously through the dark streets, stepped around and over all kinds of debris. I peered into the trashed vehicles I passed, but there was never anyone in them. Thick dust puffed up around my feet with every step, only to fall straight back again. There wasn't even a puff of wind. The cold air was still, lifeless. The sounds grew louder as I drew nearer. They were coming from more than one direction. I remembered the giant, mutated insects from my last visit and moved more slowly, more quietly. Until finally I came to the edge of a great open square, and when I saw what walked there, I shrank back into the darkest, deepest shadow I could find, holding my breath so as not to give away even the slightest sign of my presence.

It lurched across the open square, its weight cracking the ground with every step, huge and bulging like a living cancer growth, all red-and-purple striations, with rows of swollen eyes and mouths dripping pus. It stalked unsteadily forward on tall stilt legs that might have been leg-bones, once upon a time. It stopped abruptly as something else entered the square from the other side. Something tall and vague, made up of shifting unnatural lights. It surged forward in sudden spurts and jerks, spitting and sparking vivid energies, discharging lightning bolts at everything metal it passed. The two monsters howled and squalled at each other, terrible sounds, like two great Beasts disputing territory.

The hideous racket called others. They burst out of side streets and the shells of broken buildings, huge monstrosities that could never have survived and prospered in a sane and rational world. They snapped and snarled at each other, stamping and coiling and rearing up jagged heads full of teeth. Something big and brutal with too many clawed arms circled warily around something with a long scarred carapace that leaked slime. It waved long, serrated claws in the air, while something else like a massive squashed over-ripe fruit, big as a bus, humped its way across the square, leaving a trail of steaming acid that ate into the bare stone ground.

All their movements were sudden, erratic, disturbing. Their raised cries were awful, actually painful to the human ear. They struck at each other, or at nothing, or charged each other head-on, like rutting stags. They did not move or act like sane things. You only had to watch them to know that their minds had gone bad, their spirits broken by this terrible place, this end of all things. They looked as though they were sick inside, everything gone to rot and corruption, dying by inches.

I knew what they were. What they had to be. These hideous, distorted things were all that was left of Lilith's children, the last of the Powers and Beings she'd recruited from the Street of the Gods to follow her. Stripped of their might and glory, mutated and driven mad. I backed slowly away from the square, away from them, away from the world I'd made. But one of them found me anyway.

At first, I thought it was just another deep shadow, cast against the unusually high wall of a jagged building, but then it moved, lurching out into the street to block my way. It rose before me like a massive black slug, big as a building, wide as a lobby, made up of living darkness. It didn't gleam or glisten, and it had no discernable details; what light there was seemed to just fall away into it like a bottomless pit. It had no eyes, but it saw me. It knew I was there, and it hated me. I could feel its hatred, like a pressure on the air. Hatred without cause, or character, or even consciousness.

I took a cautious step backwards, and it came after me. I stopped immediately, and it stopped, too. Something else slowly manifested on the air, besides the hatred. It was hungry. I turned and ran, side-stepping and lunging across the piled-up rubbish in the street, and behind me came the Beast. I ran carelessly, taking crazy risks with my footing, not caring where I was going. I chose the narrowest streets and darted down side alleys, but it came relentlessly after me, crashing through the sides of crumbling buildings, never slowing or diverting from its path. Its bulk smashed through the material world like it was made of paper, while falling masonry bounced harmlessly off its dark hide. Dust rose in thick clouds, and I coughed harshly as I ran. I was faster, more manoeuvrable, but it was inexorable. And finally, it cornered me.

I chose the wrong turning and ended up in a side street blocked by piled-up cars. Too tall to climb and no way past. There was a door to one side. I grabbed at the brass handle and it came away in my hand, jerked right out of the rotten wood. I kicked at the door, and it absorbed my foot like spongy fungus. I pulled my foot free and turned around, and there was the great black slug, blocking the street, towering over me. I leaned forward, gasping for breath, coughing out the dust in my lungs. I had nothing on me that could deal with such a monster, no tricks or magics or last-minute escapes. I started to raise my gift, hoping it could find me a way out, then the black slug lurched forward, and my concentration shattered.

Up close, it stank of brine, of the sea. Of something that should have remained hidden at the bottom of the deepest ocean. It hung over me, impossibly huge, then it stopped, as though . . . considering me. I could have reached out and touched it, but I could no more have made myself do that than plunge my bare hand into a vat of acid. And then, slowly, a reflection formed on the flat black surface of the Beast, facing me, coming into focus like an old photo, or an old memory. An image of me. The Beast remembered me. Slow ripples spread across the black surface, increasing in speed and urgency, and it lurched backwards, returning the way it had come, until finally it disappeared back into the night.

It knew me. And it was terrified of me.

I sat down on some rubble and concentrated on getting my breathing back under control. I could feel my heart hammering like a pile-driver, and my hands were shaking. It was times like this that I wished I smoked. Eventually my composure returned, and I looked around me. I had no idea where I was. All the landmarks were gone, beaten down into mess and ruin. Everywhere looked the same. Civilisation had come and gone, and only monsters stalked old London's streets. I shuddered suddenly. It was very cold, here at the end of the world. But I still had work to do. No rest for the wicked. I got to my feet again, beat my numbed hands together, and raised my gift. There was nothing to See. The unseen world was as dead and gone as everything else. But when I concentrated, it only took me a moment to find the lair of my Enemies. Their light was feeble and flickering, but still it shone like a beacon in this darkest of nights. I shut down my gift and set off in the direction it had shown me. It wasn't far.

I kept well away from the Beasts. Or maybe they were keeping away from me. Either way, nothing crossed my path till I came to my Enemies' hideout. Again, it looked just as I remembered it. A cracked, crumbling house in a rotted tenement, with nothing obviously different about it. No light showed at any of the shuttered windows, but I could feel light and life inside, hidden, barricaded against the monsters of the night. I advanced slowly, carefully, using just enough of my gift to See the concealed protections and magical booby-traps covering all possible approaches to the house. Most were of the *Don't see me, nothing here, move along* kind, but surprisingly they were all keyed to abhuman energies. None of them would activate even if I walked right through them. Perhaps they no longer had any reason to expect human visitors. Or maybe they just needed to be able to get back inside at a moment's notice. The outer door wasn't even locked.

I let myself in and moved silently through the gloom and tension of the broken-down house. My eyes had adjusted to the gloom of the end of the world, but it was still hard to see anything inside. I trailed the fingertips of one hand along the nearest wall, to keep my bearings, and the plaster crumbled into dust under my touch. I strained my ears against the quiet, and finally I caught the first faint traces of sound, from the end of the corridor before me. I padded forward and came to a door camouflaged in the wall. It wasn't locked either. I slipped through the door, and for the first time there was light, real light. I stopped to let my eyes adjust. Butter yellow light leaked round the edges of another door, in the wall ahead. The light looked warm and comforting. It looked like life. I eased over to the door. It was a little ajar. I pushed it open a few more inches, and looked through. And there were my Enemies, just as I'd seen them before, in my vision.

They had a great haunch of unidentifiable meat cooking over an open fire, turning slowly on a rough metal spit. They were all crouched around it, utterly intent, not even aware of my presence. Such familiar names and faces. Jessica Sorrow, Larry Oblivion, Count Video, King of Skin, Annie Abattoir. All of them major players and even Powers in their time, now fallen far from what they had once been. They were huddled together, as much for companionship and comfort as against the cold that seeped through even into the hidden room. All of them small ragged figures, with fear and hopelessness written deep in their bony, malnourished faces.

Jessica Sorrow, no longer the terrible Unbeliever, looked almost unbearably human and vulnerable as she sat cross-legged before the fire, as close to the flames as she could get without burning herself. She hugged an ancient teddy bear in her skinny arms, holding it close to her shrunken chest. She wore a battered black leather jacket and leggings, that looked a lot like the ones Suzie always wore.

Next to her sat Larry Oblivion, the dead detective. Betrayed and murdered by the only woman he ever really loved, brought back as a zombie, surviving now even when he would probably rather not, because he couldn't die again. His dead pale flesh showed through the tatters of what had probably once been a very expensive suit. Unlike the others, he didn't look tired, or defeated. He just looked angry.

Count Video was a mess. He wore nothing but a collection of leather straps, and his skin was wrinkled and loose in places, from where it had been stitched back on after the angel war. Heavy black staples held him together, in places. Silicon nodules and sorcerous circuitry projected from puckered skin, soldered into place long ago to form the necrotech that powered his binary magics. Plasma lights sputtered on and off around his wasted body, and a halo of intermittent energies cast an unhealthy light on his twitching face.

King of Skin was just a man here, stripped of his once-terrible glamour. In my time he could have killed with a word or enslaved with a look, but not here, not now. He was all skin and bone, his gaze distant and unfocused. Objects of power hung about him on tangled silver chains, half-hidden under a thick fur coat with patches torn away. He rocked back and forth on his haunches, perhaps lost in memories of better times, because memory was all he had left.

And finally, Annie Abattoir; assassin and seductress, secret agent and confidence trickster, praised and feared and damned in a dozen countries. She wore what was left of a long crimson evening gown, the low-cut back showing off the mystic symbols carved deep into the flesh between her shoulder blades. She'd always been very hard to kill, though many had tried, often with good reason. Though she was six-foot-two and still mostly muscle, her face held little of its old striking charm. She looked . . . diminished. Beaten down.

I finally announced my presence with a polite cough, and they all spun round, scrambling to their feet, ready to fight. Their eyes widened, and a few jaws dropped as they recognised me, then King of Skin cried out like a hurt child and scurried away to crouch in a corner, terrified and trembling. Count Video's face convulsed with rage, and new energies crackled around him as his necrotech sparked into life.

"Don't!" I said quickly. "I'm protected! And I mean seriously protected, by major magics. Anything strong enough to break through my defences would almost certainly attract the attention of the Beasts outside. And I don't think any of us want that, right?"

Annie Abattoir looked uncertain, a glowing dagger in each hand, but after a tense moment Larry Oblivion stepped forward and put a hand on her arm and Count Video's, and they both reluctantly nodded and stepped back. Larry Oblivion studied me coldly.

"I don't see any protections . . ."

I grinned. "Of course not. That's how good they are."

I was bluffing, but they had no way of knowing that. And they didn't dare risk being discovered.

"John Taylor," Larry said slowly. "How is it that you are here? Did you bring yourself back from the dead, too?"

"Time travel," I said briskly. "For me, Lilith has only just happened. The War hasn't started yet. I'm here looking for answers, and advice."

"Let me kill him," said Count Video. "He has to die. For what he did, he has to die!"

"Yes," said Larry. "But not now. Not here."

Annie made the Count sit down by the fire again. King of Skin was still shivering in his corner, in a spreading pool of urine, crying childish tears. It hurt me to see him that way. I'd never liked him, but I always respected him. Annie Abattoir and Jessica Sorrow stood before me, on either side of Larry Oblivion. They looked at me like I was a ghost, some horrid spectre at the feast, some ancient evil from their worst nightmares. And maybe I was.

"My brother Tommy fought on your side," Larry said finally. "In the great War against Lilith. He trusted you, even though he had good reason not to. And when they struck him down you just stood there, and watched him die, and did nothing to help."

I spread my hands helplessly. "You're judging me over something I haven't even done yet. And may never do . . . That's why I'm here. I need you to tell me what I have to do to prevent all this happening." They stared back at me, unconvinced. I took a step forward. When dealing with Enemies, it's all about confidence, or at least the appearance of it. I gestured at the great haunch of meat burning over the fire. It smelled really bad. "You seem to be preparing dinner. Do you mind if I join you? There's nothing like struggling to avoid the Apocalypse to give you an appetite. What are we having?"

Larry snorted, amused despite himself. "That . . . is one of Lilith's children. Pretty much all there is left to eat, these days. Apart from the bodies. There are still a lot of dead people left over from the War, but we haven't been reduced to cannibalism. Not yet. Oh yes, they're still lying around, decades after the War. Nothing decays any more, you see. Except the buildings. All kinds of strange energies were released during the final days of your struggle with your mother. And now all the natural processes are . . . out of order. Existence follows new rules now. Sometimes we don't feel the need to eat or drink for days or even weeks at a time. And we don't sleep. Bad dreams can take on a life of their own, these days."

"It's hard to keep track of time any more," said Jessica, in a voice like a shell-shocked child's. "There's no way of measuring it, you see. There are no days, the night never ends, and watches don't work even though there's nothing wrong with them. Perhaps you and Lilith broke Time, during the War . . ." She cocked her head to one side, like a bird, still fixing me with her direct, unblinking gaze. "How did you know where to find us?"

"My gift," I said. "And a little help from an angel."

Her mouth twitched briefly. "You always did move in exalted circles, John."

"Heaven and Hell have abandoned us," Annie Abattoir said harshly. "Nothing left to fight over, any more. Do you know who we are? Why we stay together? Why we still struggle to survive, in this worst of all possible worlds?"

"Yes," I said. My mouth was suddenly dry. "You're my Enemies. You've been trying to kill me ever since I was born, striking back through Time, to kill me before I do . . . whatever it is I do that brings about the destruction of the Nightside."

"And the world," Larry said flatly. "Don't think this is just London. There's nothing else."

"We had to do it," said Jessica. "It was . . ."

"Oh please!" I said. "Don't you dare say *It was nothing personal!* You and your Harrowing have hounded me all my life! I've never been able to feel safe, feel secure, because I could never know when your bloody assassins would appear suddenly out of nowhere, killing everyone in their path for a chance to get at me! You made my life a living Hell!"

"You made the world a living Hell," said Count Video. "Everything we've done is justified by what you did."

"I haven't done anything yet!"

"But you will, John," said Jessica. "You will."

I made myself control my temper. I was here for their help. And there was still one question I hadn't asked. Something I had to know.

"Where's Suzie?" I said. "Where's my Shotgun Suzie?"

Larry looked a little surprised. "You expected her to be here?"

"She tried to kill me," I said. The words hurt, but I

forced them out. "She told me she was one of you. That's why I came here, through Time, for information. The future isn't set in stone. This doesn't have to happen. Tell me what you know. The things only you know."

"She volunteered, to be made into one of our assassins," said Larry. "You do know she volunteered, to be made over into . . . what we made her?"

"Yes," I said. "She told me. We never did believe in keeping secrets from each other."

Jessica hugged her teddy bear tightly, resting her chin on its battered head. "She never came back. We assumed you killed her, like all our other agents. What did happen to her, John?"

"Merlin ripped off her arm," I said steadily. "The one with the Speaking Gun attached to it. Then she disappeared. She was still alive, the last time I saw her. I had hoped . . . she'd made it back here."

"No," said Annie. "We haven't seen her. We have to assume she's lost to us. Another death on your conscience, Lilith's son."

"He has no conscience," said Count Video. "He's not human. Not really. Why should he have human feelings?"

"I was human enough to get past your defences," I said.

"Then we'll have to tighten them up," said Larry.

I looked at Jessica. "I see you still have your teddy."

"Yes," she said. "You found him for me. I remember. He brought me back to life, and sanity."

"I'm glad I could help," I said.

She shook her head slowly. "I'm not. This world would be so much easier to bear if I was still crazy. Still safely mad."

"Ah well," I said. "No good deed goes unpunished."

"Especially in the Nightside," she said.

And we both managed a small smile, just between the two of us.

"So," I said, looking around me, "this is the end of the

world, and it's all my fault. Now tell me why. Tell me
what happened."

"You started it" said Larry Oblivion. "When you came
back to the Nightside after five years away. That wasn't
supposed to happen. We went to a lot of trouble to or-
chestrate the events that drove you out—working behind
the scenes, always through agents who never knew whom
they were serving. It took a lot of our strength and power,
but since we'd had so little success in trying to kill
you . . . we were ready to try anything else. You were
supposed to be so traumatised by events that you would
flee to London, and the normal world, and never return.
We were so sure we'd succeeded, at last. But nothing
changed here, and when Annie investigated why, she got
a vision of you returning anyway. So we used the creature
that pretended to be a house on Blaiston Street, and set a
trap for you. If you were going to come back to the
Nightside, we wanted it to be on our terms."

"But if it hadn't been for the house, I never would have
come back," I said.

"Maybe," said Jessica. "Meddling with Time is an uncertain business. Sometimes I think the whole universe
runs on irony. By interfering, we created a rod for our
own backs and the seed of our own destruction. Doesn't
it make you want to spit?"

"And once you returned, events proceeded with predictable inevitability," said Annie Abattoir. "By insisting
on searching for the truth about your mother, though
everyone warned you against it, you set in place the chain
of events that led to the War between your forces and
hers. The two of you destroyed the Nightside by fighting
over it, like two dogs with a single bone, because neither
of you would allow the other to control it. Between you,
you sucked all the life out of the world, draining it dry to
power greater and greater magics, for your precious
War."

"You squandered your own people," said Larry.
"Throwing them into the fray, again and again. Nothing

mattered to either of you, except winning. And so the War went on, until you both ran out of people to throw at each other, and there was no-one left but you and Lilith."

"You killed each other," said Count Video, still staring into the fire. "Using the Speaking Gun. But by then it was far too late. The damage had been done."

"That's why we retrieved the Gun and bonded it to Suzie," said Jessica. "Even though the process nearly destroyed us. Because it was the only weapon we were sure would destroy you. She screamed like the damned when we fitted it to her, but she never once flinched away. Poor Suzie. Brave Suzie."

And then all our heads whipped round, and we fell silent, as we heard something impossibly huge and heavy dragging itself by, outside. We all stood very still, listening. Even King of Skin stopped whimpering in his corner. The whole house shook with each dragging movement, then the sounds moved on, fading away into the night. We all slowly relaxed. No wonder my Enemies were so diminished. To have to live like this, all the time, never free from fear, never knowing when they might be discovered and killed . . . Not unlike the life they made for me, really. But it was hard for me to feel any real sense of revenge, or satisfaction. No-one should have to live like this.

"All that remains of Humanity now," said Jessica, "is small groups like us. Those who survived the War by hiding, like frightened mice in their holes. We're still hiding, hanging on, surviving, doing what we can. Hoping against hope . . . for a miracle. But we haven't heard anything from the other groups for months now, and when we call out, no-one answers. So perhaps . . . we're all that's left. The last Redoubt of Humanity, pinning all our hopes on the death of one man."

"Who would have thought it would come down to the likes of us, to be Humanity's last hope," said King of Skin sadly, from his corner.

We all looked at him, waiting, but he had nothing else

to say. He still wouldn't look at me. But at least he'd stopped crying.

"Outside, all that lives now are the last few remnants of Lilith's children," said Larry Oblivion. "Mutated and monstrous, and quite mad. Roaming the ruins, killing everything they find, including each other. I sometimes wonder if they even know the War is over. They won't last much longer. The energies loosed during the War, by you and your mother, are still abroad in the night, changing everything, mutating everything. Soon enough they'll all be gone . . . and so will we, and what's left of the world will belong to the insects."

"But now I'm here," I said forcefully. "And we've talked, and that changes everything."

"Does it?" said Jessica.

"Yes," I said. "I have to believe that. And so do you. It's our only hope. Humanity's only hope. Use your power. Send me back into the Past, back to the time I came from. And I promise you I'll find a way to stop Lilith that doesn't involve raising an army. There won't be any War, to cause all this."

"You want us to trust you?" said Count Video. "Trust the man who damned us all?"

"Why should we believe in you?" said Larry. "Why should we trust in you, John Taylor, Lilith's son?"

"Because your brother Tommy did," I said. "Even though he had good reason not to."

Count Video rose abruptly to his feet, turning to face me. "We could kill you," he said. "Now you're here, finally, in our grasp. We could kill you, even if it meant all our deaths. It might be worth it, to know you were dead. And then maybe we could all rest peacefully."

"Do you want revenge, or do you want to stop the War?" I said. "If I die, here and now, who's going to stop Lilith? You must know she plans to remake the Nightside in her own image, kill everyone who stands against her, and remake Humanity into something more pliable, to serve her all her days. I think I'd rather be dead, than that.

I'm the only chance you've got of stopping Lilith. Of stopping this. If I can find a way to bring her down, without fighting a War . . . that has to be more important than revenge. Doesn't it?"

In the end, they only argued for about ten minutes before reluctantly agreeing. Annie Abattoir opened a vein in her arm, and used the blood to draw a pentacle on the floor, while the others worked together to raise what power remained to them. Jessica Sorrow used her teddy bear as a focus for the right place and time. Count Video swept his hands back and forth, leaving sparkling energy traces on the air, weaving description theory and binary magics, while his necrotech sparked and sputtered on his wrinkled flesh. King of Skin stood tall and proud, doing what he was born to do, evoking powerful magics with ancient Words of Power. And Larry Oblivion took it all in, his undead body the conduit for the terrible energies they were raising, absorbing all the punishment so the others could concentrate on the Working.

Annie Abattoir gestured sharply with her bloody arm, and I stepped inside the pentacle. She closed the pattern with a final flourish, and the spell ignited. The crimson lines of the pentacle blazed with power, and the world outside it began to grow dim and insubstantial to me.

And then King of Skin lifted his head, his eyes huge. "They're here!" he cried. "They followed Taylor here! They broke through our defences, and we were so preoccupied with Taylor we didn't even notice! *They're here!*"

Monsters came crashing through all the walls at once. Huge brutish forms with eager eyes and dripping mouths. Long claws and taloned hands ripped through stone and brick and plaster, while something dark and leathery smashed a hole through the ceiling. The floor jarred upwards and split apart, as a great eye looked up through the widening chasm. My Enemies ignored them all, concentrating on the Working that would send me back through Time. A barbed tentacle shot down from the ceiling and wrapped itself around Count Video. Blood spurted from his mouth as his ribs collapsed, but he still fought to pronounce the last few Words of Power. A bone spike transfixed Annie Abattoir, gutting her, but still she stood and would not fall.

I faded away, falling back through Time, and that was the last I saw of them. Had the Beasts really followed me to their hiding place? Had I brought their deaths about, after all?

No. I could still save them. Save everyone. I would find a way. That was what I did.

EIGHT

While I Was Away

I came back to fire and screams, and the thunder of buildings falling. The street was full of rubble and overturned vehicles, and there were bodies everywhere. A shop-front blew out in a soundless explosion, glass fragments flying on the air like shrapnel. I hunkered down, arms over my head, and stared quickly about me. There was fighting going on all around, mad-eyed mobs attacking each other with spells and weapons and anything that came to hand. Fires burned to every side, consuming the few buildings still standing. The air was thick with smoke, and heavy with the stench of burned flesh and spilled blood. I'd come back to a war zone.

For the first time that I could remember, all traffic on the road had stopped. The way was blocked with blazing wrecks, crashed vehicles, and piled-up cars. Some of them had bodies in them, while others leaked blood and similar fluids. A lightning bolt slammed down only a few feet away from me, buckling the pavement, and I headed for the nearest cover. I scurried over to the broken hulk of an overturned ambulance and crouched down beside it, pressing hard against its blood-smeared side. I could just make out its dying whispers, fluttering on the edges of my mind, as the vehicle's animating spirit dissipated. *I've been good . . . I've been good . . . I'm scared . . . .* The ambulance coughed once, then was silent. All around me, the fighting raged back and forth.

I sighed heavily. Some days you can't turn your back for even a moment, without everything going to hell.

It would seem Lilith had started the War without me. I peered around me, trying to make out landmarks or details through the thick drifting smoke, while various combatants ran back and forth, screaming garbled war cries. After a while, I realised I was back in Uptown, in the heart of Clubland. Or at least, what was left of it. Half of it was already demolished, and there was a firestorm raging at the end of the street. Several of the buildings were burning hotter and brighter than any earthly flames should. Dark figures came and went in the smoke, and only some of them were human. Winged shapes soared by overhead, flapping huge membraneous wings, and none of them were angels.

Some people were trying to help. Staff from the various clubs sprayed the roaring flames with fire extinguishers that probably hadn't been tested in years. Magics sparked and flared on the grimy air, and a water elemental burst up out of several manholes to drench those buildings closest to it. A group of Christian Commandos chanted a blessing over a fire hose, and used the high-pressure holy water as a weapon against the more sorcerous blazes. Stone golems strode unflinchingly into burning buildings past saving, and pulled them down, using the weight of the rubble to smother the flames. Sometimes the golems came out again, and sometimes they didn't. All around me, famous clubs with old and honoured names were already gone, reduced to cinders and blackened frames.

A large group of naked men and women, armed with axes and knives and machetes, their ungainly bodies daubed with blood and woad and ashes, came stalking down the ruined street like they owned it. They struck out at everyone they passed, and carried severed heads on poles, all the while howling praises to their god Lugh, and the glories of destruction. They all had mad, happy eyes and broad smiles. Yet many of them were still wearing wristwatches, which was a bit of a give-away that they weren't quite as primitive as they were affecting. *Well,* I thought, *I've got to start somewhere.*

I rose from behind the dead ambulance and strode forward to confront the mob. They stumbled to a ragged halt, almost falling over each other. I got the impression it had been some time since anyone had done anything but take one look at them and run away screaming. Their leader fixed me with his best mad stare, and started screaming something nasty about blasphemers, and I walked right up to him and kicked him square in the balls. I put a lot of strength and all my displeasure at what had happened into that kick, and it actually lifted him a few inches into the air before dropping him to his knees. His eyes got very big, and though his mouth was working, not a sound came out of it. He looked like he'd be pretty busy for some time, trying to get some or indeed any air back into his lungs, so I turned my attention to the crowd before me. They looked at their fallen leader, then back at me, and some actually started to shuffle their feet guiltily.

"I am John Taylor," I announced loudly, giving them my best disturbing smile. The people at the front of the mob immediately tried to press backwards, away from me, but the ones behind them were having none of it. There was a certain amount of undignified scuffling. I raised my voice again. "Whatever you've been doing, it stops, right here and now. I have work for you."

"And what if we don't feel like working for you?" said

a voice from somewhere at the back of the crowd. "You can't kick us all in the balls."

"Right," said someone else. "We can take him! He's only one man!"

I had to smile. I love it when they say things like that. "You may have heard about this little trick I do," I said. "Where I take the bullets out of guns."

Some of the mob began to stand a little straighter. Axes and machetes and knives were brandished.

"Guns?" said a woman, who would definitely have looked a lot better with her clothes on. "We don't need no stinking guns!"

I could feel my smile broadening. "I've been working on a new variation," I said.

I snapped my fingers, and all the fillings disappeared from their teeth. Along with all crowns, caps, bridges, and veneers. There were a great many howls of muted pain, an awful lot of clapping of hands to mouths, and suddenly everyone in the mob looked a whole lot less crazy and entirely willing to listen to whatever I had to say.

"Any more words of dissent," I said, "and I will show you another variation, that involves your lungs and a whole bunch of buckets."

Somewhat garbled voices hastened to assure me that they were all ready and willing to assist me in anything I might want done. So I set them to defending those people who were trying to fight the fires.

I left them to it and set off down the street, stepping carefully around and over the cracked and raised pavement. The air was painfully hot on my face from all the fires, and the smoky air was thick with floating cinders. Fighting was still going on, in fits and starts, but no-one bothered me. I stopped as I came to a club I recognized, the lap-dancing joint Not Fade Away. The ghost girls were out in force, using their smoky bodies to smother any flames that threatened their club's already scorched façade. The barker kept them moving, his tired and strained voice still rising easily over the general din. He nodded brusquely in my direction as I went over to join him.

"Club's closed, for redecoration," he growled out of the corner of his mouth. "We will reopen. Look for our ads."

"How long is it since I was last here?" I asked him.

"About a week, squire. Just before all this unpleasantness started. Now unless you've got something useful to contribute, be a nice gentleman and bog off. The ladies and I are busy."

I used my gift to find somewhere it was raining heavily, and brought the rain to where it was needed. It slammed down, a torrential downpour the whole length of the street, drowning all the fires and washing the smoke right out of the air. People shouted and cheered, and the ghost girls danced joyously in the street as the rain fell straight through them. I tipped a wink to the barker and continued down the street. I shouldn't have used my gift so blatantly. Lilith would be bound to detect it, and know I was back. But I needed to do something, and I've always had a weakness for the grand gesture.

Next, I needed to find out what had happened while I was away. It appeared my Enemies' return spell hadn't been as accurate as I'd hoped.

I eventually found the establishment I was looking for— Simulacra Corner. A discreet little joint, specialising in the sale of magic mirrors, crystal balls, scrying pools, and other less-well-advertised means of spying on your neighbour from a distance. Simulacra Corner dealt in everything from confidential connections to industrial espionage, and everything in between. The sign over the front door said FOR ALL YOUR VOYEURISTIC NEEDS. Tucked away down a side street that wasn't always there, none of the recent excitement had even touched it. As I approached the rough wooden door, an approximation of a face raised itself out of the wood. The blank eyes glared at me, and the brass letter box formed itself into a sneering mouth.

"Go away," it said, in a harsh, growling voice. "We are closed. As in, not open. Call back later. Or not. See if I care."

I've never cared for snotty simulacra. "You'll open for me," I said. "I'm John Taylor."

"Good for you. Love the trench coat. We're still not open. And you probably couldn't afford anything here even if we were."

"Let me in," I said pleasantly. "Or I'll piss through your letterbox."

The face scowled, then sniffed mournfully. "Yes, that sounds like John Taylor. I hate this job. When everyone knows you're not real, you get no respect."

The face sank back into the wood, disappearing detail by detail, and the door swung slowly open before me. I stepped inside, and the door immediately slammed shut behind me. An invisible bell tinkled, announcing a customer. The shop's interior was wonderfully calm and quiet, after the noise and chaos of the street, and the air smelled sweetly of sandalwood and beeswax. The entrance lobby was empty, apart from a few comfortable chairs and a coffee table half-buried under out-of-date magazines. The shop's owner came bustling forward to greet me, a small furtive type, badly dressed and overweight, and smiling a little bit too widely. He was already rubbing his hands together, and I stuck my hands into my coat pockets so I wouldn't have to shake hands. I just knew his would be cold and clammy. He looked like the kind of guy who always assures you the first hit is free.

"Mr. Taylor, Mr. Taylor, so good of you to grace my humble establishment with your presence! Sorry we didn't let you in straightaway, Mr. Taylor, but it's chaos out there! Absolute chaos, oh my word yes! Can't be too careful . . . Don't those fools realise what they're doing? Property values will be depressed for years after this!"

"I need to make use of some of your items," I said, declining to enter a conversation I knew wasn't going to go anywhere useful. "I need to catch up on what's been happening in the Nightside, while I was away."

"Well, I don't know about that, Mr. Taylor . . . you don't actually have a line of credit with us, and in the current circumstances . . ."

"Charge it to Walker," I said.

The shop's owner brightened immediately. "Oh, Mr. Walker! Yes, yes, one of my most valued customers. You're sure you have his . . . well, of course you do! Of course! No-one ever takes Mr. Walker's name in vain, eh? Eh? I'll just put it all on his bill . . ."

He bustled away, and I followed him through an inconspicuous door into a hall of mirrors. They hung in uneven rows on the two walls, with no obvious means of support. They were long and tall, round and wide, in silver frames and in gold, and one by one they opened themselves to me, to show me visions of the recent past.

I saw Lilith burst out of the Street of the Gods, at the head of an army of her monstrous children and maddened followers. I watched as she commanded them to kill every living thing who wouldn't bow down and worship her and swear eternal loyalty to her cause. I heard her order them to destroy every building and structure in her path. *Burn it all down,* she said. *I won't be needing it.* And I wouldn't let myself look away as the mirrors showed me bloody slaughter, ancient buildings crumbling, flames rising into the night sky, death and destruction on an almost inconceivable scale. The bodies piled up as people ran screaming through the wreckage of their lives.

I saw Walker, working desperately to organise resistance from the safe haven of Strangefellows bar. Hidden and protected, for the moment, by Merlin Satanspawn's defences. Someone had healed Walker of the injuries he'd taken on the Street of the Gods, but his face was gaunt with stress and fatigue, and there were heavy dark shadows under his eyes. For the first time in all the time I'd known him, he didn't look confident. I watched and listened as he tried again and again to contact the Authorities, to summon the armed forces that had always backed him up in the past. But no-one ever answered him. He was on his own.

I ordered the mirror before me to concentrate on a specific time and place: on what Walker was doing the day before I arrived back in the Nightside. The mirror narrowed its focus and showed me.

Walker sat at a table pushed right up against the long bar in Strangefellows, poring over reports brought to him by a series of runners, deathly tired men and women only kept going by duty and honour and the pills Walker passed out by the handful. Walker looked in really bad shape; but still he studied his reports and gave orders in a calm, unhurried voice, and his agents went straight back out into the night again, to do what was needed.

The bar had the look of a place under siege. It was dark and overcrowded, with people sitting slumped at tables or on the floor, nursing their drinks and their hurts and their remaining strength. A healer was running a rough-and-ready clinic in one corner, doing meatball sorcery on the worst wounds to get people on their feet, so they could be sent out again. The floor was stained with blood and other fluids. People were coming and going all the time, and most of them had that driven, damned, defeated look in their faces. A few were sleeping fitfully on pushed-together mattresses, twitching and crying out miserably in their sleep.

An unseen band was playing the old Punk classic "He Fucked Me with a Chain-saw and It Felt Like a Kiss." Which was worrying. Alex only ever plays Punk when he's in a really bad mood, and then wise men check their change carefully and avoid the bar snacks. Alex was behind the bar, as usual, making Molotov cocktails out of his reserve stock and complaining loudly about having to use some of his better vintages. He comforted himself by adding a splash of holy water to every bottle, to give the mixture that little extra bite. Alex had a particularly unpleasant sense of humour when he put his mind to it.

Betty and Lucy Coltrane stood poised in the centre of the bar, their bulging muscles distended, each of them holding a really vicious-looking shillelagh carved out of blackthorn root and covered in deeply etched runes. Now and again some poor damned fool would force his way past Merlin's defences and teleport blindly into the bar, hoping to impress Lilith with feats of daring, and each and every time Lucy and Betty Coltrane would pound the living shit out of him, with extreme prejudice. I didn't see what they did with the bodies afterwards, and I wasn't sure I wanted to know.

Walker got up from his table, stretched slowly and painfully, and leaned wearily against the bar. Alex sniffed loudly.

"Taking a break again, your high-and-mightyness? More Benzedrine with your champagne, perhaps, you heathen?"

"Not just now, thank you, Alex. Still no chance of Merlin's manifesting, I suppose?"

Alex shrugged. "I can't feel his presence, though I have no doubt he's keeping a watchful eye on things. Either he's biding his time, or he's keeping his head well down till it's all safely over. Trust me, when he finally does decide to Do Something, you'll almost certainly wish he hadn't. Merlin has always favoured a scorched-earth policy when it comes to dealing with problems."

"I like him already," said Walker, and Alex sniffed loudly again.

*   *   *

At the end of the outside alley that led to the bar's front door, Shotgun Suzie was standing guard. A tidal wave of Lilith's more fanatical followers came sweeping down the narrow alley towards her, and she met them with guns, grenades, and incendiaries. Explosions filled the alley with painful light and sound, throwing bodies this way and that, while shrapnel from fragmentation grenades cut through the packed ranks like a scythe. Suzie fired her shotgun again and again, blowing ragged holes in the surging mob of zealots before her, and the dead piled up into a bloody barricade that her enemies had to drag away or climb over to get at her.

The alleyway was narrow enough that only a dozen or so could come at her at one time, and none of them ever got close enough to touch her. She fired her shotgun over and over, constantly reloading from the bandoliers crossing her chest, until the gun got hot enough to burn her hands. And then she pulled on leather gloves and kept on firing until she ran out of ammunition. Blood sprayed across the alley walls, and gore ran thickly in the gutters. The screams of the wounded and the dying went ignored by both sides. And still Lilith's followers pressed forward, and still Shotgun Suzie stood her ground.

She tossed the last of her incendiaries into the thickest part of the mob, and a terrible flickering light filled the alleyway as men burned like candles. They thrashed back and forth, spreading the flames, and Suzie seized the moment to snatch up a Colonial Marines smart gun that had fallen through a Timeslip from a particularly militaristic future. She opened up with the smart gun, and thousands of rounds a minute slammed into the mob. The carnage moved up another notch as she swept the heavy muzzle back and forth, and the mob's front ranks disappeared in a bloody haze of exploding heads and bellies. There was a pause as the piled-up dead sealed off the alleyway completely, and Lilith's surviving followers had an earnest discussion over what to do next. Suzie grinned and lit herself a nasty black cigar. In the end Lilith's followers were more afraid of failing her than they were of dying, so they sent runners back to request more powerful weapons, pulled the barricade apart, and pressed forward again.

They kept coming, and Suzie kept killing them. Facing impossible odds, knowing they were bound to drag her down eventually, Suzie was still grinning broadly. I didn't think I'd ever seen her look happier.

Reluctantly, I switched to another mirror. I'd worn the other one out, and I had to see how Walker's agents were doing out on the streets against Lilith's far greater forces. The first one the mirror found was Dead Boy. He was striding carelessly down a half-demolished street, his long purple greatcoat flapping in the gusting wind, his dark floppy hat crammed down over his curly hair, while an armed crowd charged right at him. Dead Boy laughed in their faces, and didn't even bother to increase his pace. He took a deep sniff of the black carnation in his button-hole, tossed back a handful of the nasty little pills that an Obeah woman made up specially for him, drank the last of the whiskey in his bottle, and tossed it aside. His corpse-pale face was full of a dreadful anticipation.

"Come on, you bastards! Show me what you've got! Give me your best shot. I can take it!"

The mob hit him like a hammer, flailing arms wielding knives and clubs and even broken glass, but he stood his ground, and almost immediately the crowd broke around him like a wave hitting a solid outcropping of rock. Dead Boy struck about him with his pale fists, and there was a vicious strength in his dead arms. He moved impossibly quickly, thrusting himself forward into the face of his attackers, and those he hit fell and did not rise again. The raging mob struck him and cut at him, and hit him with everything that came to hand, doing their best to drag him down by sheer force of numbers; but still he stood and would not fall. His dead body soaked up ap-

palling punishment, but he felt none of it. He just kept
going, forcing his way into the heart of the mob, going to
slaughter as to a feast, laughing aloud as he crushed
skulls and stove in chests and tore limbs from their sockets. He was dead, and his strength was no longer bound
by the limitations of living flesh. Blood made his face a
crimson mask, and none of it was his.

In the end the mob simply split apart around him,
streaming past in search of easier prey. He was only one
man, and he couldn't stop a crowd. Dead Boy cried out
angrily after them, and struck out at those who passed,
but the mob quickly learned to give him a wide berth, and
soon enough they had all moved on and left him behind.
Dead Boy stood alone on a burning street, surrounded by
the dead and the dying. He shouted after the departing
mob, demanding they come back and fight, but none of
them were zealot enough or stupid enough to listen. Dead
Boy shrugged, cleaned his face with a dirty handkerchief,
then sat down on the nearest pile of bodies and opened
his tattered purple greatcoat, to check the extent of the
damage he'd suffered.

There were bullet holes, of course, but he'd dig the
slugs out later. He liked to collect the more obscure
brands. There were cuts, with pale edges but no blood,
and puncture wounds that were nothing more than puckered holes in his unfeeling flesh. He'd stitch them up
later. Or superglue them, if he was short of time. There
were some wider tears, exposing pale pink and grey meat,
and he scowled at one especially wide rip down his left
side, big and deep enough to expose half his rib cage.
Some of the ribs were clearly broken. He sniffed and
pulled a roll of black duct tape from his coat pocket. He
wrapped it round and round his torso, to hold himself together until he could perform more detailed repairs.

"Thank God for duct tape. Maybe I should invest in
one of those industrial staplers . . ." He shrugged easily
and tore off a length of the tape with his teeth. He

smoothed the tape flat, then held up one hand and glared at it. "Shit, I can't have lost another finger . . ."

He was still searching through the rubble and the bodies for his missing finger when his head came up sharply. His senses might have been dulled, but his instincts had never been sharper. One of Lilith's children was heading down the street towards him. Dead Boy stood up and pushed his floppy hat onto the back of his head to get a better look.

Lord Pestilence was a stringy grey figure in a tattered grey robe, his face so gaunt it was little more than brittle leather over a grinning skull. Thick pus oozed from his empty eye-sockets and dripped from his mirthless smile. His bare hands were covered in weeping pustules. He rode a primitive hobby-horse fashioned from human bones, and wherever he went he spread disease. All around him people fell back choking and bleeding, dying slowly and horribly from a hundred different plagues. Lord Pestilence rode his hobby-horse down the middle of the road, and didn't care whether he struck down enemy or ally; it was enough that he was free at last from his prison under the Street of the Gods, free once again to spread sickness in the world and glory in the suffering he caused.

Dead Boy saw him coming, and was the only one to stand his ground, when everyone else did the sensible thing and fled. Lord Pestilence headed straight for him, giggling like a happy child, and Dead Boy considered the old god thoughtfully. Lord Pestilence lashed out with typhoid, cholera, polio, AIDS, Ebola, and green monkey fever, and everyone for half a mile around fell twitching and choking to the ground; but not Dead Boy. He just stood his ground, waiting, his pale face impassive. Enraged, Lord Pestilence urged his bony hobby-horse on, throwing increasingly obscure diseases and maladies at the single figure that stood so contemptuously in his path. Until finally the old god made the mistake of coming within arm's reach of Dead Boy, who lashed out with a move too fast for living eyes to follow. He clubbed Lord Pestilence right off his hobby-horse and sent the old god crashing to the ground. He lay there a moment, crying out at the unthinkable indignity, and Dead Boy stamped on his chest. Old bone cracked and splintered under the force of the blow, and Lord Pestilence unleashed all his awful power in one terrible blow at the grim figure standing over him.

A hundred thousand diseases issued from the old god, every fever and blight and growth that had ever vexed mankind, and none of them could touch Dead Boy. Diseases were for the living. Thwarted, the magic recoiled and turned back upon its sender. Lord Pestilence screamed and howled horribly as the diseases took hold in him, all at once, eating him alive. Cursed to know at last all the pain and horror he'd spent lifetimes imposing on others. His leathery skin cracked and bubbled, and finally ran away like watery mud. He fell apart, bit by bit, crying out like an animal now as the diseases turned his insides to soup, and his bones cracked apart into shards and splinters, and finally dust. In the end, there was nothing left of that old god Lord Pestilence but a grinning misshapen skull. Dead Boy stamped it into pieces, just to be sure.

"It's not easy being dead," he said solemnly. "But sometimes it does have its advantages."

I moved to another mirror, and ordered it to show me Larry Oblivion. The dead detective, the post-mortem private eye. I'd heard a lot about him, most of it uncanny or unsettling, but I'd never met him in my own time. Only in the future, as one of my Enemies. And now there he was in the mirror before me, and looking very different. He looked . . . so much more alive. He strode purposefully down a smoke-streaked street, looking fine and sharp and so stylish with his Gucci suit, his manicured hands and his razor-cut hair. He had the look of a man who always travelled first class, and didn't have a care in the world. Except for being some kind of zombie. I never did get the full story about that.

A crowd of minor godlings with animal heads and in-human appetites broke off from raping and feasting on the running people, and spread out to block his path. Blood dripped thickly from their clawed hands and furry mouths. And Larry Oblivion disappeared. Vanished into thin air, gone in the blink of an eye. I didn't know he could do that. Neither did the godlings, apparently, as they heaved themselves about, this way and that, stamp-ing their hoofed feet on the ground. They weren't used to being cheated of their prey.

Blood flew abruptly on the air, gushing from a severed throat, and one of the godlings crashed to the ground, kicking spasmodically as its life-blood flowed away. More and more of the godlings cried out as they were at-tacked by something none of them could see, striking im-possibly quickly, killing them with contemptuous ease. One by one they fell, old gods brought down by a more recent power. The dead detective, Larry Oblivion.

At first I thought he must be using some kind of invis-ibility, but the mirror said otherwise. It would have been able to see through that. So I got the mirror to slow the image right down, and sure enough there was Larry Oblivion, moving too quickly for the eye to follow. He was here, there, and everywhere, come and gone in a mo-ment, appearing out of nowhere to strike down an unsus-pecting godling with a shimmering silver blade and already disappearing before his victim hit the ground. He flickered on and off, only present for such small fractions of time that even the mirror had trouble keeping up with him. *I'm getting such a headache,* it complained, but I drove it ruthlessly on. I needed to know what was hap-pening.

In the end all the godlings were dead, and Larry Obliv-ion appeared out of nowhere next to the bodies, looking as immaculate and stylish as ever, with not one hair out of place. He'd moved so quickly there wasn't even a single drop of blood on his Gucci suit. But he was holding a Faerie wand. I smiled, satisfied. A lot of things about the mysterious Larry Oblivion and his impossible exploits made sense now. He'd been using the wand to bring Time to a halt, while he kept moving. Very useful little toy, that. Of course no-one ever suspected, because wands were so passé, these days. Everyone had just assumed he had a gift like mine, or his brother Tommy's.

And then Larry looked up sharply from adjusting his silk tie, as something far worse than a pack of minor godlings came crashing down the street towards him with murder on its mind. It was thirty feet tall if it was an inch, a giant mechanical apparatus stamping down the street on giant multijointed steel legs. It was all bits and pieces pressed into use and held together by unknown forces, all kinds of metal revolving around glowing sources of power. Everything about it shouted brute force. It was roughly humanoid, with mismatched arms and legs and a bulging brass head with two huge eyes that glowed red as hellfire. It had a long jagged slit for a mouth, its rising and falling edges sharper than any teeth.

It swung down the street with long ungainly steps, swaying from side to side, stamping the living and the dead to pulp under its heavy steel feet. Its long arms ended in fists as big as wrecking balls, and it struck out casually at every building it passed, smashing through stone and brick with equal ease. The ground shook with its every step. I had no idea what it was, god or construct or some mechanical ideal run by an animating spirit. The Spirit of Crap Robots Past, perhaps.

Certainly Larry Oblivion didn't look at all impressed by the huge clunky thing as it tramped and crashed its way down the street towards him. Everyone else hurried to get out of its path, at least partly because it didn't look too steady on its flat steel feet, but Larry just shot his immaculate white cuffs, brushed an invisible fleck of dust from one shoulder, and stood his ground. He waited until the huge construct was practically on top of him, then he gestured almost negligently with his wand, and disappeared. The massive contraption reared back, roaring like a deep bass steam whistle, swivelling its great brass head back and forth in search of its elusive prey.

A blur of motion surrounded the metal thing, swift glimpses of something appearing and disappearing too fast to be tracked, then bits of the construct began flying off in all directions. It took Larry Oblivion less than five minutes to dismantle the metal construct and reduce it to its component parts. Larry reappeared next to the detached brass head and kicked it down the street like an oversized football. I'm pretty sure people would have cheered, if there'd been anybody left to witness it.

Larry checked his suit carefully for signs of stress, then continued down the street.

The next mirror showed me King of Skin, slouching down a wide thoroughfare in all his sleazy glory, looking proud and potent and confident. His eyes were bright with a terrible aspect as he sallied forth, undoing probabilities and spreading nightmares through the power of his awful glamour. Even through the distance of the mirror, I still couldn't stand to look at King of Skin directly. These were his glory days, and he was still a Power to be reckoned with. Even following his progress out of the corner of my eye was almost too much to bear. Look at him for too long and I started to see . . . unbearable things. When King of Skin walked abroad, wrapped in his glamour, everyone saw what they feared most, and his power reworked probability to make those nightmares real, and solid. No man can stand to face his own nightmares, made flesh and blood. Hideous things manifested around King of Skin as he slouched along, the dreadful King with his dreadful Court.

He went where he would in the besieged city, surrounded by awful shapes, rich with terrible significance for those who saw them, like the monsters we see in the dark bedrooms of our childhood. They reared and roared and swaggered in the night, attacking everything within reach, broken free at last from the restraints of unreality. King of Skin went where he pleased, and all the Powers and Forces and Beings of Lilith's court ran screaming from him. King of Skin smiled and sniggered and continued on his way.

Until someone dropped a building on him, from a safe distance. He disappeared under a mountain of rubble, and although I watched the mirror for a long time, I didn't see him again.

Although I knew I would, in a certain, terrible future.

By now I'd exhausted all the mirrors. The scenes they showed me became hazy and blurred, and some couldn't even muster the strength to show me my own reflection. I tried the crystal balls, but their range was very limited, and half of them had gone opaque from the traumas of what they'd witnessed. Reluctantly, I moved on to the scrying pools. They weren't much to look at, just a selection of simple stone grottos in an underlit room, each holding pools of clear water. I knelt beside the first pool, pricked my thumb with a prepared dagger, and let three big fat drops of blood fall into the water. Scrying is old magic, with old prices and penalties. The clear water swallowed up my blood without taking on the faintest tinge of red, but the ripples kept spreading and spreading, until finally the pool focused in on what I wanted to see, and then the ripples cleared to show me an image almost painfully bright and clear.

Razor Eddie, the Punk God of the Straight Razor, walked through what was left of the Street of the Gods, and if he was at all affected by the destruction around him, the burned-out churches and demolished temples, it didn't show in his sharp, pinched face. A thin intense presence wrapped in a filthy old greatcoat, he strolled unconcerned past the bodies of dead gods and didn't give a damn.

A crowd of spiked and pierced zealots looked up from desecrating a sacred grove as Razor Eddie approached, and they swaggered out into the Street to block his way, laughing and calling out suggestively to him. They didn't know who he was, the fools. When he showed no fear of them, or any intention of doing something amusing, like running or begging for his life, the zealots grew sullen and angry, and sharp objects appeared in their hands. They were vultures, feeding on the carrion left behind by Lilith's crusade, hyped up on adrenaline and bloodlust and religious fervour.

They went to meet Razor Eddie with torture and horror and murder on their minds, laughing and squealing with delight, and the Punk God of the Straight Razor walked right through them. When he came out the other side they were all dead, nothing left of them but a great pile of severed heads. None of them had any eyes. I don't know how he did it. No-one does. Eddie might be an agent of the good these days, but even the good looks the other way sometimes. Razor Eddie is a mystery as well as a god, and he likes it that way.

He looked round interestedly at a sudden loud clattering sound, and a huge creature something like a millipede came writhing and coiling up out of the ruins of an ancient temple. It was impossibly huge and seemingly without end, its vast shiny bulk propelled along by thousands of stubby little legs. Hundreds of yards of it came hammering along the Street towards Razor Eddie, easily a dozen feet wide and made up of curving segments of shimmering carborundum, gleaming dull red in the light of a hundred simmering fires. It darted forward impossibly quickly, its bulging head covered with rows of compound eyes, its complicated mouth parts clacking expectantly. It could sense the power in Razor Eddie, and it was hungry. I don't know what it was. Some old nameless god from out of the depths, perhaps, no longer worshipped by anything but the worms of the earth.

Razor Eddie went forward to meet it, frowning slightly as though considering an unfamiliar problem. His pearl-handled straight razor was in his hand, shining bright as the sun. The creature reared up, its blunt head rising high above the surrounding buildings, then it slammed down again and snatched up Razor Eddie in its pincered mouth. Razor Eddie struggled briefly, his arms pinned helplessly to his sides, and the giant millipede swallowed him whole. He was there one moment, and gone the next. The millipede tossed back its carapaced head, and a series of slow ripples passed down the bulging throat as it gulped Razor Eddie down. The great head nodded a few times, as though satisfied, then it continued on its way down the Street of the Gods.

Only to pause, just a few yards later. Its head swayed uncertainly back and forth, its mouth parts clacking loudly, then it screamed like a steam geyser as its belly exploded outwards. The gleaming segments cracked and splintered and blew apart as Razor Eddie cut his way out from the inside. The huge millipede curled and writhed and slammed back and forth, demolishing buildings all around it, smashing stone and concrete and pounding the rubble to dust in its agonies, but still it couldn't escape from the awful, remorseless thing that was killing it. In the end, Razor Eddie strolled unhurriedly away from the wreckage of the dead god, ignoring the last spastic twitches of the cracked and broken body. He was smiling slightly, as though considering even more disturbing things he intended to do to his fellow gods.

Another pool, another three drops of bloods, another vision. Those of Walker's agents not strong enough to take on Lilith's offspring, or enter maddened mobs single-handed, had banded together to take on smaller targets, doing what they could to make a difference. Sandra

Chance, the consulting necromancer, stabbed about her with her aboriginal pointing-bone, and wherever she pointed it, people crashed convulsing to the ground and did not rise again. When she'd exhausted the bone's power she tossed handfuls of carefully pre-prepared graveyard dirt from the pouches hanging at her waist into the air, and all around her Lilith's zealots fell choking, as though buried alive.

Annie Abattoir watched Sandra's back. A huge muscular presence and a head taller than most, she stalked the night in her best opera gown, tearing people limb from limb, biting out their throats and cramming the flesh into her ravenous mouth. Her crimson smile dripped blood and gore.

The Nightside's very own transvestite super-hero, Ms. Fate, the man who dressed as a super-heroine to fight crime, finally came into her own. She stamped and pirouetted through crowds of maddened zealots, felling them with vicious kicks and blows as she moved gracefully from one martial art to another. No-one could stand against her, and no-one could touch her. Now and again she'd throw handfuls of razor-edged shuriken where they would do the most good. She might not have been making a whole lot of difference in the great scheme of things, but at long last Ms. Fate was the dark avenger of the night he'd always wanted to be.

The three fighters roamed far and wide, combining their efforts to break up mobs, save those under threat, and do what they could for the wounded and the lost. Walker sent more of his agents to back them up, when he could spare them, but there were never enough to do more than slow Lilith's advance into the Nightside. Scene followed scene in the pool's clear water as Lilith's growing army marched in triumph through burning streets and devastated districts. Everywhere Lilith went, people flocked to join her growing army—either because they fell under the spell of her powerful personality, or because they were desperate to be on the winning side . . .

or just because they were afraid Lilith's people would kill them if they didn't.

She walked up and down in the Nightside, and buildings exploded where she looked. Fires burned at her word, and the street cracked apart where she walked. Bodies piled up because there was no-one left to take them away, and people ran screaming or sat huddled in the doorways of burned-out homes, driven out of their minds by shock and suffering. The mad and the desolate staggered whimpering through streets they no longer recognised, retreating endlessly before Lilith's advancing forces. Walker's people did their best to guide Lilith away from those areas where she could do the most damage, by goading her with hit-and-run tactics, falling back just slowly enough that she would be sure to follow them.

Still the Nightside was a big place, much larger than its official boundaries suggested, and there was a limit to how much death and destruction even Lilith and her forces could bring about. Walker's people set up roadblocks, barricaded narrow passageways, and set up distractions, trying to herd Lilith into areas they'd already evacuated. Lilith didn't seem to care where she went, as long as she got to kill or destroy everything she saw. She knew sooner or later she'd reach the people and places that really mattered. She was in no hurry. For the moment, she was just playing, indulging herself. If she had an overall plan, Walker couldn't see it.

And neither could I.

I watched as Walker discussed his most recent stratagems with Alex Morrisey. They sat together round a small table, talking softly in a quieter, darker Strangefellows. It wasn't crowded any more. Anyone who could was out fighting in the streets. People lay on bloody mattresses, quietly dying. Betty and Lucy Coltrane sat slumped in a corner, leaning on each other for support, their faces slack and exhausted. There was blood all over them, not all of it from their victims. Alex and Walker didn't look much better. Their faces were drawn and gaunt, older than their years. There was no music playing in the bar, and from outside I could hear the baying of monsters and the screams of their prey. Strangefellows didn't look like a bar any more; it looked like somewhere people went to wait to die.

"Tell me you've got a plan, Walker," said Alex, too tired even to scowl properly. He took off his sunglasses to rub at his tired eyes, and I was actually shocked. It was like seeing him naked. He looked like he'd been hit so many times he was broken inside. "Tell me you've got a really good plan, Walker. Even if you haven't."

"Oh, I have a plan," Walker said calmly. His voice tried hard to sound confident, but his face was too tired to cooperate. "You might remember a certain creature from Outside that pretended to be a house on Blaiston Street. It called people to it, then consumed them. After Taylor destroyed it, I had my people collect scrapings of the alien cell tissues and preserve them for analysis. As a result of what they discovered in their labs, I was eventually able to grow a new house, in a setting of my own choice. I had it lobotomized, of course, so it would only eat what I chose to feed it. Never know when you'll need a secret weapon to use against your enemies."

Alex looked at Walker. "Enemies? Like John Taylor, perhaps?"

"Of course," said Walker.

"Do you think he'll ever come back?" said Alex.

"Of course," said Walker. "The murderer always returns to the scene of his crime, and the dog to his vomit. Anyway, my plan is to lure Lilith inside the alien house and see what happens. I doubt very much it will be able to consume her completely, but it might be able to leach off a considerable amount of her power. Make her easier to deal with."

"You'll need to bait your trap," said Alex, peering listlessly at the almost empty glass before him. "She's bound to suspect something. What have we got, that she wants badly enough to walk into certain ambush for?"

"Me," said Walker.

The scene faded out, as the pool's waters went opaque. I fed it more blood, but it didn't want to know. It was tired and scared, and it didn't want to see any more. But I did. So I raised my gift and thrust it into the pool. The two magics combined, and the scrying pool screamed pitifully in my mind as I made it show me what happened next. I had no time for kindness. I'd almost caught up with what had happened while I was gone, and time was running out. The pool's waters shook and trembled, but finally showed me what Walker did next.

I saw Lilith parade through a burned-out business district, at the head of an army so large I couldn't see its full extent. I saw Walker step calmly out of an alleyway at the end of the street to confront her. Lilith stopped abruptly, and all the monsters and zealots jammed up behind her. A slow sullen hush fell across the empty street, broken only by the sounds of distant screams and the low crackle of guttering fires. Walker stood perfectly poised before Lilith, in his smart suit and bowler hat, as though he'd just stepped out of a tea room or a politician's office, to discuss the time of day with an old acquaintance. He'd pushed the tiredness away from him by an effort of will, and looked just like the Walker of old. He smiled easily at Lilith, and tipped his bowler to her.

"Walker," said Lilith, in a voice just like poisoned wine. "My dear Henry. You do get around, don't you? I thought you might take the hint from our last little encounter that I have nothing more to say to you. But you always were a stubborn soul, weren't you? I have to say, you heal remarkably quickly, for a human."

Walker shrugged easily. "Needs must, when the Devil drives. I'm here to take you in, Lilith. Surrender now, and no-one need get hurt."

Lilith laughed girlishly, and actually clapped her hands together before her. "Dear Henry, you were always able to surprise me. What makes you think you can take me in?"

Walker reached inside his jacket and pulled out a gun. It was a bright shining silver, with coloured lights flashing all over it. Walker handled it casually, but his eyes were very cold. "Don't make me have to use this, Lilith."

"Now you're just boring me, Henry."

"Really? Try this."

Walker raised the gun and shot Lilith in the face. The paint capsule hit her right between the eyes. Paint exploded all over her shocked face, a thick evil-smelling purple slime liberally spiked with Alex's holy water. Lilith actually fell back a pace, spitting and sputtering and clawing frantically at her face with both hands. Walker chuckled nastily, turned, and ran. White-hot with rage, Lilith chased after him. I have to give it to Walker; I'd never seen him move so fast in his life. He was already down the street and round the corner before Lilith was even up to speed. I don't think she was used to having to exert herself physically. Walker ran, and Lilith followed, and her somewhat confused army brought up the rear.

Walker paused outside the front door of a house that looked no different from all the others around it, then he darted inside, leaving the door that wasn't a door standing open. Lilith charged through the opening a few moments later, and it slammed shut after her. The army stumbled to a halt outside. One of the leaders tried the door, but it wouldn't open. One of Lilith's children pushed forward, placed an oversized hand on the door and pushed, then cried out in shock and pain as the door tried to eat his hand. The front ranks of the army looked at each other, and decided to stay where they were until Lilith emerged from the house to give them orders.

The scene in the scrying pool changed to show me a rear view of the house that wasn't a house, as Walker came running full pelt out the back door. He ran through the overgrown garden to the back gate, then leaned on it for a while, breathing heavily. He looked back at the house, shuddered once, and immediately regained his

composure. The back wall of the house seemed to heave,
and swell, twisting black veins standing out suddenly in
sharp relief in the fake brickwork. First the wall, then the
whole structure of the house began to shake and shudder.
Black and purple splotches of rot and decay appeared,
and the two windows ran away like pus. Holes like
ragged wounds opened up all over the sloping roof, and
the back door slumped, running away in streams of liquid
foulness. The house hadn't stood a chance against Lilith.
She'd barely been in it a few moments, and already it was
dead and rotting.

Maybe he shouldn't have lobotomized it, after all.

"Damn," said Walker, quite succinctly. He produced a
Strangefellows Membership Card from his pocket,
pressed his thumb against the embossed surface, said the
activating Word, and was gone, teleported back to the relative safety of the bar. I shut off the scene in the pool. I
didn't want to see Lilith's rage when she emerged from
the trap Walker had set for her. I was actually a little jeal-
ous that Alex had given Walker one of his Cards. They
were supposed to be reserved for close friends and allies.
I was also just a bit concerned about what Walker might
do with the Card, in the future. I really didn't like the idea
of his being able to just drop in at the bar, whenever he
felt like it.

Of course, that assumed any of us had a future . . .

The scrying pool was sobbing quietly to itself, but I
made it show me one last vision—what Lilith did next.

Raging mad at being mocked and outmanoeuvred by
Walker, Lilith transported herself and all her great army
straight to the Necropolis. The main building was barricaded, boarded up, and rendered positively indistinct behind a dozen layers of magical defences, but Lilith
ignored them. She tore the air apart with her bare hands,
breaking all the barriers set between this world and that
of the Necropolis's private cemetery. Nothing was hidden

from her, and nothing was safe. The final barrier screamed as it went down, and the cobbled street in this world split from end to end. Through the ragged tear Lilith had made in reality, the grim and grey world of the Necropolis graveyard could clearly be seen. Long streamers of fog drifted out. Lilith gestured sharply for her followers to stay put and stalked forward into the private cemetery.

The vision followed her. The graveyard looked just as cold and depressing as I remembered it, with row upon row of graves and tombstones stretching away to the distant horizon. Lilith looked around her and sniffed contemptuously. The Caretaker reared its earthy head to observe her, took one look, and sank back into the ground again, diving for deep cover. It wanted nothing to do with her. It knew when it was outmatched.

Lilith walked among the graves, glaring about her, and finally stopped and stamped her bare foot impatiently. When she spoke, her voice cracked like a whip on the still and silent air.

"You can all stop lying around, right now! I want every single one of you up and out of those graves, and standing here before me! Why should you lie quietly, when there is work you could be doing for me? Up, now! And the Devil help anyone who dares to keep me waiting!"

She snapped her colourless fingers, and immediately every grave and mausoleum gave up its occupant. They stood in endless rows, in the good suits and gowns they'd been buried in, looking around them in a confused sort of way. Even I was shocked, and not a little impressed. There were major spells defending the private graveyard, but to a Power like Lilith, Life and Death were very similar states.

It had to be said, the returned from the dead didn't look at all happy about their new condition. They'd paid good money in advance, precisely to avoid being disturbed from their rest like this. But they still had enough sense not to argue with Lilith. Even those who had been major players in their day knew better than to cross the ancient and terrible Power standing before them.

"These are your orders," she said crisply. "I want all of you out of here, and back in the Nightside. Snip, snap, no dawdling. Once back in your home territory, you are to kill every living thing you see and destroy everything in your path. No exceptions. Any questions?"

One man raised his hand. Lilith snapped her fingers again, and the reanimated man exploded into a thousand twitching pieces.

"Any more questions?" said Lilith. "I just love answering questions."

There were no more questions. Some of the returned even stuck their hands deep into their pockets so there wouldn't be any unfortunate misunderstandings. Lilith smiled coldly and led her new army back into the Nightside. The newly revived dead didn't object, being ready to do whatever was required of them, as long as they could go back to the comfort of their graves afterwards. Anything for a little quiet resting in peace. Still, some of them did feel the need to discuss their new condition, in guarded whispers and mutters.

"She said kill everyone," said one voice. "Does that mean we're supposed to eat their brains?"

"No, I think that's only in the movies, darling."

"Oh. I think I'd quite like to try eating some brains, actually."

"Now that's just gross," said a third voice.

"Do we have to eat them raw, sweetie; or are we allowed to add condiments?"

"I think it's probably a matter of personal taste, dear."

The ranks of the returned dead streamed through the streets of the Nightside, falling upon every living thing they encountered. Some of them with more enthusiasm than others, but all of them bound to Lilith's will. They couldn't be hurt or stopped, and their sheer numbers overwhelmed any and all defences. A hell of a lot of people had died in the Nightside, down the centuries. Walker sent a small army, under Sandra Chance, of his best people to try and contain the returned dead, but they couldn't be everywhere at once.

Many people were distressed to find themselves fighting off deceased friends and relatives, now intent on killing those who had once been closest to them. There were tears and screams, sometimes on both sides, but the reanimated dead did what they had to, and so, eventually, did the living. The risen dead were burned, blasted, and dismembered, but still they pressed forward. Walker's barricades were soon overrun, and the defenders forced to run for their lives. Walker was forced to order a general retreat, just so he could control it. He ordered the demolition of whole areas, to seal off the better defended sections from those already fallen. There was fighting everywhere now, and fires wide as city blocks raged fiercely, unconfined.

There were those who still had the guts to fight. The Demonz street gang, minor demons who claimed to be political refugees from Hell, poured up out of their nightclub the Pit to defend their territory. Eight feet tall, with curling horns on their brows and cloven hoofs, scarlet as sin and twice as nasty. The reanimated dead stopped in their tracks. They knew real demons when they saw them. Lilith just laughed at the Demonz, said *Children shouldn't stray so far from home,* snapped her pale fingers, and sent all the Demonz back to Hell again.

After that, she went to Time Tower Square, deserted but almost untouched by the chaos all around. Lilith struck a mocking pose before the blocky stone structure that was the Tower, and called loudly for Old Father Time to come out and face her. She had work for him. Minutes passed, and Lilith snarled and stamped her feet as she realised Old Father Time wasn't coming out. She ordered her offspring to tear the Tower apart, and drag Old Father

Time from the ruins to face her displeasure. But, as I knew to my cost, the Tower was seriously defended. The first few Beings to touch the Tower with bad intent just disappeared, blown out of existence like the flame of a candle. Other, greater Powers advanced on the Tower. A terrible stone Eye opened in the wall facing them, and the Powers froze in the glare of that awful regard. The life seeped out of them, and left behind only a handful of ugly stone statues, in awkward poses. The great stone Eye slowly closed again.

Lilith cried out a single angry Word, and the whole stone structure blew apart, until there was nothing left of the Time Tower save a pile of smoking rubble. Lilith glared at what she'd achieved, shaking with effort and re-action, while her army watched carefully to see what would happen next. In the end, it was clear that Old Father Time was either dead or trapped. Either way, he wouldn't be coming out to obey Lilith's wishes, so she spat and cursed, turned on her heel and led her army on to other ventures.

And that brought me up to date. The scrying pool had gone cloudy with shock and trauma, and I left it sobbing quietly to itself. The shop's owner trailed behind me as I left his emporium, complaining bitterly and wringing his hands over what I'd done to his best merchandise. I told him again to send the bill to Walker.

Outside the shop, it was relatively quiet. The fires had run out of things to burn, and the survivors were keeping their heads down and quietly licking their wounds. I walked slowly through deserted streets, and no-one bothered me. Just as well. I had some thinking to do. Why had Lilith been so determined to control Old Father Time? Could there be something about Time travel, or perhaps Time itself, that would be a danger to Lilith's plans? I smiled mirthlessly. It beat the hell out of me. I needed advice and information, which meant . . . I needed to talk to Walker.

I pulled my Strangefellows Membership Card from my pocket, activated it, and called for Walker. After making me wait a little while, to keep me respectful, Walker's face looked out of the Card at me. He looked calm and poised and completely confident. He might have got away with it, if he hadn't also looked like hell.

"Taylor!" he said brightly. "Back at last, after your extended vacation? I should have known you'd turn up for the main event. I didn't know these Cards could be used for communication."

So Alex didn't tell you everything, I thought, a little smugly. "I'm back," I said. "We need to talk."

"Couldn't agree more, old chap," said Walker. "I need to know everything you know."

"We don't have that much time," I said. I never could resist a good cheap shot. "Right now, we need to talk to the Authorities. Get their resources behind us. They need to hear what I have to tell them. I need you to set up a meeting."

"I've been trying to contact them ever since this whole mess started," said Walker, just a little tartly. "No-one's returning my calls."

"Call them again," I said. "Drop my name, and set up a meet. We need to do this in person. They'll talk to Lilith's son."

"Yes," said Walker. "Yes, they just might. Very well, I'll arrange a face-to-face, at the Londinium Club."

"Of course," I said. "Where else?"

NINE

Thrown to the Wolves

I found an undead Harley Davidson lurking in an alleyway, and persuaded it to give me a lift to the Londinium
Club, in return for squeezing the essential juices out of
several nearby corpses into the undead machine's fuel
tank. I swear other people don't have days like this. The
motorcycle carried me smoothly through the Nightside,
weaving in and out of crashed and overturned vehicles
littering the abandoned road. The air rushing into my face
was hot and dry, thick with drifting smoke and ashes. It
stank of burned meat. Even above the roar of the bike, I
could still hear distant screams. Riding through the deserted streets, lit by the intermittent glow of burning
buildings rather than the sleazy flush of hot neon, reminded me uncomfortably of the devastated future Nightside that was coming. A future coming true in front of my
eyes, despite everything I did to try and stop it.

You're trying to steer again, said the Harley. *Don't. I know what I'm doing.*

"Then I envy you," I said. "Really. You have no idea."

That's right; condescend to me, just because I'm undead. You wait until the mystical Vampire Lords of the Twenty-seventh Dimension descend in their crimson flying saucers to make me Grand High Overlord of the Nightside . . . Oh. Damn. I said that out loud, didn't I? Sorry. I've not been taking my medication, lately.

"It's all right," I said. "We've all got a lot on our minds at the moment."

The Harley mournfully sang Meatloaf's "Bat out of Hell" as we cruised through the deserted streets. There were hardly any people around now. They were either hiding, or evacuated, or dead. There were bodies everywhere, and sometimes only parts of bodies. I saw piled-up severed heads, and dozens of severed hands laid out in strange patterns. Something had strung a web of knotted human entrails between a series of lamp-posts. I didn't raise my Sight. I didn't want to understand. I didn't want to see all the new ghosts.

The motorcycle dropped me off outside the Londinium Club, then disappeared into the night at speed. It thought there was still somewhere safe to go, and I didn't have the heart to disillusion it. I wasn't blessed with the same delusion. I knew better. Walker was already waiting for me, of course. He stood at the foot of the Club's steps, looking sadly down at the dead body of the Doorman. The Londinium's most faithful servant lay sprawled across the steps, before the entrance he'd guarded for so many centuries. Something had ripped the Doorman's head off and impaled it on the spiked railings. The expression on the face was more surprised than anything.

"He was supposed to be immortal," observed Walker. "I didn't think anything could kill him."

"Now that Lilith's back, all bets are off," I said. "It is a pity."

Walker gave me a hard look. "You know very well you couldn't stand the man, Taylor."

"I gave him a rose once," I said.

Walker sniffed, unconvinced, and led the way up the steps to what was left of the Londinium. The oldest Gentleman's Club in the Nightside had seen better days. The magnificent façade was cracked and holed, smoke-blackened and fire-damaged. It looked like the outer wall of a city that had finally fallen to its besiegers. The huge single door had been burst inwards, forced off its hinges. The great slab of ancient wood lay toppled on the floor of the lobby, torn and gouged with deep claw marks. The once-elegant lobby had been thoroughly trashed and befouled. The statues had been shattered and the paintings defaced. The delicately veined marble pillars were cracked and broken, and the unknown Michelangelo painting that covered the entire ceiling was now half-hidden behind smoke stains and sprayed arterial blood.

Bodies littered the wide floor, left to lie where they had fallen. Many were mutilated, or half-eaten. Most of them looked to have been unarmed. Important men and servants lay together, probably killed fighting back-to-back, equal at last in death.

"Something got here before us," I said, because I had to say something. "You think any of the bastards are still around?"

"No," said Walker, kneeling beside one of the bodies. "The flesh is cold, the blood-stains are dry. Whatever happened here, we missed it." He looked at the dead man's face for a long moment, frowning slightly.

"Did you know him?" I asked.

"I knew all of them," he said, rising to his feet again. "Some were very good, some were very bad, and none of them deserved to die like this."

He stalked across the lobby, his back very straight, stepping carefully round the scattered bodies. I followed him, my shoulders tense with the anticipation of unseen watching eyes. Someone had gone to a lot of trouble to trash the Nightside's most visible symbol of power and authority. Walker finally came to a halt facing the right-hand wall, and solemnly considered a part of it that looked no different from any other part. I stood beside him, looking hard for any sign of a concealed door or panel, but I couldn't see anything. And I'm usually really good at spotting things like that. Walker fished in his waistcoat pocket for a long moment, but when he finally brought his hand out, it was empty. He held the empty hand up before me, the fingers pinched together as though holding something.

"This," he said, "is a key that isn't a key, that will open a door that isn't a door, to a room that isn't always there."

I considered his empty hand. "Either the strain is finally getting to you, or you're being cryptic again. This secret room . . . it's not by any chance going to try to eat me, is it?"

He smiled briefly. "It's a real key. But invisible. Feel it."

He put something I couldn't see into my hand. It felt cold and metallic. "Okay," I said. "That's creepy. If the door is as invisible as the key, how are we going to find it?"

"Because it isn't invisible to me," Walker said airily, taking the key back again. "I serve the Authorities, so I get to see everything I need to see."

"Show-off," I said, and he smiled briefly again.

He thrust the key only he could see into the lock only he could see, and part of the wall before us disappeared. I was staring so hard by now that my eyes were beginning to hurt. Walker strolled into the newly revealed room before us with just a hint of smugness, and I sighed and followed him in. It figured that the Authorities would have their very own special room to hold their meetings in, exclusive even from other members of the Nightside's most exclusive Gentleman's Club.

"The Authorities don't agree to meet with just any-one," Walker murmured. "You should feel honoured."

"Oh, I do," I said. "Really. You have no idea."

Walker actually winced. "Somehow, I know this isn't going to go well."

The wall reappeared behind us, sealing us in, and the room abruptly snapped into focus. It was protected by very powerful magics. I could feel them, crawling on my skin like living static. The room itself was something of a cliché, the very essence of a private room in a Gentleman's Club. Oversized but no doubt extremely comfortable chairs, rich furnishings, and splendid decorations. Far more splendid, indeed, than the expensively tanned, personally trained but still sloppy, overdressed men sitting slumped in their big chairs, with their big drinks and their big cigars. I took my time looking them over, the ten powerful men who ran the Nightside, inasmuch as anyone did. You wouldn't know their names. You've never seen their faces in the glossies. These men were above that. They all had the same casual arrogance of people used to getting what they wanted when they wanted it. Somehow, I just knew we weren't going to get along.

Walker introduced me to the Authorities, then moved aside to stand leaning against the William Morris wallpaper, his arms folded, as though to indicate he'd done all that could reasonably be expected of him. Maybe he simply wanted to be out of the line of fire, for when everything inevitably went wrong. And though he must have had many questions of his own for his absentee masters, he seemed content to leave the lead to me. For the moment, at least.

"So," I said finally, "you're the grey men, the businessmen, the faceless men who only ever operate behind the scenes. Somehow, I always thought you'd be . . . bigger. Talk to me, Authorities. Tell me what I need to know. While there's still time."

"I am Harper, and I speak for us all," said the man nearest me. His face was far too old for his jet-black hair, and his waistcoat strained over a bulging stomach. It was covered with cigar ash that he couldn't be bothered to brush away. Presumably he had someone to do that for him, in his own world. He stared coldly at me with piggy, deep-set eyes. "Our ancestors made their fortunes operating in the Nightside of Roman times, during their occupation. Our families have spent generations building on those fortunes. We own all the businesses here, at one remove or another. There's nothing that happens that we don't take our cut. The Nightside belongs to us."

"Not for much longer," I said. "If Lilith has her way. This isn't just a corporate take-over she'd proposing, she plans to kill us all. Or hasn't that penetrated your thick skulls yet?"

My voice must have got a little sharp, because that was when the Authorities' bodyguards decided to make themselves known to me. They manifested abruptly, one on each side of the room, and I studied them warily. Two basically humanoid forms, large and overpowering, one made of pure light, one of pure darkness. It would be hard to say which was more unpleasant to the eye. They were presences rather than physical forms, and I could feel power radiating off them. It was like standing in front of a furnace when someone unexpectedly opened the door.

"They used to be angels," said Harper, with more than a hint of smugness. "From Above, and Below. Now they work for us."

"How are the mighty fallen," I said, just to be saying something. Never let the other side know when you've been seriously impressed. "I suppose that's why they don't have wings any more. Or halos."

"You cannot conceive how much we have lost," said the figure of light, its voice like cracking ice floes.

"But we have also gained much," said the figure of darkness, in a voice like a burning orphanage. "We are here because we developed . . . appetites. Tastes for things that can only be found in the material world. Our new masters . . . indulge us."

"We take our comforts here," said the light. "To our eternal shame."

"To our endless satisfaction," said the dark.

"But why serve the Authorities?" I said. "Even as diminished as you are, you must know they're not worthy of you."

"We have to serve someone," said the light.

"It's in our nature," said the dark.

"Enough," said Harper, and immediately both figures fell silent. Harper glared at me, and I glared right back. He raised his voice a little, to convince both of us who was really in charge here. "Normally, we run the Nightside from outside. We live in London proper, in the sane world. We're only here now because Walker summoned us with your name. What do you want with us, John Taylor?"

"Answers, to start with," I said, meeting his gaze unflinchingly. "Why haven't you sent your armies to support Walker? Don't you know how bad things are here?"

"We know," said Harper. "But what help could we send that could hope to stand against Lilith and her followers? We're not in the business of throwing good lives away after bad."

Walker stirred for the first time. "Bad? Those were my people!"

Harper didn't even look at him. "Not now, Walker. I'm talking."

"If not now, then when?" said Walker, and his voice was colder than I'd ever heard it before. "How many years have I and my people served you here, protecting your interests in the Nightside? Is this how you reward us—by throwing us to the wolves?"

Harper finally looked at him, but only to smile condescendingly. "You mustn't take it personally, Walker. It's just business."

"You look nervous," I said suddenly. "All of you. Uncomfortable. Sweating. You don't like being here, do you?"

"As you said, the Nightside has become a dangerous place." Harper took a long draw on his cigar. "Before Walker contacted us with your name, we had been preparing to seal off the Nightside, closing every entrance and exit until all this . . . unpleasantness has run its course."

"You're abandoning us?" I said.

"Why not? You're only a business interest. A cash cow, from which we squeeze every penny we can. We are aware of the powerful men and women who come to your little freak show, to indulge in the pleasures and excitements they can't find anywhere else, but we . . . We have only ever cared about the profit they made us. For us, the Nightside is simply a commodity, that we exploit. Correct, Walker?"

"Don't look at me," said Walker, surprisingly. "I see things differently, these days."

I looked at him for a moment. There was something in his voice . . . but that would have to wait. I turned back to Harper.

"If the Nightside falls to Lilith, then so does the rest of the world. You can't hope to contain a Power like her. She will break out, then there'll be nowhere far enough or safe enough for you to hide."

"So we have come to believe," said Harper, reluctantly. He glared at his cigar, as though it had failed him in some way, and stubbed it out in an ashtray with quick, angry movements. "So, it seems we have no choice but to make a deal with Lilith. Very well. We can do that. We're good at making deals. It's what we do, after all. That is why we agreed to meet with you here, John Taylor. Lilith's son. You will be our agent, our representative, in these negotiations. Talk to your mother and promise her . . . whatever it takes, to reach an accommodation. We have already revealed our presence to her and summoned her here to talk with us."

Walker stood up straight, pushing himself away from the wall he'd been leaning on. "What? Why didn't you consult me first? Do you know what you've done, you bloody fools . . ."

"Not now, Walker!" Harper didn't even look at him.

He was still doing his best to intimidate me with an imperious stare. "We are rich beyond the nightmares of avarice, Taylor. We can afford to be flexible, if we have to. Better to share the wealth of the Nightside with your mother than risk seeing it destroyed. It's just a matter of finding out what she wants . . . We're all reasonable people, after all. I'm sure we can come to an understanding with Lilith, with your help."

"Lilith isn't reasonable," I said. "She isn't even people. You have no idea what you're dealing with. She isn't interested in money, or even in power, as you understand it. She just wants to wipe the whole slate clean and start again. And replace Humanity with something more suited to her needs."

One whole wall of the private room suddenly disappeared, ripped away by an outside force. We all looked round, startled, to discover that the room now looked directly out onto the Nightside. Nothing stood between us and the dark, the blazing buildings, and the streets filled with smoke and screams. And there before us stood Lilith, naked and magnificent, with all her monstrous Court ranked behind her. The Authorities rose to their feet, stumbling and awkward, staring with wide horrified eyes.

The two former angels surged forward, to stand between the Authorities and Lilith, their power shimmering on the air around them like a heat haze. Lilith smiled at them and said *Go home*, and the light and dark figures both disappeared in a moment, banished from the material planes by the sheer force of her will. I had a good idea where she'd sent them, and I doubted either of them could expect much of a welcome back.

"So," said Lilith, stepping gracefully forward into the private room, her voice light and teasing, "you're the Authorities. The Secret Masters of the Nightside, the Big Men . . . We meet at last. Only, I have to say, you don't look very big to me. You look much more like little boys,

way out of their depth. Come to me. Come to Mommie . . ."

Her presence ignited, filling the whole room, vast and
overwhelming. I had to look away, retreating behind my
strongest mental shields, while the ten most powerful
men in the Nightside, and therefore the world, fell to their
knees and went to Lilith on all fours, like swine before a
goddess. Walker started forward. I grabbed him by the
arm and hustled him towards the invisible door. He found
the key and opened the door, his hand steady even though
his face was torn with conflicting emotions. I looked
back, briefly.

Lilith laughed, to see the high-and-mighty Authorities
cringe and fawn at her colourless feet. "Why, you're so
cute! I could eat you up . . . but I think you'd probably
make me sick. Fortunately, my children have far more ro-
bust appetites . . ."

She laughed again, as her horrid offspring surged forward. I pushed Walker through the door, following him
into the relative safety of the Club's lobby. As the door
swung slowly shut behind us, I looked back one last time.
And saw Lilith's monstrous children fall upon the
screaming Authorities and tear at them hungrily, like
wolves let into the fold.

TEN

A Chance for Revenge

I ended up having to drag Walker back through the lobby and out onto the steps of the Londinium Club. His eyes weren't tracking properly, and he was mumbling to himself. Once we were safely outside, I glanced quickly around to be sure we were alone, then sat down on the steps to get my composure back. With the invisible door shut again, Lilith shouldn't be able to come after us. For a while, anyway. Walker sat down suddenly next to me, all his usual poise and confidence gone. I suppose it's not an easy thing, to see the lords and masters you've followed all your life revealed as cowards and scumbags, then turned into monster food. The night seemed relatively quiet, and no-one came by to bother us. I looked at Walker. A pain in my arse for most of my life, I'd often wanted to see him brought down, but not like this. He was staring out into the night as though he'd never seen it before.

"The Authorities are dead," he said abruptly. "What do I do now?"

"Be your own man," I said. "You can still give the orders that need giving, kick the arses that need kicking. Get things done. Someone's got to lead the resistance. Who's got more experience than you? You're needed, Walker; now more than ever."

Walker turned his head slowly to look at me. "You're Lilith's son," he said finally. "You're the King in waiting. You're the legendary John Taylor, who always snatches victory from the jaws of defeat. Maybe you should be in charge."

"No," I said. "I've never wanted that. I have enough trouble being responsible for myself, never mind anyone else. And I've got other things to do. Don't ask what. It would only upset you. You've always been The Man, Walker. So suck it up and solider on."

He smiled briefly. "You sound very like your father sometimes, John." He stood up, and just like that all his old poise and confidence were back again. "I suppose someone's got to turn you rabble into a disciplined fighting force. So, I'm going back to Strangefellows. Where will you go?"

"In search of some heavy-duty backup," I said, getting to my feet. "We need more big guns on our side."

"And if there aren't any?"

I grinned at him. "Then I'll improvise. Suddenly and violently and all over the place."

He nodded. "It's what you do best."

He took out his Membership Card, activated it, and stepped through into the relative safety of Strangefellows bar. The Card disappeared with a soft sucking sound and a brief flurry of sparks, and I was left standing alone on the steps of the Londinium Club. I pushed my hands deep into the pockets of my trench coat, and looked out into the night. All the buildings around me were wrecked or burned out. Bodies everywhere. Screams in the distance, strange lights flaring on the horizon. The Nightside was going down for the third time, and I was running out of ideas. There had to be someone else, some Power or major player who still owed me a favour, or could be fooled into thinking they did . . . but I couldn't think who. I couldn't do this on my own. I needed someone powerful enough, or tricky enough, to stop this War in its tracks before it got out of hand. Before it led to the terrible future that was becoming more real, more inevitable, by the minute. Unfortunately there was only one name left on my list, the one I'd been trying so hard not to think of. Because he scared the crap out of me.

The Lord of Thorns. The Overseer of the Nightside, appointed directly by God to keep an eye on things.

Mostly, he didn't intervene personally. He was the last judge of all disputes, the Nightside's court of last resort, the one you only went to when everything else had failed and you were tired of living anyway. I'd been half-expecting him to turn up and start smiting everything in sight for some time now. Since he hadn't, it looked like I was going to have to give him his wake-up call. Lucky old me. The Lord of Thorns lived in the World Beneath, the miles and miles of caverns, catacombs, and stone galleries that lay deep below the Nightside. The place where you went, when the Nightside wasn't dark enough for you. The Lord of Thorns slept his sleep of centuries in a crystal cave in the deepest, darkest part of the World Beneath, and God help anyone who disturbed him unnecessarily.

I had only met him once, and that was more than enough. *I am the stone that breaks all hearts,* he'd said. *I am the nails that bound the Christ to his cross. I am the necessary suffering that makes us all stronger* . . . God's power flowed through him, the power over life and death and everything between. He could save or damn you with a word or a glance, and his every decision was binding. I was pretty sure he didn't approve of people like me, even though he'd been friendly enough, in a distant sort of way, at our last meeting.

Why hadn't he come forth to confront Lilith?

I wasn't at all keen on descending into the World Beneath, to talk to him. It was a foul and dangerous place, and a hell of a long way to travel, besides. Especially if he had already surfaced somewhere, to show Lilith the error of her ways . . . I pushed the thought back and forth for a while, but I was only putting off what I knew I had to do, so in the end I just sighed heavily, took the risk, and raised my gift. Wherever the Lord of Thorns was, in or under the Nightside, my gift would find him.

My inner eye, my third eye, opened wide and soared up into the night sky, my Sight spreading out for miles in every direction, till the whole of the Nightside lay sprawled below me like a twisted and convoluted map. Whole areas were burning, out of control, while monsters roamed the streets and panicked mobs ran this way and that. I forced my Sight to focus in on the one individual soul I was searching for, and my mind's eye plummeted down, narrowing in on a single speck of light in the dark. I'd found the Lord of Thorns. Just as I'd thought, he had left the World Beneath for the surface; but much to my surprise, the most powerful man in the Nightside was currently hiding out in St. Jude's, the only real church in the Nightside.

I quickly shut down my Sight, and dropped back into my head. I took a few moments to make sure all my mental barriers were safely in place again. I really didn't want Lilith to know where I was till I was ready to face her. I considered what to do next. St. Jude's wasn't anywhere near the Street of the Gods, because it was the real deal. An ancient place of worship, almost as old as the Nightside itself, older by far than the Christianity that had given it its present name. (St. Jude is the patron Saint of lost causes, in case you were wondering.) It was the one place in all the world where you could go to speak with your Maker and be sure of getting a reply. Which is why most people didn't go there. Unless they absolutely had to.

St. Jude's was located way over on the other side of the Nightside, a long way from anywhere, and separated from me by miles and miles of very dangerous territory. Walking was not an option. I wished I'd told the Harley to stick around. I took my Membership Card out of my pocket, fired it up, and called for Alex Morrisey in a loud and demanding voice. There was a pause, just to keep me from getting above myself, then his face appeared, glowering out of the Card at me.

"Taylor! About time you turned up again. If only so you can pay your bar bill before the world ends. And what have you done to Walker? He showed up here a few minutes ago looking like someone had put the fear of God into him. I don't think I've ever seen him so pissed off at the world. He's currently charging round my bar yelling orders at everyone like Captain Kirk on crack, and organising everyone within an inch of their lives."

"Probably just a midlife crisis," I said. "Put Tommy Oblivion on, would you, Alex? I need to ask him something."

Alex sniffed loudly, just to remind me he was no-one's servant, and his face disappeared from my Card, which then played me a tinny Muzak version of Prodigy's "Firestarter" while I was on hold. Tommy's face finally peered out of the Card at me, frowning suspiciously.

"What do you want, Taylor?"

"You," I said.

And I reached into the Membership Card, grabbed him by the front of his ruffled shirt, and dragged him through the Card to where I was. The Card expanded hastily to let him through, but even so it was a tight squeeze for a moment. Tommy sat down suddenly on the Club steps as his head spun from the sudden transfer, and the Card shrank back to normal size and shut itself off, possibly in protest at such rough handling. I put it away, and helped Tommy to his feet.

"Son of a bitch!" he said.

"Yes," I said. "That just about sums me up."

He glared at me. "I didn't know you could do that with a Card."

"Most people can't," I said. "But I'm special."

Tommy sniffed. "I suppose that's one way of putting it." He brushed himself down here and there, repairing his appearance as best he could, then looked at the headless Doorman, lying on the steps beside him. He moved fastidiously a little further away from the blood. "Been busy, I see."

"For once, not my fault." I filled him in on what had been happening, or at least as much of it as I thought he could cope with, and explained my need to get to St. Jude's in a hurry. He really wasn't keen on the idea, but I can be very persuasive when I have to be. Not to mention downright threatening. I only had to mention a certain video that had come into my hands, featuring him and a very athletic exotic dancer, who happened to be married to someone exceedingly scary, and suddenly he was only too willing to help me out. (I didn't actually have the video. I'd just heard of it and run a bluff. The guilty flee . . .)

Tommy Oblivion's gift manifested subtly on the air around us, and everything became uncertain. Tommy was an existentialist, and his gift allowed him to express his uncertainty about the world in a real and very physical way. The more he thought about a thing, the more possibilities he could see, and he fixed on the reality he preferred and made it solid. By concentrating hard enough, Tommy was able to convince the world that not only were we not where it thought we were, but actually we were somewhere else entirely.

And so, in the blink of an eye we left the Londinium Club behind us and materialised outside the Church of St. Jude. A dodo wandered past, hooting mournfully, a flock of passenger pigeons flapped by overhead, and an ostrich with two heads looked confusedly at itself, but they were only a few odd possibilities generated by Tommy's gift. He concentrated on shutting his gift down, while I looked around us. Everything but the church had been razed to the ground, for as far as the eye could see. It stood alone, an old squat stone structure in the middle of a wasteland. A wide-open plain of ash and dust, where thick curls of glowing ground fog surged this way and that under the urging of a fitful wind. It was very dark, with just the blue-white glare of the oversized moon shining off the church walls. In the distance, fires leapt up briefly, screams rang out, but it was all very far away. The War had come and gone here, and left nothing behind but the church.

"I'm trying very hard to be existential about this," Tommy said finally, "But this really is a god-awful place. I'd like to say something like . . . from the ashes of the old shall arise a brave new Nightside . . . but my heart isn't in it."

"If a new Nightside does arise, I doubt it would be anything you or I would recognise, or would want to," I said. "Not if Lilith has her way."

"God, you're depressing to be around, Taylor. My brother's more cheerful than you, and he's dead. Who are we here to see, anyway?"

"The Lord of Thorns."

"Right," said Tommy. "I am leaving now. Good-bye. Write if you get work. I am out of here . . ."

"Tommy . . ."

"No! No way in Hell! There is absolutely nothing you can say or do or threaten me with that would persuade me to have anything to do with Him! I would rather eat my own head! The Lord of Thorns is the only person who actually scares me more than Lilith! She only wants to kill me; he wants to judge me!"

"You could leave," I said. "But it's a really long walk to anywhere civilised. All on your own, in the dark. And if you try to teleport back using your gift . . . I'll just have the Lord of Thorns drag you back again."

"You know the Lord of Thorns?"

"I know everyone," I said airily.

Tommy kicked at the dusty ground. "Bully," he muttered, not looking at me.

"You're my ride home, Tommy," I said, not unkindly. "You don't have to come into the church with me, if you don't want to. You can guard the door."

"It'll all end in tears," said Tommy.

I tried the church's only door, and it opened easily at my touch. I left Tommy sulking outside, and went in. The bare stone walls were grey and featureless, with only a series of narrow slits for windows. Short stubby candles that never went out burned in old lead wall holders, casting a cold judgemental light. Two rows of blocky wooden pews, without a cushion in sight. The altar was just a great slab of stone, covered with a cloth of spotless white samite. A single silver cross hung on the wall over the altar. And that was it. You didn't come to St. Jude's for frills and fancies.

This was a place where prayers were answered, and if you didn't like the answers you got, that was your problem.

A single ragged figure sat slumped on the cold stone floor, leaning against the altar, embracing it with desperate arms. It was the Lord of Thorns. He looked like he'd been crying. He also looked like he'd been dragged through Hell backwards. Instead of the grand Old Testament Prophet I remembered, he looked like one of the homeless, like a refugee. The Overseer of the Nightside had been reduced to a man in torn and bloodied robes. His long grey hair and beard had been half–burned away. He didn't look up as I walked down the aisle towards him, but he flinched at the sound of my footsteps, like a dog that's been kicked once too often. I knelt before him, took his chin in my hand, and made him look at me. He trembled at my touch.

"What are you doing here?" I said. I didn't mean for it to come out as harshly as it did, but that's St. Jude's for you.

"It's all gone," he said, in a distant, empty voice. "So

I'm hiding. Hiding out, in the one place where even Lilith's power can't touch me. I believe that. I have to believe that. It's all I've got left."

I let go of his chin, and made an effort to soften my voice. "What happened?"

His eyes came up to meet mine, and a Vision appeared in my mind's eye, showing me Lilith's descent into the World Beneath. She came in force, with all her monstrous Court, smashing through ancient defences and protections as though they weren't even there, and set her people to destroying everything and everyone. As above, so below. Just because she could. She wiped out the Eaters of the Dead, the Solitudes in their cells, the Subterraneans in their sprawling city of catacombs. A warning went out ahead of her, echoing from gallery to gallery, and some came out to fight and some dug themselves in deeper; but none of it did any good. Lilith and her terrible offspring pushed relentlessly on, destroying whole nests of vampires and ghouls and Elder Spawn, and even the worms of the earth in their deep deep tunnels.

The Lord of Thorns came forth from his crystal cave, wrapped in power and a cold, awful anger, to set his faith and authority against Lilith. For he was the Voice of God, and she was but a name out of the past. He had his staff of power, its wood taken from a tree grown from a sliver of the original Tree of Life itself, brought to Britain long and long ago by Joseph of Arimathea. The Lord of Thorns stood in Lilith's way, and she slapped him aside contemptuously. She took his staff and it shattered into pieces in her grasp. She walked on, leaving him lying helpless in the dirt, and not even the least of her offspring would deign to touch him. The killing continued, and there was nothing he could do to stop it. He made himself watch, as a penance. And when it was all over, the Lord of Thorns made his way up from the World Beneath and came to St. Jude's. To hide.

"You have to understand," he said, as the Vision faded from my mind. "When Lilith appeared, I thought I'd finally discovered my true purpose, my reason for being in the Nightside. That this was my destiny—to stop Lilith when no-one else could. But I was wrong. I was nothing, next to her. After so many years of judging others, I was judged . . . and found unworthy."

"But . . . you're one of the greatest Powers in the Nightside!"

"Not compared to her. I forgot . . . in the end I'm just a man, blessed with God's power. And my faith . . . was nothing compared to her certainty."

"All right," I said. "We need backup. Can we use St. Jude's to call for Heavenly help? For direct divine intervention?"

"What do you think I've been doing?" said the Lord of Thorns. "The Nightside was expressly designed from its first conception so that neither Heaven nor Hell could intervene directly. And it was decided long ago in the Courts of the Holy that this Great Experiment would be allowed to continue, to see where it would lead. I was placed here to Oversee the Experiment, to keep it on track. But now that the Nightside's creator has returned, it seems my time and my purpose are at an end. There will be no outside help. The Nightside must save itself. If it can."

"There is a resistance," I said. "Come with me. You can be a part of it."

But the Lord of Thorns just sat where he was, shaking his grey head. "No. I am not who I thought I was. So I will stay here and pray for guidance."

I tried to argue with him, but I don't think he really heard me. Lilith broke him when she broke his staff. So I left what was once the most feared man in the Nightside, sitting mumbling to himself, in the one place he still felt safe.

I went outside and found myself facing a crowd of hard-faced and heavily armed individuals. Their expressions lit up at the sight of me, and not in a good way. At their head stood Sandra Chance, resplendent in her thick crimson swirls of liquid latex and not much else. Though the old-fashioned pistol holstered on her bare hip was a new addition. She grinned at me, very unpleasantly. I looked at Tommy Oblivion, who was standing very very still, with his back pressed against the wall of the church.

"Sorry, old sport," he said miserably. "Didn't even hear them coming. Just popped out of nowhere."

"Have you at least asked them what they want?" I said.

"Oh, I'm pretty sure they want to speak to you, John. In fact, they were most insistent on it being a surprise."

"It's all right, Tommy," I said, trying to hide the fact that internally I was hyperventilating. "I know who they are. They're bounty hunters. How did you find me here, Sandra?"

"I can get answers from the dead, remember?" She was still smiling, not at all pleasantly. "And there are a lot of dead up and about just at the moment. The dead know many things that are hidden from the living. They have . . . an overview. And I can get them to tell me anything."

"Yes," I said. "And I know how. It's one thing to love the dead, but you take it far too literally. You coffin chaser, you."

"Am I understanding this correctly?" said Tommy. "You mean she actually . . ."

"Oh yes," I said.

"Now that's just tacky. I can't believe I shared a picnic with her."

"Shut up, Tommy," said Sandra, not taking her eyes off me.

"In case you hadn't noticed, there is a War going on," I said. "This really isn't the time . . ."

"There's always a war going on somewhere in the Nightside," said Sandra. "You should know—you've started your fair share of them. My associates and I have decided that we don't care. We want the reward on your head. It's a really big reward; one of the biggest bounties ever posted in the Nightside. The very well connected families of the thirteen Reasonable Men you slaughtered want you dead, John, and they don't care how much it costs them. There's enough money on the table to buy all of us a way out of the Nightside and into some distant dimension where even Lilith can't reach. And still leave enough cold cash for all of us to live like royalty, in our new home. So, revenge, escape, and all our dreams come true. In return for your head, preferably no longer connected to your body. See how neatly it all works out?"

"I thought you said you owed me," I said carefully. "For saving your life in the Necropolis graveyard?"

"Whatever small debt I may have owed you, I more than paid it off being a good soldier for Walker and defending the Nightside during your absence. I want you dead, John. I can't even breathe easily while you're still among the living. You murdered my sweet Saint of Suffering, my beloved Lamentation. You have to pay for that. I put together this little band of bounty hunters, some of the very best in the business, just so I could be sure you wouldn't dodge your death this time. Try your little bag of tricks against professionals, Taylor, and see where it gets you."

She had a point. I considered the dozen or so bounty hunters fanned out in a wide semicircle before me, covering all the possible escape routes. Most were vaguely familiar faces, and three of them were actually famous, almost in a class with Suzie Shooter herself. At least she wasn't here. Then I really would have been in trouble. The tall scarecrow figure in Sally Army cast-offs was Dominic Flipside, a short-range teleporter. Frighteningly quick and sneaky, you never knew from which direction he'd come at you next. Whispering Ivy was a rogue anima from Wales, made up entirely from flowers and thorns, an ever-shifting montage of natural forms in the vague shape of a woman. When she moved, it sounded like the whispering of owls. And Cold Harald, dressed as always in the starkest black and white, with a mind like a calculating machine. He always worked the odds, his logic unclouded by any trace of emotion or humanity. He held a machine pistol in each hand and looked like he knew how to use them. Any one of these three would have worried me, but all of them together . . . and Sandra Chance . . . I thought about running back into the church and screaming for sanctuary, but I knew I'd never make the second step.

"Don't even think about the church," said Sandra. "Or we'll shoot your friend."

Tommy looked at her, hurt. "After we worked together, such a short time ago? Have you no shame? You wound me, madam."

"If you don't shut up, I'll wound you somewhere really painful," said Sandra. "It's up to you, Taylor. Surrender, and we'll make it quick. You can go out with some dignity, at least. Make us work for your head, and we'll all take turns expressing our displeasure on your helpless body."

"Come and take it," I said. "If you can."

"I was hoping you'd say that," said Sandra Chance. "Remember, people, do what you like to the body but don't damage the head. Our patrons won't pay up unless the face is unquestionably his. I think they want to take turns pissing on it. Otherwise, anything goes."

Tommy Oblivion stepped forwards. He'd always been a lot braver than people gave him credit for. His gift manifested very subtly on the air, making his words seem the very epitome of reasonableness and good sense.

"Come," he said warmly, his arms reaching out to embrace everyone. "Let us reason together . . ."

"Let's not," said Cold Harald, in his flat, clipped voice, and he shot Tommy half a dozen times in the stomach. Tommy staggered back under the impact, slamming up against the church wall, then slid slowly down it until he was sitting on the ground. The whole bottom half of his ruffled shirt was slick with blood.

"Oh dear," he said quietly. "Oh dear." He bit his lip against the pain, and I could see him trying to concentrate, trying to raise his gift, so he could find a possibility where the bullets hadn't hit him. But his face was already white and beaded with sweat, his breathing hurried and shallow. I could feel his gift sparking on and off, but pain and stress were getting in the way of his concentration.

I couldn't expect any help from him. I was on my own.

I palmed an incendiary from out of my sleeve and tossed it into the midst of the advancing bounty hunters. Fire and smoke exploded noisily, and two of the bounty hunters fell broken and bleeding to the ground. The rest scattered. Dominic Flipside giggled, a long knife suddenly in each hand, then he disappeared, air rushing in to fill the space where he'd been. I felt as much as heard him reappear almost immediately behind me, and spun round, one arm raised. He cut me open from wrist to elbow, and disappeared again. Blood soaked the length of my coat sleeve.

Cold Harald stepped forward, raising both machine pistols to target me. Dominic Flipside was already gone. I fired up my gift, used it to find where he'd reappear, and stepped forward to meet Cold Harald. He hesitated, expecting some trick, some magic. Dominic Flipside appeared behind me, and lunged silently forward with his long knife. I stepped aside at the last moment, and Dominic plunged on to stab Cold Harald through the heart. His fingers tightened on the triggers of his machine pistols, and blew a dozen holes through Dominic Flipside. Both of them were dead before they hit the ground.

There was a rustling of plants, and the murmuring of dreaming owls, as Whispering Ivy stretched out a hand made of petals and thorns. She sprouted fierce tendrils of barbed greenery, her shifting shape rising up and towering over me, then she stopped abruptly. There was the sound of crackling flames, the smell of smoke. She looked back, turning her flowery head impossibly far round. While she was fixed on me, Tommy had crawled around behind her and set fire to her with his mono-grammed gold lighter. Whispering Ivy shrieked as the flames shot up incredibly fast, consuming her construct body, and she ran off across the open ashy plain, howling shrilly, a shrinking flickering light in the gloom.

I looked at the remaining bounty hunters. They were all frozen in place, horrified at how quickly I'd taken out their star players. They all looked at Sandra Chance, to see what she would do. To her credit, she'd already thrown off any surprise or shock she might have felt, and had drawn the old-fashioned pistol from its holster. It was an ugly, mean gun, built with function in mind, not aes-thetics. The metal was blue-black, the barrel unfashion-ably long. It looked like what it was—a killing tool.

"This is an enchanted pistol," Sandra Chance said steadily. "It never misses. It belonged originally to the famed Western duellist, Dead Eye Dick, renowned hero of dime novels and at least one song. I dug up his grave and broke open his coffin to get this gun. I had to break his fingers to make him let go of it. I'd been saving it for a special occasion. You should feel honoured, John."

"People keep telling me that," I said.

She pulled the trigger while I was still speaking, and shot me three times in the chest. It was like being kicked by a horse, an impact so great it knocked all the breath out of my lungs and sent me stumbling backwards. The pain was remarkably focused; I could feel each separate bullet hole. There was a roaring in my head, and I still couldn't breathe. I bent forward over the pain, as though bowing to my killer, to the inevitable, and then, suddenly, I could breathe again. I sucked in a great lungful of air, and it had never tasted so good. My head cleared, and the pains faded away to nothing. I straightened up slowly, not quite trusting what I was feeling, and pulled open my bullet-holed trench coat to look underneath. There were three more holes in my shirt, but only a little blood. I put my fingers through the holes in my shirt, and found only unbroken skin. I felt great. I looked at Sandra Chance, and she stared blankly back at me, open-mouthed.

"Honest," I said. "I'm just as surprised as you are. But I think I know what's happened. I once put werewolf blood into Suzie Shooter, to save her from a mortal wound. And later she put her blood into me, for the same reason. So it seems I have acquired a werewolf's healing abilities. The blood's probably too diluted to do anything else to me, but . . ."

"It's not fair," said Sandra. "You bastard, Taylor! You always have a way out."

I had a feeling silver bullets might still get the job done, but I didn't think I'd mention that to Sandra. I turned to the other bounty hunters, who were still as statues, watching with gaping mouths, and gave them my best nasty smile. Five seconds later all I could see was their backs, heading for the nearest horizon. They knew when they were outclassed. I turned back to Sandra Chance, and she shot me in the head. The impact whipped my head round, and for a moment it seemed like all the bells in the world were ringing inside my skull. I then felt the weirdest sensation, as the bullet crept slowly back out of my brain, the hole healing behind it, until it popped out my forehead and dropped to the ground. The bone healed with only the faintest of cracking sounds, and that was that.

I smiled at Sandra. "Ouch," I said, just to be sporting.

She stamped her foot. "Don't you ever play by the rules?"

"Not if I can help it," I said.

We stood and looked at each other for a long moment. Sandra lowered her gun but didn't put it away. I knew she was considering the possibilities of a bullet to a soft target, like an eye or my groin.

"We don't have to do this," I said. "All this kill or be killed bullshit. I don't want to kill you, Sandra. There's been enough death in the Nightside."

"I have to kill you, John," said Sandra, almost tiredly. "You murdered the only thing I ever loved."

"The Lamentation isn't actually dead," I said. "I only returned it to its original human components."

"They weren't the Lamentation," said Sandra. "They weren't what I loved. So I killed them. And now I have to kill you."

"I never understood what you saw in it," I said carefully. "Even allowing for your well-known death fetish, and your preference for . . . cold meat. You must know the Lamentation didn't love you. It couldn't, by its nature."

"I knew that! Of course I knew that! It was enough . . . that I loved it. The only creature something like me could ever love. It made me happy. I'd never been happy before. I'll kill you for taking that away from me."

"I won't kill you, Sandra," I said. "And you can't kill me. Forget this shit. We've got a War to fight."

"I don't care," she said. "Let it all burn. Let them all die. That's the world I live in anyway. I'll find you, and I'll kill you, John. There's always a way. Wherever you go, I'll be there in the shadows, hunting you. And one day I'll step out of a door or an alleyway and kill you dead, when you're least expecting it. I'll watch you choke on your own blood and laugh in your face as you die."

"No you won't," said Suzie Shooter.

We both spun round, startled, and the roar of the shotgun was like thunder. Sandra Chance took both barrels in the chest, at close range. The blast tore half her upper torso away, and she was dead long before she hit the ground. Suzie nodded calmly, lowered the double-barrelled shotgun, and reloaded it from her bandoliers, and only then looked at me.

"Blessed and cursed ammo. If one barrel doesn't get you, the other will. Hello, John."

"Thank you, Suzie," I said. There was nothing else I could say. She wouldn't have understood. "How did you know to find me here?"

Suzie nodded at Sandra's sprawled body. "She was dumb enough to approach me when she was putting her little army together. She thought the sheer size of the bounty would sway me. I won't say I wasn't tempted, but I like to think I've moved beyond that, where you're concerned. So I came here. I thought you might need some backup."

"I had the situation under control," I said. "You didn't have to kill her."

"Yes I did," said Suzie. "You heard her. She'd never give up. That's why you'll always need me around, John. To do the necessary things you're too soft to do."

"That's not why I keep you around," I said.

"I know," said Suzie Shooter. "My love."

She extended a leather-gloved hand to me, and I held it lightly in mine, for a moment.

"Excuse me for butting in on such a tender scene," said Tommy Oblivion, "But I do happen to by dying here. I would appreciate a helping hand."

He was lying on his side on the ground, both hands at his stomach, as though trying to hold it together. Suzie knelt beside him, pushed his hands aside, and checked the extent of the damage with experienced eyes.

"Gut shot. Nasty. If the bullets don't kill him, infection will. We need to get him out of here, John."

"I can't use my gift," said Tommy. His voice was clear enough, but his eyes were vague. "Can't concentrate through the pain. But I absolutely refuse to die in such a drab and depressing location as this."

"Don't worry," I said. "I'll take us back to Strangefellows through my Membership Card, and Alex will fix you up. You can put it on my tab."

"Oh good," said Tommy. "For a minute there, I was almost worried."

I took out my Membership Card, activated it, then almost dropped the bloody thing as Lilith's face looked out of the Card at me.

"Hello, John," she said. "My sweet boy. My own dear

flesh and blood. I haven't forgotten you. I'll come for you soon, then you'll be mine, body and soul, forever and ever and ever."

I shut down the Card, and her face disappeared. I was breathing hard, as though I'd just been hit. Suzie and Tommy were looking at me, and I realised they hadn't heard a thing.

"Bad news," I said. "We're going to have to do this the hard way."

ELEVEN

Truth and Consequences

I stripped off my trench coat and gingerly inspected my injured arm. Dominic Flipside really had sliced it open from wrist to elbow, and blood was coursing down my arm. It hurt a lot more once I saw how bad it was. It also showed absolutely no signs of healing on its own. Suzie bandaged my arm with practised skill, brisk efficiency, and a bedside manner that bordered on distressing. She kept her gloves on the whole time. I would have liked to make a lot of noise, or at least indulged in some impassioned cursing, but somehow I couldn't when Tommy Oblivion's wounds were so much worse, and he wasn't making a sound. Suzie tied off both ends of my bandaged arm, and I flexed it carefully.

"You'll need stitches later," said Suzie.

"That's right, cheer me up." I glanced at Dominic's body. "Trust a sneak assassin like him to use a blade with a silver edge. It's lucky you were carrying bandages, Suzie."

"Lucky, hell. I always carry a full med kit. Tools of the trade, when you're in the bounty-hunting business. Even though the powers that be won't let me claim them as a business expense, the bastards."

I put my trench coat back on. The slit sleeve flapped loosely around my injured arm. "I suppose," I said thoughtfully, "they won't let you claim because the med kit could be used by you, or your victims."

"Don't be silly, John. You know I always bring them in dead. Less paperwork that way."

We looked over at Tommy Oblivion, who was still sitting with his back propped against the wall of St. Jude's. Suzie had pushed his guts back into place, then wrapped his stomach with half a mile of bandages, but they were already soaked through with fresh blood. Tommy's face was grey and beaded with sweat. His eyes were wide and staring, and his mouth trembled. There was no way in Hell he was going to be able to concentrate hard enough or long enough to heal himself.

"We have to get him back to Strangefellows," Suzie said quietly. "And fast."

"I can't use my Membership Card, or his," I said, just as quietly. "Lilith has found a way to hack into it. She's closing in on me, Suzie, and I can't afford to be found."

Suzie looked out over the wasteland of ash and dust. Strange lights flared briefly on the horizon. "We're a long way from the bar, John. A long way from anywhere civilised. Tommy won't make it if we have to travel through the war zones on foot. Hell, I'm not even that sure we'll make it. Things are bad out there . . . How about if we go into St. Jude's, and pray for a miracle?"

"How about you go in?" I said. "Tommy and I will watch. From a safe distance. St. Jude's has a famously zero-tolerance policy when it comes to sinners."

"Could you two please keep the noise down?" Tommy said hoarsely. "I'm dying here, and I have a headache."

"He's delirious," said Suzie.

"I wish," said Tommy.

Suzie leaned in close to me, her mouth right next to my ear. "It might be kinder to kill him here, John. Rather than let him die by inches, dragging him through the war zones. His screaming would be bound to attract attention. I could do it. I'd be very humane. He wouldn't feel a thing."

"No," I said. "I won't let him down. I won't let him die. He saved my life. He crawled twenty feet in the dirt with half a dozen bullets in his gut to set fire to that rogue anima. Bravest thing I've ever seen. I wasn't the hero he wanted me to be, on our trip into the Past. But he was a hero for me."

I remembered Larry Oblivion's words, from the pitiful last redoubt of my Enemies in the future. *He trusted you, even though he had good reason not to. And when they struck him down you just stood there, and watched him die, and did nothing to help.*

I looked at Suzie. "How did you get here?"

"Razor Eddie cut a door in the air with his razor, opening up a breach between there and here. All I had to do was step through."

Suzie fixed me with her cold, unwavering gaze. "You want to save him, there's only one thing left. Use your gift, John. *Find* us a way back to the bar."

"Using my gift is like using the Card," I said reluctantly. "It's another way for Lilith to find me. If I keep pushing my luck, it's bound to run out. But . . . right now, I'd have to say Tommy's chances are much worse than mine. So."

I fired up my gift, concentrating as hard as I knew how on finding a way out of this mess. Not for me, but for my friends. Because they both came through for me, when I needed them. I pushed hard, gritting my teeth until my jaw ached. Sweat rolled down my face. I could feel some chance, some possibility, close at hand. Something we'd all overlooked. I concentrated till my head ached, a vicious pounding beat of pain, forcing my inner eye, my private eye, to focus in on what I needed. And finally my Sight showed me a door, or at least the essence of a door, hanging before me. It was the opening Razor Eddie had made, with his godly will and his awful straight razor. The door had closed behind Suzie when Eddie stopped thinking about it, but the rift he'd made was still there, if only potentially. I felt my lips pull back in a death's-head grin that was as much a snarl as anything else. I was back in the game again. I sensed Suzie moving in to stand very close to me, comforting me with her presence, but I couldn't see or hear her.

I hit the potential door with every bit of willpower I had, all my muscles locked solid from the strain, my stomach clenching so painfully I almost cried out; and slowly, inch by inch and moment by moment, the door grew more real and more definite. Sweat was pouring off me now, my whole body aching from the tension, and my head felt like it would fly apart at any moment. Blood poured from my nose and ears, and even oozed up from under my eyelids. I was doing myself some serious damage, pushing my gift harder than I ever had before. My breathing came harsh and rapid, my heart hammered in my chest, and my vision narrowed till all I could see was the door, as real to me as I was, because I made it so. I couldn't feel my hands. Couldn't feel my wounded arm. A terrible chill spread through me. I fell to my knees, and didn't even feel the impact. I could sense Suzie kneeling beside me, yelling my name, but even that was faint and far away.

The door swung open, and I cried out, a harsh rasping cry of victory. The door hung on the air before us, an opening, a window through space itself. I shut down my gift, and the door remained. I'd broken it to my will. Sight and sound and sensation returned in a rush. Suzie was kneeling beside me, shaking my shoulder with her gloved hand and yelling right into my ear. I slowly turned my head and grinned at her, blood spilling out over my lips, and said something indistinct. She saw I was back and stopped shouting. She produced a surprisingly clean handkerchief from inside her leather jacket and wiped the blood and sweat and tears from my face. When I was ready, she helped me up onto my feet again.

Through the gap in the air I could see right into Strangefellows. Walker and Alex Morrisey were looking back through the gap, their faces slack with almost comic expressions of surprise. I waved cheerfully at them, and they both recovered quickly. Suzie started to help me towards the door.

"No," I made myself say. "Tommy first. I'll heal. He won't."

She nodded and let go of me. I swayed a little, but stayed upright. Suzie picked Tommy up in her arms as though he was a child, and carried him towards the door. He cried out once at the sudden new pain, but that was it. Tough little guy, for an effete existentialist. Suzie took him through the opening into the bar, then came back for me. I walked through the door under my own steam, but it was a near thing. I'd pushed myself too hard this time, and I had a strong feeling I'd have to pay for it, later. I might have werewolf blood in me, but God alone knew how diluted it was, having passed through Belle and Suzie on its way to me. Suzie stuck close to my side, ready to catch me if I fell.

Is there a better definition of love?

We came home to Strangefellows, and I felt the door close very firmly behind me. Alex already had Tommy Oblivion laid out on a table-top, while Betty and Lucy Coltrane hurried to get Alex the repair spells he needed. Tommy's breathing didn't sound at all good. I started to go to him, but I was suddenly hot and cold at the same time, and the bar swayed around me. Suzie lowered me onto a chair, and I collapsed gratefully. I checked myself out as best I could. I didn't seem to be bleeding from anywhere any more, and feeling was flooding back into all parts of my body. It hurt like hell. Suzie snapped her fingers imperiously for some clean water and a cloth, and set about cleaning the last of the mess off my face. The cool water felt good on my skin, and my head settled down again.

Razor Eddie stood before me, an intense grey presence in his filthy overcoat, regarding me thoughtfully with his fever-bright eyes. He was holding a bottle of Perrier water. Flies buzzed around him, and up close the smell was really bad.

"You reopened a door I made," he said finally, in his quiet, ghostly voice. "I didn't know you could do that. I didn't think anyone could do that."

"Yeah, well," I said, as casually as I could, "nothing like having your mother around to inspire you to new heights."

Walker brought me a glass of wormwood brandy. I'd actually have preferred a nice ice-cold Coke, but I appreciated the thought. I nodded my thanks to him, and he nodded back. Which was about as demonstrative as we were ever likely to get. It did seem we were becoming closer, whether we liked it or not. Suzie stopped dabbing at my face with her damp cloth, inspected her work critically, then nodded and tossed the bloody cloth aside. She sat down on the edge of a table facing me, and concentrated on cleaning her double-barrelled shotgun.

At another table, not too far away, Tommy Oblivion thrashed about while Alex did necessary, painful things to him. Betty and Lucy Coltrane held Tommy down, using all their considerable strength, while Tommy used the kind of language you didn't expect to hear from effete existentialists. Alex's remedies tended to be swift, brutal, but effective. He chanted something alliterative in Old Saxon, while pouring a thick blue gunk into Tommy's exposed guts, while Dead Boy peered over his shoulder, watching interestedly.

"I could lend you some duct tape, if you like," he said. "I've always found duct tape very useful."

"Get the hell away from my patient, you heathen," said Alex, not looking up from what he was doing. "Or I'll use this superglue to seal your mouth up."

"Superglue?" gasped Tommy. "You're putting me back together with superglue? I demand a second opinion!"

"All right, you're a noisy bugger, too," said Alex. "Now shut the hell up and let me concentrate. Superglue was good enough for the grunts in Vietnam. It's not like you needed all that lower intestine anyway . . . There. That's it. Give the glue a few minutes to bond with the spells, then you can sit up. I've got the bullets here. Do you want to keep them for souvenirs?"

Tommy told Alex exactly where he could stick the bullets, and everyone managed some kind of smile. I looked around me, studying the small crowd gathered in the bar. My only remaining allies in the struggle to stop Lilith. It really was a very small crowd. I looked at Walker, who shrugged. He'd got his equilibrium back, but he still looked very tired.

"All my other agents are either out in the field, doing what they can, or they're missing, presumed dead. What you see . . . is all that's left."

There was Alex Morrisey, cleaning his bloody hands on a grubby bar cloth, all in black as usual, in perpetual mourning for the way his life might have gone, if only he hadn't been Alex Morrisey. He glowered at me, and said something about the mess I'd made of his place, but I could tell his heart wasn't really in it. Tommy Oblivion was already sitting up on his table-top, ruefully inspecting the tattered and bloodied remains of his ruffled shirt. He nodded almost cheerfully to me and gave me a thumbs-up. Betty and Lucy Coltrane had chosen chairs from where they could keep a watchful overview of the bar, ready to deal with any and all intruders. They looked muscular as ever, but there were deep black smudges of fatigue under their eyes.

Dead Boy struck a casual pose in his flapping purple greatcoat, while Ms. Fate struck an heroic pose in his leather superhero outfit, mask, and cape. Standing proudly at his side was my teenage secretary, Cathy Barrett, in an oversized black leather jacket covered in badges. I stopped and looked at her closely.

"Cathy . . . why are you wearing a black domino mask?"

"Ms. Fate made me his sidekick!" Cathy said cheerfully. "I thought I'd call myself Deathfang the Avenger, or maybe . . ."

I shut my eyes, just for a moment. Teenagers . . .

Razor Eddie was standing a little off to one side, as he always did. Eddie wasn't a people person. Julien Advent was nursing a glass of champagne and smoking a long black cheroot. As always, he was every inch the elegant Victorian, but his opera cloak was torn and tattered and even burned through in places. Of us all he looked the most like a real hero, tall and brave and unbending. Because he was. Larry Oblivion, in a soiled and battered Gucci suit, stood supportively beside his brother, and nodded briefly when my gaze landed on him.

"You saved my brother's life," he said. "Thank you."

"You're welcome," I said.

I hadn't let Tommy die. The thought warmed me. I'd finally broken one clear link between my present and the devastated future, and it felt good, so good. And then I felt guilty, for caring more about that than for saving the man who'd risked his life to save mine. I do try to be a good man, but my life gets so damned complicated, sometimes . . .

"We're all glad you're back, Taylor," said Walker, a little tartly. "But you'd better have some really good ideas, because we're all out. We're losing, John."

Outside the bar, I could hear the roar of unchecked fires and the rumble of explosions, running feet, human screams, and the cries of monsters loose in the streets. Merlin's shields were apparently still holding, but the War was edging closer. It occurred to me that this might be the last safe haven left in the Nightside. I remembered my Enemies, huddled together in their last refuge, and shuddered despite myself.

"What is there left for us to do?" said Walker. "We've tried open confrontation, manning the barricades, hit-and-run tactics, and guerrilla warfare, and none of it has ever done more than slow down Lilith's advance. Now there's just us . . . We're all good, in our own ways, but she's Lilith. Even her children were worshipped as gods for centuries. Lilith represents a kind of Power that's almost beyond our comprehension. And her army of followers is growing all the time. I like to think most of them have been terrorised into joining, and would cut and run if given a chance, but . . ."

Everyone looked at me, and the silence stretched, because I had nothing to say. I had no plans, no schemes, no last trick up my sleeve.

"Can't you use your gift, to find out what Lilith will do next?" said Cathy. It was hard for me to look at her. She still had faith in me. "Couldn't your gift find us a way to defeat her?"

I shook my head slowly. "I know you're trying to help, Cathy, but my gift doesn't work like that. And every time I raise my gift now, it's like running up a flag to tell Lilith exactly where I am."

"But you're always finding new things you can do with your gift," said Cathy.

"Specific questions lead me to specific answers," I said tiredly. "The vaguer the question, the harder it is to get any kind of answer that makes sense."

"Where did you get this gift, anyway?" said Ms. Fate, in his rough, smoky voice. "I would have loved to have a gift to help me. I had to create myself through hard work and long training."

"I won my gift in a poker game," said Tommy Oblivion, unexpectedly.

"It's true, he did," said his brother Larry. "And he was bluffing, with a pair of threes. I couldn't believe it."

"My gift was a legacy, inherited from my inhuman mother," I said. "My only legacy."

"Now that's interesting," said Julien Advent. "Why that

gift, in particular, and no other? I mean, when your mother is an ancient Power and a Biblical myth, I think you could reasonably expect to inherit at least half of that power, simply through the operations of chance. If all you got was one specific gift, it's because that's what your mother intended. She wasn't prepared to risk your becoming powerful enough to challenge her, but she wanted you to have this gift for finding things. Why?"

An earthquake shook the bar. Tables rattled and chairs shimmied across the heaving floor. The walls creaked, and the long wooden bar groaned out loud. Everyone clung to each other, to keep from falling. Bottles toppled and crashed behind the bar, and the lights swung crazily. My first thought was that Lilith had found us at last, and was smashing her way through Merlin's defences, but as quickly as it started the disturbance faded away, and everything grew still again. We were all standing, prepared to defend ourselves in our various ways.

"The cellars!" Alex said abruptly. "I can hear something moving, down in the cellars!"

We all fell silent, listening. Nothing good could come from the cellars under Strangefellows. Finally, we heard faint but definite footsteps, coming up the stairs under the bar. Slow, measured, inexorable footsteps. And then the trap-door behind the bar flew open with a crash, and that ancient sorcerer, Merlin, came up into the bar. Merlin of Camelot, the Devil's only begotten son, risen up in his own dead body with the dirt still on him from where he'd burst up out of his own grave. I'd known that giant crucifix wouldn't hold him down if he wanted out.

Merlin strolled out from behind the bar, taking his time, enjoying the shock and apprehension in all our faces. Alex stared, open-mouthed. He'd never seen his ancestor before, because up till now Merlin had always manifested through him. This was the real deal, Merlin's dead body up and about again, raised from its long rest through an effort of supernatural will.

Merlin Satanspawn. A man born out of Hell who became a warrior for Heaven. And scared the crap out of both sides.

His face was long and heavy-boned, unrepentantly ugly, and two flames leapt in the empty sockets where his eyes should have been. (*He has his father's eyes,* they said . . .) His long grey hair and beard were stiff and packed with old clay. His skin was taut and cracked and stained with grave-moss, but still he looked in pretty good shape for someone who'd been dead and buried for fifteen hundred years. He wore the magician's robe they'd buried him in, a long scarlet gown with golden trimming round the collar. I remembered that robe. He'd been wearing it when I killed him, back in the Past. The robe hung open to reveal a bare chest covered in Druidic tattoos, interrupted by a great gaping hole, from where I'd torn the living heart out of his chest with my bare hands. For what seemed like good reasons at the time. As far as I knew, he didn't know I'd taken it.

Merlin came striding through the bar, and the tables and chairs drew back to get out of his way. His dead body made low, creaking sounds with every movement, and gravedirt fell off him. He wasn't breathing. He ignored Razor Eddie, standing ready with his straight razor shining impossibly bright in his filthy hand. He ignored Suzie Shooter, with her double-barrelled shotgun following his every movement. He ignored Dead Boy and Julien Advent and all the others. He came straight for me, his dead lips drawn back in a mirthless smile that showed brown teeth and grey leathery tongue.

He stopped right before me, and actually bowed slightly. "Here we are at last," he said, in a voice like everyone's favourite uncle. "Two sons of distinguished parents, who only ever wanted to be left alone to work out their own destinies. I was born to be the Antichrist, but I declined the honour and went my own way. And much good it did me. We've always had a lot in common, you and I, John Taylor."

"What brings you up here, sorcerer?" I asked. I kept my voice calm and easy through an effort of will. (First rule of operating in the Nightside—never let them see they've got you scared or they'll walk all over you.) "What brings you up out of your grave, after all these centuries?"

"To tell you things you need to know," he said, still smiling his unnerving smile. "I know why your mother bestowed only the one gift upon you, when she could have made you one of the greatest Powers in the Nightside. I am old and wise and I know many things I'm not supposed to. Being dead didn't stop me listening, and learning. Lilith gave you that one gift and no other because she intended to make use of you and it, on her return. Your gift will find for her the one thing that will make possible her control of the whole Nightside.

"I would have thought you'd have worked that out by now. If she could remake the Nightside by will alone, she would have done it by now, don't you think? But her creation has grown and changed so very much during the long centuries of her absence, become something far greater and more intransigent than she ever intended . . . Why else would a Power like Lilith need an army to subdue the Nightside?"

"Why haven't you manifested before?" Walker said sharply. "We could have used your help. Why wait till now, when it's almost too late?"

"I'm here now because you finally asked the right question," said Merlin, still looking only at me. He pulled up a chair and sat down before me, and his manner made it seem like a throne. His presence dominated the room, pulling all eyes to him. "Now I'm up and about again, Lilith will know I'm back. She'll know where to come, to find me. She has to face me, because I'm her only real rival. She'll never feel safe until she's seen me utterly destroyed and cast down."

"Can you stop her?" said Julien Advent.

Merlin ignored him, his fiery gaze fixed on me. "The protections I have set in place around this bar won't keep her out forever. She'll be here, very soon now. And if she finds me in my present condition, she'll strike me down with a look and a word and laugh while she does it. And then she'll take you over, John, make you her puppet, and use your gift as though it were her own. Just as she's planned from the very beginning."

I considered him for a long moment, letting the silence build. "But now you're here, to save the day. Because you have a plan, too, don't you, Merlin?"

He nodded. "Yes. I have a plan."

"Of course you do. You're Merlin Satanspawn, and you always have a plan."

"Don't drag my father into this," said Merlin. "You know very well we never got on. Now, John Taylor, I need you to use your gift for me. I need you to find my missing heart and bring it here to me. I will place it back in my breast, and then . . . Ah then, I will show you wonders and miracles beyond your wildest dreams! I will live again, my body made new and vital, and all my old power will return! I shall be the greatest magician of this Age, and walk out of this bar, free at last . . . to teach Lilith the error of her ways."

There was a long pause. I looked around, and it was clear that no-one except Merlin thought this was a good idea.

"You might win against Lilith," I said finally. "Or you might not. But even if you did . . . who's to say you might not prove as great a threat as she?"

Everyone looked at me, then at Merlin. He rose slowly up out of his chair, his dead body creaking and groaning, and I stood my ground, facing him unflinchingly.

"I could make you find my heart," said Merlin.

"No you couldn't," I said.

We stared at each other, both of us very still. I looked into the flames that were his eyes, and I'd never felt colder in my life. And in the end, Merlin looked away first. He sat down heavily on his chair. I sat down quickly, too, so no-one would see how badly my legs were shaking. There were impressed murmurs all around me, but I just nodded stiffly. I was the only one there who knew for sure that I'd been bluffing.

"I've had enough of this," I said harshly. "Enough of guesses and warnings and prophecies of doom. It's time to get to the heart of the matter, time to find out the truth, once and for all. You were right all along, Cathy. The only way to find out what I need to know, is to use my gift. So, gift, *Why did Lilith give you to me?*"

I was ready for another fight, another concentrated effort of will that would half kill me, but in the end it was as easy as taking a deep breath. As though my gift had been waiting all my life for me to ask of it the one question that really mattered. My shadow stood up before me, separating itself, taking on form and substance until it looked exactly like me, right down to the white trench coat with the flapping sleeve. Exactly like me, in every detail—except my doppleganger's eyes were full of darkness. It leaned against a table and folded its arms across its chest, smiling mockingly at me.

"Took you long enough," it said. Its voice was smooth, assured, and only just short of openly taunting. "Well, here I am, John. Your gift personified, ready to answer all your questions."

"All right," I said. My mouth was very dry. "How do you work? How is it you're always able to find the things that are hidden from everyone else?"

"Easy. I tap directly into reality itself. I see everything that is, all at once. I'm really so much more than you ever allowed me to be, John."

"Damn," Tommy said quietly. "That is . . . really spooky."

"Why did Lilith give you to me?" I said.

"Because she intends to use you to find the Speaking Gun. The most powerful weapon in the world. It was originally created to kill angels and demons, but it can do so much more than that. Lilith will use the Speaking Gun to remake the Nightside in her own image. Return it to what she originally intended it to be, before Humanity infested and perverted it from its true purpose and nature. She was responsible for the Gun's creation, long and long ago. Adam gave of his rib and his flesh to make Eve, and after Lilith came back up from Hell, having lain down with demons and given birth to monsters, she also gave of her rib and her flesh, to make the Speaking Gun. With the help of Abraxus Artificers."

"Yeah," Suzie said suddenly. "That was engraved on the stock of the Speaking Gun; *Abraxus Artificers, the old firm, solving problems since the beginning.* I've always been very good at remembering things, where weapons are involved."

"Very good," said my double. "Now shut up and listen, and you might learn something. Abraxus Artificers were the descendants of Cain, the first murderer. How else do you think they could fashion such marvellous weapons of destruction?" My double paused. "You do all realise that I'm talking in parables, representing a far more complicated reality? Good. I shall continue. The Speaking Gun was designed to speak backwards the echoes of the original Word of Creation, which resonates on in everything, giving each separate thing its own true secret name. By speaking this secret name backwards, the Speaking Gun can thus unmake or uncreate anything. But the Speaking Gun could be used, by someone with enough power, someone who gave of their own flesh to make it, to *respeak* those secret names, and thus change their essential nature. Lilith will use the Speaking Gun to respeak the Nightside, making it over into whatever she wants it to be. Personally, I can't wait to see what she's going to do . . ."

"That's enough," I said, and shut down my gift. It didn't fight me, just collapsed back into darkness, and my shadow was nothing more than my shadow. I wondered if I'd ever look at it in the same way again. Or ever really trust my gift, knowing that it lived within me like a parasite.

"So," Walker said finally, "who has the Speaking Gun? My people lost track of it some time back."

"I last saw it here, in this bar, with the future Suzie Shooter," said Alex, glancing apologetically at Suzie. "Before Merlin banished both of them."

"Don't look at me," said Merlin. He sounded a lot smaller, since I'd stared him down. "I only sent them away. They could be anywhere now. Or anywhen."

"The last time I saw it, in the Present, Eddie had it," I said. I looked at him. We all looked at him, and he nodded slowly. "You were using it to kill angels from Above and Below, in the angel war," I said, being careful to sound not at all challenging or confrontational. "What did you do with it, Eddie?"

"I gave it away," said Razor Eddie, quite calmly. "To Old Father Time. The only Being I knew powerful enough to control it and not be corrupted by it."

"I thought all you cared about was smiting the bad guys?" said Suzie.

"No," said Razor Eddie. "I wanted to do penance. There's a difference. All the time I had the Speaking Gun, I could feel it working on me, trying to seduce me with its endless hunger for death and destruction. But I have been there, and done that. I am something else now."

"According to my agents' last reports, Lilith has destroyed the Time Tower," Walker said heavily. "Reduced it to nothing but rubble. Old Father Time is dead, and the Speaking Gun buried under the rubble with him."

"No," I said, feeling hope rise anew within me. "Time's domain isn't actually in the Nightside. The Tower was just how people got to speak to him. There is another way to reach him . . . . So, who's up for one last suicidal charge for glory? Don't all speak at once."

TWELVE

Last Train to Shadows Fall

I explained what I had in mind. Everyone looked at me. And somehow I knew they weren't too keen.

"You're crazy!" said Larry Oblivion.

"And if you think we're going along with you, you're crazy, too!" said Dead Boy.

"Hold everything," said Walker, holding up his hand, and it was a measure of the man that everyone else fell silent, like children when the teacher speaks. "Let me be sure I've grasped all the details of this cunning plan of yours, John. You want us to go out onto the streets full of madmen and monsters and run interference for you, at the risk of all our lives, so you can get safely to the nearest Underground station and catch a train to take you safely out of the Nightside? Is that it? Have I grasped all the nuances correctly?"

"I love it when you get all sarcastic, Walker," I said. "But actually, you're pretty much right. Look, Old Father

Time resides in Shadows Fall, that small town in the back of beyond that's an elephants' graveyard for the supernatural. He only commutes into the Nightside to work. When Lilith destroyed the Time Tower, all she did was cut off his access to the Nightside. He's still safe in Shadows Fall, with the Speaking Gun. If I can get safely to the Underground, I can take a train straight to him. And just maybe I can persuade him to give me the Speaking Gun, to use against Lilith."

"Or, you could just run out on us," said Larry, fixing me with his cold unblinking gaze. "Even Lilith would think twice about going after you, if you were hiding out in Shadows Fall."

"He may be dead, but he has a point," said Walker. "You've never been the most trustworthy soul, Taylor. Why should we risk our lives to save your selfish skin?"

"Oh ye of little faith," I said. "We need the Gun, and I'm the only one he might give it to. Do you have any means of communicating with Shadows Fall, Walker? Any way we can talk to Time, and save me the journey?"

"No," Walker admitted reluctantly. "All outgoing communications have been jammed. Scientific and supernatural. We're completely cut off from the rest of the world."

"Then I have to go in person, don't I?" I said. "Is there anyone else here who thinks Old Father Time might surrender the most powerful weapon in the world to them? No, I didn't think so."

"Why should he give it to you?" said Julien Advent. From him, it was a fair question.

"Because I'm Lilith's son. Because he knows I'm the only one who can stop her now."

"I say!" Tommy Oblivion said suddenly, and we all jumped a little. "I've just had a brilliant idea! Taylor, why don't you get Old Father Time to send you back into the Past again, to before all this started, so you can warn yourself about what's coming?"

"I can't," I said patiently, "because I didn't."

Tommy frowned, his lower lip pouting out sullenly. "I

can't help feeling there should be more to the argument than that." He pulled a notepad out of his pocket and started jotting down equations and Venn diagrams, muttering about divergent timetracks, opposing probabilities, experiment's intent, and whether or not someone's pizza had anchovies on it, so we left him to get on with it. In my experience, Time travel just complicated things even more.

"The Speaking Gun is what matters," I said forcefully. "It's the only weapon we can be sure will work on Lilith, because it's made out of her flesh and bone. I can use it to speak her name in reverse, and uncreate her."

"Or perhaps to respeak her?" said Walker. "Remake her into some more acceptable form? She is your mother, after all."

"No," I said. "As long as she lives, she'll always be a threat. For everything she's done, and for everything she intends to do, she has to die. She was never my mother. Not in any way that mattered."

Alex produced a rather grubby and much-folded map of the local Underground system out from behind the bar, along with half a dozen cards from local taxi firms, a stuffed cat, and a dead beetle or two, and after a certain amount of argument and calculation (because the streets around Strangefellows aren't always there when you need them), we finally decided the nearest Underground station entrance had to be Cheyne Walk. Within walking distance from the bar, under normal circumstances, which these weren't, but still . . . it was reachable.

"I don't like this," said Ms. Fate. "It's a war zone out there."

We all stopped and listened to the chaos raging outside the bar. Even behind the shuttered windows and the locked doors, even behind Merlin's ancient defences, we could still hear screams and howls, the rage of fires and the rumble of collapsing buildings. Raw hatred ran loose in the streets, and it was hard to tell what sounds were human and which weren't, any more.

"So," I said, trying hard to sound confident, "who's coming with me?"

"I am," said Suzie Shooter. "But you knew that already."

"Yes," I said. "My love."

"I may puke," said Alex.

"I can't go with you," said Walker. "I have responsibilities, to my people. Many of them are still out there, fighting. Someone has to stay here, to organise the resistance. In case you don't come back. I will do my best to keep Lilith distracted while you make your run to Shadows Fall."

"I'll go with you, old thing," said Tommy Oblivion, throwing his notebook aside. "I feel fine again. Honest! And I owe you more than I can ever repay. I was so wrong about you."

"If you're going, then I'm going, too," his brother Larry said immediately. "You'll need someone to watch your back. You always do."

"You're not coming, and that's final!" snapped Tommy. "I don't care if you are dead, one of us has to survive this mess, to look after Mother."

Larry subsided, muttering under his breath. Razor Eddie drank the last of his designer water, tossed the bottle carelessly over his shoulder, and nodded to me.

"I'll go. I've always wanted to see Shadows Fall."

"I'm not going, and you can't make me!" said Alex Morrisey. "I've got a bar to run. And no, you can't have the Coltranes either. I need them, to protect the place."

Alex couldn't leave Strangefellows. The bar's geas held him there. We all knew that, but he had a reputation to keep up.

"I cannot go to Shadows Fall," said Merlin. "And no, I'm not going to tell you why. I'll just say . . . you'd think such a proud, ancient, and legendary town would have more of a sense of humour about . . . certain things. I'll stay here and keep Lilith's attention focused on me. I'm pretty sure I can set up a glamour, to fool her into thinking Taylor's still here with me. For a while, anyway . . ."

I looked at Julien Advent. "I really could use your help on this one, Julien . . ."

But he was already shaking his head. "I'm sorry, John. It's my responsibility to protect the Nightside, not risk my life on such a long shot. I'll help Walker run the resistance. I have contacts and associates and Beings who owe me favours that even he doesn't know about."

"I wouldn't put money on that," said Walker. "But thanks, Julien. I could use someone level-headed around here."

"Who's he looking at?" Alex said loudly. "I don't know what he's talking about. Like to see him run a dive like this. I can feel one of my funny turns coming on."

In his own way, he was trying to cheer us up. I looked at Cathy before she could say anything.

"No," I said, "you can't come with me. You'd have to kill or be killed out there, and I won't have that on my conscience."

She nodded jerkily. Her eyes were full of tears she refused to shed. "You come back safe," she said. "Or I'll never forgive you."

"I'll keep an eye on her," said Ms. Fate. "She's stronger than you know."

"You keep her safe," I said. "Or I'll come back from my death to haunt your Bat-cave."

"You probably would, too," said Ms. Fate. "I wish I could go with you, but I know my limitations. Good luck, Taylor."

And that left Dead Boy. He scowled, shook his head, and finally shrugged. "Oh hell, why not? I could use a little excitement. Where did I put that duct tape . . . ?"

"I could use my gift to transport you right to the station entrance," Tommy said suddenly.

"No, you couldn't," I said. "Lilith will be looking for

that. If she even guesses I'm heading for Shadows Fall, she'll stop me."

And that was that. People finished their drinks, said their good-byes, and set about preparing themselves for what was to come. Shotgun Suzie took me to one side, and looked at me solemnly. She put a leather-gloved hand on my chest and let it rest there, like a butterfly on a wall.

"I wanted us to have a moment together," she said, in her cold calm voice. "Because . . . things can always go wrong, and we might not get a chance to say a proper good-bye, later. We've been through so much together, and if this is it, well . . . I need to say something to you, John. You . . . matter to me. No-one's mattered to me for a long time. Not even me. Perhaps especially not me. But you . . . made me want to live again. So I could share my life with you. I care for you, John. I wanted you to know that."

"I knew that, Suzie . . ."

"Shut up and let me say this. It isn't easy. I love you, John Taylor, and I always will."

She made herself hug me. Her leather jacket creaked loudly as she put her arms around me, and her bandoliers of bullets pressed hard against my chest. She put her head forward, and deliberately pressed her unscarred cheek against mine. Flesh to flesh. I held her gently, as though she was brittle and might break. I could feel the effort involved, in what she was doing, of how much strength it took her to do a simple thing like this, and I was so proud of her I could hardly get my breath.

"If we do both make it out of this alive," she said, very quietly, her mouth right next to my ear, "I can't promise I'll ever be able to be a woman for you, John. But I will try."

"Suzie . . . it doesn't matter . . ."

"Yes it does! It matters to me. Do you love me, John?"

"Of course I love you, Suzie. Now and forever, and all the times between. I'd die for you, if I had to."

"I'd much rather you lived for me."

She let go of me and stood back. I let go of her immediately. I knew better than to push it. She looked at me, her face apparently entirely unmoved.

"I know about the future Suzie. I know what happened to her, here in this bar. You can't keep secrets in a dump like this. You mustn't worry about it, John. The future is what we make it."

"That's what worries me," I said.

And so, finally, I led my brave little band of heroes out of the bar. Shotgun Suzie, Razor Eddie, Tommy Oblivion, and Dead Boy. I eased open the door, slowly, silently, and one by one we crept out into the narrow cobble-stoned back alley. It smelled really bad. The piled-up bodies I'd expected from Suzie's defence were gone, and it was best not to wonder where, but the blood and gore remained, splashed up the alley walls and soaking the cobbled ground. The air was hot and heavy, thick with old smoke, and an overbearing sense of a world running down, of things coming to an end. There were screams and roars and howls, all the sounds of death and destruction, horror and fury. The Nightside might be going down for the last time, but it sure as hell wasn't going down quietly. I set off down the alley at a steady pace, ignoring the blood splashing under my shoes, trying hard to radiate confidence and a strong sense of purpose.

Suzie was right there at my side, shotgun at the ready, happy and smiling like a woman on her way to a really good party. Tommy and Eddie and Dead Boy moved along with us, and together we made our way to the end of the alley and looked cautiously out into the main street.

Fires blazed everywhere. Dead vehicles sprawled the length of the road, overturned and abandoned. A hearse had been broken apart from the inside out, and a taxi lay on its side with a wooden stake hammered through its engine block. Maddened crowds swept back and forth under a flickering twilight of burning buildings and half-smashed neon signs, attacking everything in sight. The noises they made didn't sound human any more. Reason had been blasted from their minds, by loss and horror and Lilith's will, leaving them only the most basic instincts and emotions. Men and women killed and ate each other, while monsters roamed freely, killing where they would and exhausting their various appetites on the fallen. Lilith was softening the Nightside up, before she went in for the kill. And because she enjoyed it.

"How the hell are we supposed to get to Cheyne Walk through *that*?" said Tommy.

"I'd suggest running," said Suzie.

"I'd also strongly suggest killing anything that isn't us," said Dead Boy.

"Works for me," said Razor Eddie. "But . . . loath as I am to be the voice of reason in this group, I really don't like the odds out there. Too many of them, too few of us. Enough hyenas will bring down even the strongest lions. If we have to fight for every step of the way, they'll drag us down long before we get anywhere near Cheyne Walk."

"We can't hit them head-on," I said. "In fact, we can't afford to be noticed at all. Lilith is bound to have people out there looking for me. Once she knows I've left Strangefellows and Merlin's protections, she'll come straight for me. So, Tommy, you're up."

"What?" said Tommy. "What?"

"Use your gift to hide us. Or at least hide our identities. Such a small use of your gift should slide past Lilith unnoticed."

"Yes," said Tommy, after a moment. "I think I could do that . . ."

He frowned, concentrating. It took him a while, to force his mind to deal with only one thing and ignore the madness and horror around him, but finally I could sense his gift firing up, as he imposed his existential will upon the world. Slowly and carefully, moment by moment, we became as uncertain as he thought we were, until the world couldn't decide whether we really were there or not, and even if we were, it couldn't make up its mind about who we were. I could feel Tommy's gift all around us, like a fog of possibilities. Everywhere I looked, it was like seeing through a heat haze, as though we were out of synch with our surroundings. I took that as a good sign and made myself concentrate on the only thing that really mattered—getting to Cheyne Walk Station.

I took a deep breath and led the way out onto the main street, walking openly, taking my time, doing nothing to attract attention. The others came with me, sticking close but not crowding. No-one even looked at us. Crazed mobs rioted up and down the street, and swept right past us without even slowing. I led the way down the street, through chaos and murder and foulness of all kinds, and no-one touched us. Sometimes they'd step out of our way, without even realising they were doing it. Suzie stayed at my side, the others spread out behind us. I tried to keep track of where they were without looking at them directly, but Tommy's gift made that difficult. It was hard to be sure of anything under the concentrated field of uncertainty he was generating. Terrible things happened, but none of them seemed real, or close, or threatening. Until a familiar face came running frantically out of a side alley.

Sister Morphine cared for the homeless and down-and-outs of Rats' Alley, trying to keep them fed and warm and alive, and save a few souls where she could. A good woman in a bad place, watching over those the world had abandoned. And now she came running out of the night, her nun's robes torn and tattered and soaked in her own blood. Her tear-stained face was dull with exhaustion and shock and the sight of too much horror. A mob was coming right behind her, screaming for her head. She burst out of the side alley and looked right at me. And even Tommy's gift was no match for her honest gaze.

"John! John Taylor! Help me! For God's sake, help me!"

The mob fell upon her and dragged her down, and she disappeared under a mass of flailing bodies. Knives flashed brightly in the night. She kept on screaming long after she should have stopped. And I let it happen, torn between the need to help her and the greater need to get to Cheyne Walk. I let a good woman die because I had somewhere more important to be. I walked on down the street, staring straight ahead, not even allowing myself to hurry in case that called attention to me. The screaming finally stopped, but I knew I'd be hearing it for the rest of my life. Suzie and the others stuck a little closer to me, but none of them said anything. They'd made the same choice I had. I could see the sign for the Cheyne Walk Underground Station up ahead, right at the end of the street. On a normal day, I could have walked it in a few minutes.

But the damage had already been done. Sister Morphine had called me by name, undermining Tommy's uncertainty. All around us, heads were slowly turning in our direction, not all of them human, not all of them sane. Perhaps that helped them see us, see me, more clearly. Someone pointed. Something said my name. The word flashed up and down the packed street, and men and monsters stopped the awful things they were doing to look for me. For Lilith's son.

"What do we do?" said Suzie.

"Run," I said.

And so we ran, pushing ourselves hard, ploughing through the crowds and slamming people out of our way if they didn't move fast enough. The press of bodies grew thicker as people came surging down the street towards us. My people formed a protective ring around me, without my asking. Suzie blasted a bloody hole in the crowd ahead, using both barrels, and bodies fell this way and that. Razor Eddie moved forward to take the lead while Suzie reloaded, gliding along like an angry ghost, his pearl-handled straight razor blazing fiercely in the twilight, as though it had come home. Eddie cut about him without even looking, and no-one could stand against him.

Suzie kept up a steady fire against anyone who even looked like they were getting too close, reloading on the run, though her bandoliers were almost empty now. She tossed the odd grenade or incendiary where she thought it'd do the most good, but from the unusually sparing way she was using them, I guessed she was running low on them, too. She was still grinning broadly, like she was having the best time, and maybe she was. Dead Boy hit anything that came within reach, while Tommy tried his best to wrap the last tatters of his gift around us, frowning fiercely with concentration as he ran. It must have been working. No-one seemed able to lay a hand on us.

We were all running full out, but the station entrance didn't seem to be getting any closer. My heart hammered in my chest, my lungs burned with the need for air, and my legs ached fiercely. It had been a long, hard day, and I was running on fumes now. It didn't seem fair that the world should require more effort from me, after everything I'd already done. I put my head down, and sweat dripped off the end of my nose. I concentrated on running. I could do this. I'd run harder, and longer, when Herne and his Wild Hunt chased me through the primordial forest of old Britain.

Mobs and monsters descended on us from all sides, from everywhere at once, driven by hate and bloodlust and the fear of Lilith's wrath if they let me escape. She knew I had to be stopped, before I stopped her. I ran hard, we all ran hard, sticking very close, striking out viciously at our many enemies, and Dead Boy was the first of us to fall. Hands from a faceless mob of howling savages caught hold of his flapping greatcoat and dragged him down by sheer weight and force of numbers. He was still lashing about him with his powerful dead hands as he fell, handing out death with every blow, but there were just so many of them.

We ran on, leaving him behind. We had no choice. I looked back anyway. The mob boiled around Dead Boy, stamping and kicking him and stabbing him with any number of weapons. I knew he wouldn't feel any of it, but that didn't make the sight any easier to bear. He was still struggling, the last time I saw him. I'm sure I heard him yell out to me, to keep going. I'm almost sure I heard him call out. I turned my head away, and kept running.

Razor Eddie fell back to cover our rear. Perhaps because there were more enemies behind than in front. Perhaps because even he was getting tired. Certainly even the most crazed individuals showed a marked reluctance to get too close to his infamous straight razor. He cut through the madness like a grim grey ghost, or a grim grey god, and no man and no monster came close to touching him. The street was full of people now, and things not at all like people, coming at us from every alley and side street, brandishing all kinds of weapons, yelling my name like a curse. Creatures loped through the crowds, or hovered above in the smoky night sky. I saw fangs and claws and membraneous wings, and shapes that made no sense at all, bursting out of the sides of crumbling buildings as though they weren't even there.

And then I swear I heard my mother's voice, abroad in the night, speaking Words of Power from a language so ancient it predated any human tongue or meaning. A trap-door opened up in the pavement right in front of Razor Eddie, a hole in our world, a door to somewhere else. Long tentacles with crocodile hide and suckers like barbed mouths shot up out of that other place and wrapped themselves around Razor Eddie. He cut viciously about him with his razor, but for every tentacle he severed a dozen more burst up through the trap-door. They finally whipped around both his arms, pinioning them to his sides, then they dragged him down into the hole, out of our world and into theirs. He never cried out, not once. The trap-door slammed shut, and Razor Eddie was gone.

I kept running. We all did. The Punk God of the Straight Razor could take care of himself. He'd find his way back. I believed that. I had to believe it.

The Cheyne Walk entrance was really close now. The crowds were thickening up before us, desperate to block our way. Suzie's shotgun fired again and again. The barrels were so hot that steam rose up from her leather gloves where she held the gun. Tommy was speaking gibberish, forcing his gift to manifest through sheer force of will. His face was very pale, his breathing laboured, his eyes dangerously wild. He wrapped the three of us in a cloud of uncertainty, and the mobs couldn't find us. And then a whole building collapsed as we ran past it, the smoke-blackened wall bowing suddenly outwards and slamming down like a hammer. Suzie and I forced out one last burst of speed, but Tommy was so focused on his gift he didn't realise what was happening until it was too late. The crumbling brickwork swept over him like a jagged tide, enveloping him in a moment, and we lost sight of him in a dark, billowing cloud of dust.

I stopped to look back, and through the settling dust I saw Tommy lying half-covered by rubble. He was hurt, but still conscious, still alive. Suzie was at my side, tugging my arm, calling my name. I looked at Tommy, and he looked right back at me. His gift was gone, and everyone knew exactly where we were. Voices were calling my name. Suzie pulled me away, and I turned my back on Tommy and started running again. The station entrance was right there. Tommy called out my name once, then I heard him scream as the mob found him.

I left Tommy Oblivion to die. I hadn't saved him after all. And all I could think was *What will I tell his brother?*

We came to the Cheyne Walk underground station entrance, and I started down the steps. It took me a moment to realise Suzie wasn't there with me. I looked round, and she'd taken up a position at the top of the steps, blocking the entrance. She glared at me.

"Go on, John. I've got your back."

"Suzie, no . . ."

"Someone's got to hold them off long enough for you to catch your train out of here. And I'm the only one left. Don't take too long, John. I'm seriously low on ammo and almost out of dirty tricks."

"I can't just leave you!"

"Yes you can. You must. Now get the hell out of here, John. And don't worry. I can look after myself, remember?"

She smiled once, then the mob came surging forward. She met them with both barrels and a handful of shrapnel grenades. I carried on down the steps into the Underground. She'd been right before, as usual. There hadn't been time for a proper good-bye.

Down in the tube station, it felt a lot later than three o'clock in the morning. The place stank of blood and sweat and desperation and far too many people. They sat huddled on the steps in filthy blood-stained clothes, rocking back and forth and hugging themselves tightly, as though that was the only thing holding them together. They didn't look at me as I squeezed my way past. Down in the tunnels they were packed even more tightly, refugees from the War above. The floors were filthy, wet and slick with every kind of waste. A recent attempt at graffiti on a tiled wall said *The End Is* but it finished abruptly in a splash of dried blood.

I forced my way through the increasingly packed tunnels and down the escalators, none of which were working. Half the lights were out, too, and the air was hot and close and clammy. People were shoulder to shoulder down on the platform, and I had to force my way through. No-one had enough strength left to object. The destination board on the wall opposite said STREET OF THE GODS,

HACELDAMA, CARCOSA, SHADOWS FALL. I looked up and
down the platform, hoping to spot someplace I could sit
down and get my breath back, but there was nowhere.
Only people, packed a lot closer than people can usually
stand, their faces empty, their eyes dead. There was no
energy left in them, no hope. They'd found a place to hide
from the War, and the horror they sensed coming, and that
was enough. Natives and tourists sat huddled together,
equally traumatised, equally lost, giving each other what
comfort they could. Every now and again, some especially loud roar or explosion would reverberate down
through the tunnels from the street above, and everyone
would flinch or shudder, and huddle just a little closer together.

There was a lot of dust in the air, and the taste of
smoke, and I would have killed for a cool drink. All the
food and drink machines had been smashed open and
emptied, though I doubt their contents went far, among so
many. A woman was talking tearfully on a courtesy
phone, even though it was obvious there was no-one on
the other end of the line. There were no quarrels or shov-
ing matches anywhere, or even any raised voices. The
people were all too tired or hurt or beaten down to cause
any trouble. One area at the end of the platform had been
set aside for the wounded and the dying, and a handful of
assorted nurses and doctors did what they could, though
they had damn all to work with. Blood and offal and
other, worse things pooled on the floor, and the smell
drifting down the platform was the stench of despair.

I asked people around me when the next train was due
in. Most didn't answer. Some were so far gone they didn't
even seem to understand the question. Finally, a man in a
torn and scorched business suit, still clinging protectively
to his briefcase, informed me that no-one had seen a train
in ages. The general feeling was that all the trains had
stopped running the moment the War began. I could understand that. The trains were frightened. (They might
have started out as purely mechanical creations, but

they'd evolved down the years, and now they were all quite definitely alive and sentient, in their own way.) They were probably hiding somewhere outside the Nightside, afraid to enter.

I powered up my gift, found the nearest train, and called it to me. I didn't have to worry about Lilith's finding me through my gift any more. By the time she got here, I planned to be long gone. Using my gift felt easier than ever before. Now that I knew the truth about it. As though . . . it had stopped fighting me. I called, and the train came, protesting loudly all the way. I shut down my gift, silencing the train's querulous mental voice.

It finally roared into the station, shaking the whole platform with its arrival, a long, shining, silver bullet, cold and featureless. The long steel carriages had no windows, and only the heavily reinforced doors stood out against the gleaming metal. But still there were scuffs and scrapes down the long, steel sides, and even a few deep gouge marks. People stirred and murmured, astonished. The trains were supposed to be untouchable, by long tradition. The first carriage slowed to a halt, and its door opened, right in front of me. I stepped inside. People on the platform surged after me, but I turned and glared at them, and something of my old legend stepped them in their tracks, just for a moment. Long enough for the door to hiss shut again. Fists hammered on the outside, while raised voices cursed and pleaded.

I ignored them all and sat down. They couldn't go where I was going. It felt good to sit down and take the weight off my feet. Rest my aching back against the leather seat. Tired, so tired . . . I let my head roll forward until my chin rested on my chest . . . but I couldn't let myself sleep. I had to stay alert. The train was already off and moving, leaving behind the angry and disappointed howls from the platform.

The air in the carriage was still and clear, almost refrigerator cool. I breathed deeply, savouring it. There were a few splashes of blood on the steel grille floor, and some scorch marks on the wall opposite, but hardly worth the noticing after what I'd been through. I relaxed further into the support of the dark leather seat, and raised my voice.

"You know who I am, train, so no arguments. Take me straight to Shadows Fall. No stops, no detours."

"Don't want to," said a quiet voice from concealed speakers. It sounded like a traumatised child. "It's not safe any more. Come with me, and hide in the sidings. We'll be safe there, in the dark."

"No-one's safe any more," I said, not unkindly. "I have to go to Shadows Fall."

"The badlands aren't secure, any more," said the train, sadly. "The places between destinations are all stirred up, by the War. Don't make me do this, John Taylor."

"I don't want to do it either," I said. "I'm scared, just like you. But if I can get to Shadows Fall, there's a chance I can stop all this."

"You promise?"

"I promise," I lied.

The train left the Nightside, gathering speed.

The badlands were very bad, now. In the places that lay between places the train was attacked over and over again, in defiance of all old pacts, customs and protections. At first it was only loud noises, and the occasional buffet as the train hit something on the tracks that shouldn't have been there, but then something hit the outside of the carriage I was travelling in, something big enough and heavy enough that the impact made a sizeable dent in the reinforced steel wall. I sat up straight, jerked out of the half doze I'd fallen into in spite of myself. Something hit the carriage again, and again; first from this side, then from that, and it even stomped about on the roof for a while, leaving deep dimples in the steel. The blows grew harder, and the indentations grew deeper, the steel forced inwards by the impact. I stood up, feeling my muscles creak, and moved to the aisle between the rows of seats, just in case.

The carriage wall on my left cracked open, splitting apart, a long, jagged rent stretching from floor to ceiling. For the first time I heard voices from outside, saying *Let us in! Let us in!* There was nothing human in those voices, nothing so small. They sounded like mountains crashing together, like old gods grown senile and vicious. The rent in the steel wall slowly widened, as something forced it open from outside. And through the rent, filling the gap from top to bottom, I saw a single huge monstrous eye, somehow keeping pace with the speeding train, staring in at me. And there was nothing in its fixed gaze but an awful, malicious madness.

I made myself walk towards the terrible eye, staring right back into that monstrous gaze, and when I was close enough I punched the eye as hard as I could. There was a scream like an insane steam whistle, and the eye was suddenly gone. Outside the rent in the wall there was only darkness, and an air so cold just a moment's exposure left hoarfrost on my face. There were no more voices, and no more pounding on the carriage walls.

The train kept going, and we left that place behind. The new silence had a weight all its own, as though it was but a precursor for something even worse. I didn't feel like sitting down, so I paced up and down the narrow aisle, peering out of the long rent now and again. A strange unearthly light streamed suddenly into the carriage as we entered another phase, another dimension. The light grew increasingly harsh and bright, until it burned my exposed skin where it touched, and I was forced to retreat from it. Thin shafts of the fierce light stabbed through unsuspected smaller rents in the walls and ceiling, and I was hard put to avoid them all.

From outside came sounds of a kind I couldn't place or recognise. They reminded me most of birds made of machinery, and the sound grated on my nerves like fingernails on the blackboard of my soul. The exterior atmosphere began seeping in through the jagged steel rent, driven by the greater pressure outside. It smelled like crushed nettles, thick and choking. It burned inside my mouth and nose, and I backed away from the crack in the wall, fighting an urge to vomit. I yelled for the train to go faster and curled up in a ball on the floor.

We left that place for somewhere else, and slowly the poison in the air diminished, left behind with the awful trip-hammer songs of mechanical birds. New air built up, flat and stale, from the carriage's reserves. I gulped it down anyway and slowly uncurled from my protective ball. My hands and face were still smarting from their brief exposure to the fierce light. I sank down onto the nearest seat, slumped and almost boneless. Too much was happening too quickly, even for me, with never a chance to rest. So tired . . . I think I'd have sold my soul for a good night's sleep.

Luckily, no-one was listening.

I looked up sharply as the quality of air in the carriage suddenly improved. Light from a bright summer's day came flooding in through the jagged rent in the wall, bringing with it new sweet air, rich in oxygen. It was hot and humid, thick with perfume, like the crushed petals of a thousand different flowers. The extra oxygen made me feel light-headed, and I grinned stupidly as I took in one deep breath after another. I got up and wandered over to the rent in the carriage wall, and that was when a hundred heavy vines with barbed thorns thrust their way into the carriage from outside. Decorated here and there with thick pulpy flowers like sucking mouths, they lashed around, thrashing and coiling with dreadful energy.

More and more of the vines forced their way in, twisting around each other, flailing back and forth in the confined space, taking up more and more of the carriage while I backed cautiously away. My feet made a scuffing sound on the grilled floor, and immediately every vine reached out in my direction. The flowered mouths screamed shrilly, a vile hungry sound. I cut at the nearest vine with the Kandarian sacrificial dagger Cathy gave me for my last birthday, and the slender blade sheared right through the vine, thorns and all. All the flowered mouths howled with rage and pain. The severed vine bled a clear oozing sap, and the stumpy end just kept coming after me. Half the carriage was full of the roiling, thrashing vines now, and more were forcing their way in, widening the steel rent in the process.

I slashed open one of the leather seats with my dagger, pulled out a handful of stuffing, and set fire to it with a basic elemental spell I normally only use for lighting friends' cigarettes. The stuffing flared up eagerly, yellow flames leaping high in the oxygen-rich air. I tossed the blazing mass into the midst of the crashing vines, and a dozen caught alight all at once. The pulpy flower mouths screamed in unison as the fire spread quickly through the vegetable mass. All the untouched vines whipped back out the rent, leaving the others to burn and die. The flowers howled like damned souls as they burned.

Thick black smoke filled the carriage. The vines and flowers were all dead, but they'd spread the fire to the carriage seats. The train screamed through its hidden speakers as flames took hold of the carriage. I yelled back at the train to keep going, then had to break off as a harsh coughing fit from the smoke took hold of me. I backed away from the growing inferno and crouched on the floor where the air was still clearest. Thick tears ran down my face from my smarting eyes. I couldn't see anything, but I could hear the roar of the fire drawing closer.

And then the whole carriage shook and shuddered as the train ground to a sudden halt. The carriage door cracked itself open, a few inches at a time, while I crawled towards it on my hands and knees. I forced the door open the last of the way with the last of my strength, and half fell out of the carriage, my lungs straining for air, my eyes blurred with tears. I could feel a hard floor underneath me, and I crawled forward, away from the smoke and fire. I heard the carriage door straining to close behind me, then the train sped off, heading for sanctuary. Its roar faded slowly away, along with its telepathic screams in my mind. Poor thing. Still, needs must when your mother drives. I lay there on the hard floor, shaking with reaction, waiting for my lungs and head to clear. Hoping I'd made it all the way to Shadows Fall.

I finally sat up and looked around me. I wasn't on any train platform. I got to my feet, a little unsteadily. The train had dropped me off at a huge, old-fashioned Hall, with towering wood-panelled walls and a raftered ceiling uncomfortably high overhead. The Hall stretched away to my left and to my right for as far as my smarting eyes could see, and it was wide enough to hold a football game in. The sheer size and scale of the Hall should have made it seem overpowering, but somehow it wasn't. If anything, it felt almost . . . cosy. Like coming home, after too long away from family and loved ones. The light was a cheerful golden glow, though there didn't seem to be any obvious source for it. And no shadows anywhere. No windows either, or doors, and no portraits or decorations on the walls. Only a single stone fireplace, right in front of me, with a banked and quietly crackling fire, as though it had been set just for me. It seemed to me that I could hear a great wind blowing, outside. Something about that sound made me shudder, though I couldn't say why.

I knew where it was. What it had to be. I'd done a lot of reading about Shadows Fall. Most people in the Nightside have, because Shadows Fall is the only place on this earth that's stranger, more glamorous, and more dangerous than the Nightside. The place where legends go to die, when the world stops believing in them. Or perhaps when they stop believing in themselves . . . And since the world has believed in some pretty strange things in its time, and because not everything that comes to Shadows Fall is ready to lie down and die just yet, this little town in the back of beyond can be scarier than anything you'll

find in the Nightside. We all read everything we can find
about Shadows Fall. If only because we have a sneaking
suspicion we might end up here someday.

I was in the Gallery of Bone, in All Hallows' Hall. The
house at the heart of the world. The place where Time
lives.

On the mantelpiece over the fireplace, there was a simple clock set in the stomach of a big black bakelite cat. As
the clock ticked, the cat's red tongue went in and out, and
its eyes went back and forth. It looked like something
you'd win at a cheap carnival. Standing on either side of
the cat were stylised silver figures of a lion and a unicorn.
And on either side of them, a series of small carved figures that made me think of chess pieces, though they
clearly weren't. I moved forward, for a closer look.

They were carved out of a clear, almost translucent
wood, and I had no difficulty in recognising who the figures were. Razor Eddie, Dead Boy, Walker, Shotgun
Suzie. I wondered if I kept looking . . . would I find one
of me? I deliberately turned my back on the figures, and
found that the centre of the floor was now taken up with
a huge old-fashioned hourglass. It was easily a foot taller
than I, and two feet in diameter, with sparkling clear glass
supported by more of the strange translucent wood. Most
of the sand had fallen through, from the upper glass to the
lower, and something about that made me feel very sad.

I walked slowly round the massive hourglass, and met
someone coming the other way, even though I was sure
no-one else was there when I started. I stopped short, and
so did she, and we regarded each other suspiciously for a
while. Tall and almost painfully slender, with long cords
of muscle on her bare arms, she was a teenage punk, in
battered black leathers adorned with studs and chains,
over a grubby white T-shirt and faded blue jeans. Her hair
was a spiky black Mohawk, shaved high at the sides, and
her face was almost hidden behind lashings of black and
white makeup. A safety pin pierced one ear, while a rusty
razor blade dangled from the other. Her eyes were fierce,

her black-lipped mouth a snarl. She glared at me, two large fists resting on her hips. She had HATE tattooed on both sets of knuckles.

"I'm Mad," she announced abruptly, in a deep harsh voice.

"Of course you are," I said, keeping my voice calm and soothing.

"It's short for Madeleine, you divot!" She brought up her right hand, and suddenly there was a flick-blade in it, the blade snapping out with a nasty-sounding click. I think I was supposed to be impressed, but then, I knew Razor Eddie. And Shotgun Suzie. The punk girl snarled at me. "What are you smirking at? You think I won't use this? This is Time's house. I look after him, because, well . . . someone has to. Otherwise, he goes wandering . . . Look, we don't like unexpected, uninvited visitors, so you can just turn around and go straight back where you came from. Or there's going to be trouble."

"Actually, I'm afraid I'm stuck here," I said. "I came by train. From the Nightside."

She sniffed loudly. "That shit-hole? I wouldn't go there on a bet."

"Yes, well, a lot of people have been known to feel that way, but . . . I really do need to speak to Old Father Time."

"Well he doesn't need to see you, so piss off, before I decide to start cutting lumps off you."

I thought for a moment. "Is there anyone else I could talk to?"

"No! I'm Mad!"

"Yes, we've already established that . . . Is there perhaps someone who looks after you, makes sure you don't hurt yourself, that sort of thing?"

"Right! That's it! You're going back to the Nightside inside thirty-seven chutney jars!"

I think we were both about to do something unfortunate at that point, so it's just as well Old Father Time finally decided to make himself known. He appeared out of

nowhere, looking exactly the way I remembered him
from our last encounter in the Time Tower. A tall gaunt
man in his late fifties, dressed to the height of Victorian
fashion. Julien Advent would have loved it. Time wore a
long black frock coat of a most severe cut, over severely
tailored grey trousers, and, except for the gold watch
chain stretched across his waistcoat, the only splash of
colour in his outfit was the apricot cravat at his throat. He
was handsome enough, in an old-fashioned way, with a
determined chin held high, a steely smile, and old old
eyes. A thinning mane of long white hair had been
brushed back from a noble brow, and left to lie where it
fell. An air of quiet authority hung about him like an old
comfortable cloak, only slightly undermined by a certain
vagueness in his gaze.

"It's all right, Madeleine," he said calmly. "I know who
this is. I've been expecting him. Now go and find something useful to do, there's a dear, while I tell this gentleman things he almost certainly doesn't want to hear."

Madeleine sniffed loudly again, and made her flick
knife disappear. "Well, that's something, I suppose. Are
you sure you can trust him?"

"Absolutely not, but it's been that sort of a day for several centuries now."

Madeleine walked around the hourglass and disappeared, leaving Time and me alone in the great Hall. He
smiled briefly as he looked down at himself.

"I really should change this image for something more
appropriate. I am a Transient Being, after all . . . but so
many of you seem to find this appearance comforting,
these days. I think I know why, and the Travelling Doctor
has a lot to answer for . . ."

"Quite," I said, because you have to say something,
into pauses like that. "I'm sorry to intrude, but . . ."

"Yes, yes, my boy, I know. Lilith has come to the
Nightside at last, and it's all falling apart at the seams.
But unfortunately, I can't intervene. I can't help you. No-
one can."

"Ah." Not what I wanted to hear. "I came here because . . ."

"Oh I know why you're here, John Taylor. I know what you want from me. I've got it right here. But you won't like it."

He gestured vaguely with his left hand, and there floating on the air between us was a small black case with a dull matte surface. The lid rose up on its own, revealing the Speaking Gun, lying nestled in bloodred velvet. It lay there quietly, for the moment, the ugliest gun ever made. Just looking at it made me feel as though a mad dog had just entered the Hall. The Gun had been fashioned from meat, from flesh and bone, with dark-veined gristle and shards of cartilage, all held together with strips of colourless skin. Living tissues, shaped into a killing tool. Thin slabs of bone made up the handle, held in place by tightly stretched skin with a hot sweaty look. The trigger was a long canine tooth. The red meat of the barrel gleamed wetly. I wondered just how much of my mother's body had gone into making this awful thing, this Speaking Gun. Up close, the ancient weapon smelled like an animal in heat. And I could hear it, breathing, in its case.

"I really don't care for the thought of such a powerful weapon in the hands of the infamous John Taylor," Old Father Time said sharply. "Far too much temptation for any mortal. Let alone you. But . . . I'm going to give it to you anyway." He looked briefly at the huge hourglass. "Partly because time is running out for the Nightside. Partly because try as I might, I can't seem to find anyone else more fitting to give it to . . . But mostly because a future version of myself came back in time to tell me to give it to you, and I really wish I wouldn't do things like that to myself."

The lid of the case snapped shut, and the black box dropped unceremoniously into my hands. Time sighed heavily, shook his head, and snapped his fingers. And all at once, I was somewhere else.

THIRTEEN

Mother Love

I was back in the Nightside, in Time Tower Square, and my first thought was how quiet and peaceful everything was. I looked slowly around me, and no-one looked back. The mobs and monsters had all moved on, probably because there was nothing left in the Square to destroy, and no-one left to kill. The buildings were fire-blackened frameworks, collapsed inwards or outwards, cracked stone and broken bricks. There were bodies lying everywhere, men and women and others so damaged or torn apart it was impossible to tell who or what they might have been originally. They looked like so many broken toys someone had got tired of playing with. Nothing moved, anywhere. There weren't even any rats nosing among the bodies. Maybe they'd all been killed, too. Out beyond the Square, the War was still going on, in the distance. I could hear faint cries and roars and explosions, and now and again there'd be a sudden surge of light, pushing back the darkness. But the Square was still, and silent.

I couldn't help thinking of the devastated future Night-side I'd seen so many times. The dead lands, the broken world, and all because of me. A future that insisted on edging nearer, no matter how hard I worked to push it away, becoming more real, more imminent, detail by detail. Maybe some futures are inevitable, after all.

I slowly became aware of a soft, repetitive sound, and I looked round to see my mother, Lilith, sitting at her ease on the pile of rubble that was all she'd left of the Time Tower. In her large colourless hands she held a severed human head. Its face had been ripped away, leaving only a bloody mess, but that didn't seem to bother her. She was pulling out the teeth, one at a time and tossing them aside. And all the time her black mouth was moving silently, saying *He loves me, he loves me not* . . . She looked up abruptly and stared right into my eyes. She smiled brightly and rose to her feet, casually throwing the head to one side.

"John, darling! My most treasured son . . ."

"Don't move any closer," I said. "I'm armed. I have the Speaking Gun."

"Of course you have, sweetie. That's why I'm here."

She walked towards me. I held the black box up where she could see it, and she stopped just out of reach. She was calm, collected, utterly at her ease, and a slow anger burned within me. I gestured roughly at the bodies, at the wrecked buildings, at the War still going on in the distance.

"How could you do all this?"

She shrugged easily. "It's mine. I made it. I'll do what I want with it."

"Where are your children?" I said. "All your monstrous offspring? Where are your precious followers, your madmen and murderers?"

"Keeping themselves busy. I don't need them here. I

thought it was time you and I had a nice little chat, in private."

I frowned, as something else occurred to me. "How did you know to find me here? Even I didn't know I was going to be here."

She nodded at the flat black case in my hands. "The Speaking Gun called to me. I always know where it is. It is flesh of my flesh, after all, and as such my child, every bit as much as you. It's your brother, John, in every way that matters. Thank you for bringing it back to me. I have a use for it. Just as I have a use for you."

I opened the black box, snatched out the Speaking Gun, and pointed it at Lilith. She didn't flinch, or back away. I let the box fall to the ground as the Speaking Gun thrust its poisonous presence into my thoughts. It felt hot and sweaty in my hand, and burned like a fever in my mind, vicious and raging, like an attack dog tugging at its leash. It breathed wetly in my hand, wanting to be used. It needed to kill, to destroy, to tear down the whole world and everything that lived in it. The Speaking Gun hated, but it couldn't operate without someone else to pull its trigger, and it hated that most of all. Its filthy thoughts wormed through my mind, stoking the anger and outrage it found there . . . but I had felt its corrupting nature before, and I fought it back. I hadn't come this far to bow down to a spiteful machine.

And yet, even under its madness and its rage, I could feel the Speaking Gun yearning for my mother's touch. It wanted to go to her and nestle in her hand, and do terrible, awful things for her. I gripped the Gun so tightly my whole hand ached, and never once took my gaze off Lilith. She laughed soundlessly at me, and took a step forward. I aimed the Speaking Gun carefully, and pulled the trigger.

And nothing happened.

I tried again and again, but the long canine tooth that served as the Speaking Gun's trigger wouldn't budge. I shook the Gun, and even hit it with my other hand, but it did no good. In my mind, I could hear it laughing.

"The Speaking Gun won't work on me, John," Lilith said calmly. "It will never operate against the wishes of its creator. Just a little safeguard I had built into it, back at the Beginning. It loves me, you know. It aches to serve me, and make me happy. Such a good son . . . Unlike you. Give me the Gun, John. It was never meant for you. And in my hands it will respeak your most secret name and remake you into the respectful, obedient son I always intended you to be."

She held out her hand, and the Speaking Gun jerked in my grasp, as though desperate to go to the one who would let it do what it had always wanted to do.

I couldn't let her take the Gun. So I raised my gift, and forced it to find the one way in which the Speaking Gun could be destroyed. The answer was simple: by making it speak its own secret name backwards, and uncreate itself. My gift fought me, and the Gun fought me, but I had come a long way in the past few years, down a long hard road, perhaps to prepare me for moments like this. I bent all my will and all of my soul against the gift and the Gun, beating them down step by step and inch by inch, until finally the Speaking Gun choked out a single awful sound, then howled in despair as its very existence was reversed and undone. Uncreated.

My hand was suddenly empty, and I staggered and almost fell, wiped out by such a tremendous effort. I felt as though I'd just lifted a mountain with my bare hands, and turned it over on its side. Lilith grunted suddenly with surprise, and clapped one hand to her bare side. I studied her warily, but she just smiled back at me.

"Why thank you, John. For returning my flesh and bone to me. I'd forgotten how much I missed that rib till I had it back again. You always give your mother the best presents."

"The Speaking Gun is gone," I said. "You can't remake me without it, which means you can't remake the Nightside. So, it's over. Your precious scheme is dead in the water. Stand down your armies. This isn't your Nightside any more. You don't belong here. Just . . . go away, and leave us alone."

But she was already smiling and shaking her head. "You always did think too small, John. The Speaking Gun was never that important to me. It was just there to make things easier for you. It would have been a more . . . merciful method, that's all. Now I'll just have to do it the hard way. And don't you dare cry. You brought this on yourself. The Speaking Gun was never intended to be my main weapon against the Nightside, John. That was, and is, you. That is why I gave birth to you, after all."

"What?" I said. My mind was numb, from too many reverses. "I don't understand . . ."

"Of course you don't. I arranged for you to inherit one particular gift from me, John, so I could make use of it when the time was right. I will make you do what you were born to do. I will make you use your gift to find for me the perfect form of the Nightside, the original uncontaminated model that I always intended it to be, and when you've found that for me I will enforce that version on all the world."

"I won't do it," I said. I tried to look away from her, from her deep dark eyes, and couldn't. "I won't do that!"

"You don't have any choice, sweetie. I decided your fate before you were even born, working on you while you were still forming in my womb. All through the first few years of your childhood, I built a geas deep within your mind, so I'd be able to use it in this place, on this day. A geas to bend your will to mine. That's why you've never been able to remember your early years with me. It became necessary for me to leave the dear bosom of my family before I was quite finished with you, but there's enough there to do the job. I can see it, squirming deep in your mind, wrapped around your soul."

"You do love the sound of your own voice, don't you?" I said. *Never let them see they've got you rat-*

tled . . . "Why didn't my gift tell me any of this, when I questioned it earlier?"

"Because it's not your gift, it's mine. I gave it to you, to do my will." She pirouetted slowly, arms outstretched, mistress of all she surveyed, smiling like a cat with a small bird in its jaws. "Time to redecorate, I think. The old place has become terribly infested. I will spread my Nightside across all the Earth, freeing it from the influence of Heaven and Hell. I'll steal the world away from both those Tyrants, and make the Earth my playground, for all time. And everything that lives on it, including Humanity, that bothersome breed, will be swept aside and replaced with something more to my liking. Including you, my dearest boy. You'll be so much happier when I've remade you in my own true image. You will kneel at my feet and sing my praises through all eternity. Won't that be nice? A mother and her son, together, forever."

And I had just destroyed the Speaking Gun, the only weapon that might have stopped her.

Unless . . . the last time I went face-to-face with Lilith, long and long ago, back at the very creation of the Nightside, I'd found a way to hurt and weaken her. I grinned nastily, inside. I'm John Taylor. I always have one more trick up my sleeve. I fired up my gift, driving it ruthlessly with the last of my will, and used it to find the link between my mother and me. The physical, mental, and magical connections between a mother and her only son. A trick I'd used before, to drain the life energy right out of her.

But when I reached out through the link, she was right there waiting for me. Her will slammed through the link, slapping me aside, monstrously strong and utterly overpowering. I cried out and fell to my knees as she drained the life energy out of me, despite everything I could do to stop her. She smiled down at me.

"You didn't really expect to catch me with the same trick twice, did you? Not when I've had so many years to think about this day, this moment, planning it all down to the very last detail . . . Poor boy. This isn't your story, John; it's mine. Time to start your makeover, I think. And then what fun we'll have, tearing down everything you ever believed in. Open wide and say *aaah!*, John. It'll only hurt for a moment . . ."

FOURTEEN

The Things We Sacrifice, for Love

Time slowed, cranking down to a crawl. The hand Lilith was extending towards me ground to a halt, inches short of my face. Her voice became a long growl and then cut off abruptly as the Collector appeared out of nowhere, in an improbable device. Trust him to bring Time itself to a stop, just so he could make an entrance. The Collector, con man, thief, and snapper up of anything collectible that wasn't actually nailed down or guarded by enraged wolverines. An old acquaintance of mine, but not what you could call a friend. I don't think the Collector had friends any more. They got in the way of his collecting.

A portly middle-aged man with a florid face, the Collector was currently wearing a stylish dark blue blazer with white piping, and a large badge on his lapel bearing the number six. He was crouching inside a strange contraption that hovered uncomfortably close above my head. It looked like an overcomplicated climbing frame, made up of long quartz-and-crystal rods that sparked and shimmered against the night sky. The whole framework couldn't have been more than ten feet wide, but there was something more to it, as though it extended away in more than just the usual three dimensions. The air was thick with the smell of discharging ozone.

The Collector reached down out of his contraption and grabbed the collar of my trench coat. He hauled me up into the framework with him, and immediately I could move again. I grabbed at the nearest rods to steady myself, and they squirmed unpleasantly in my grasp as though they weren't fully there. I wasn't entirely sure whether I might have been dragged out of the frying pan and into the fire. The Collector has always been famous for not being on any side but his own. Below us, Lilith was slowly turning her head to look in our direction.

"Shit," said the Collector, "the field's collapsing. Brace yourself, Taylor, we are out of here!"

He wrapped both his plump hands around a control like a fragmented crystal flower, and the whole structure tilted sideways through space. Time Tower Square disappeared abruptly as we spun round and round, dimensions of space snapping in and out of focus. I tried closing my eyes, but it didn't help. I was sensing the movement on some basic spiritual level, and my stomach really hated it. I clung desperately to the crystal rods, which seemed to be deliberately trying to slip out of my grasp. I could still hear Lilith's voice, screaming *No . . .* in a howl that seemed to go on forever. The crystal contraption actually buckled under the force of her rage, and solid crystal rods cracked and shattered. The Collector fussed over his controls, swearing and blaspheming, and suddenly the whole device crashed to a halt, and I fell out of it into Strangefellows bar.

I sat there for a long moment, enjoying the solid support of a floor that stayed still, then I hauled myself painfully slowly to my feet. I don't know when I've ever felt so tired. I looked across at the Collector, who was walking round and round his crystal contraption and cursing loudly as bits fell off it. He actually chattered with rage and kicked spitefully at the pieces on the floor.

"Bloody thing! I'll never get another one like this! Not after the extra security they've installed since my last visit . . . This trip had better have been worth it, Henry!"

Walker strolled over to pat him soothingly on the shoulder. "Leave strategy to me, Mark. You know I've always been the devious one. You never did explain. What is this thing, exactly?"

"Well, originally it was a four-dimensional climbing frame for really gifted children in the thirtieth century. I acquired it when no-one was looking, and adapted it for interdimensional travel. Not as accurate as some of my other Time travel mechanisms, but just basically weird enough to sneak in and catch Lilith by surprise. And now look at it! I'd better get compensation for this, Henry."

"I'll see you're provided with the correct forms," Walker said briskly. "And how are we, Taylor?"

"We feel like shit," I said, collapsing into the nearest chair. "Why did you send that creep to rescue me?"

"Because you were obviously incapable of rescuing yourself, you ungrateful little turd!" snapped the Collector. "We watched you talking with Lilith through one of Merlin's visions, once he detected your reappearance, and a right balls up you were making of it. So Henry sent me in as the cavalry. And if you're wondering why someone of my good sense has joined this doomed resistance, reluctantly and very much against my better judgement, I can only put it down to emotional blackmail."

"I simply pointed out that if Lilith has her way with the Nightside, there will be nothing left to collect," said Walker.

"Bloody vandal!" said the Collector. "I haven't spent the best part of my life putting together the greatest collection of treasures and wonders in this or any other universe, just so the Great White Bitch can wipe it all out. Women never appreciate the true value of collectibles . . ."

"I knew you'd come, if I asked," said Walker. "What are old friends for?"

The Collector looked at him coldly. "Don't push it, Henry. We haven't been friends for over twenty years, and you know it. You've been doing your best to have me arrested, ever since that unfortunate incident over the dome of St. Paul's Cathedral. Hell, I haven't seen you in the flesh since Charles's funeral." He looked at me, then back at Walker. His voice softened, just a little. "You've got old, Henry. Respectable."

"You got fat."

I left them to their somewhat prickly reunion, forced myself up out of my chair, and stumbled over to the bar. Lilith had taken a lot out of me. Alex was in his usual place behind the bar and actually had a large wormwood brandy waiting for me. He'd put a little umbrella in it, just because he knew I hated them. He didn't want me to think he was getting soft. I threw the umbrella away, took a long drink, and nodded gratefully to him. He nodded back. We've never been very demonstrative.

"Did any of my people make it back here?" I said finally.

"Only me," said Suzie Shooter.

I turned around, and there she was. Shotgun Suzie, her black leathers almost falling apart from tears and slashes, and soaked with dried blood. Her bandoliers were empty of bullets, and all the grenades were gone from her belt. Even her shotgun was missing from its holster on her back. She half sat, half collapsed onto the bar stool beside me, and Alex put a bottle of gin in front of her. I was too tired to do more than smile at her, to show how glad I was to see her still alive, and she nodded in return.

"You should have seen the shape she was in, when she came back without you," said Alex. "Took three of my best repair spells to put her back together again. I put them on your tab, Taylor. Though given the way things are going, maybe you should settle up now, while there's still time."

"I broke my shotgun," said Suzie, ignoring Alex with the ease of long practice. "Had to use it as a club when I ran out of ammo. And I left my best stiletto in some bastard's eye. All my weapons are gone. I feel naked."

"How did you make it back here, through all those mobs?" I asked.

"A variety of blunt instruments and a whole lot of bad temper," said Suzie.

"Have you seen any of the others?"

"No," said Suzie, staring at her bottle of gin without touching it. "But Dead Boy was dead to begin with, and Razor Eddie's a god. I wouldn't be surprised to see either of them stroll back in here, eventually."

"But not Tommy Oblivion," I said.

"No. His brother Larry went out to look for him, as soon as he heard what happened. No-one's heard anything from him since."

"Julien Advent is out and about," said Alex. "Supposedly pulling Walker's remaining people together into an army, for one last desperate assault on Lilith's forces."

"No!" I said. I pushed myself away from the bar, and stalked over to confront Walker. He deliberately ignored me, continuing his talk with the Collector, so I grabbed him by the shoulder and hauled him around. I don't know which of us was more surprised. It had been a long time since anyone had dared treat Walker like that. "You can't fight Lilith's army with an army of your own," I said, as forcefully as I could. "You'll destroy the Nightside, fighting over it. Nobody wins. I've seen it."

"You're sure of this?" said Walker.

"Oh yes. I've talked to people in the future, people who lived through it. They were the only ones left. You'd know some of the names if I said them, but trust me on this, Walker, you really don't want to know. Believe me, you can't win this with an army."

"Then what do you suggest?" said Walker, and I swear his voice was just as calm and courteous and civilised as ever, even though I'd just kicked away his last hope. "What else can we do, except fight?"

"You have to do something," said Merlin, his voice just a harsh rasp. "And you'd better do it soon. My defences are under constant attack. I don't know how much longer I can maintain them."

I looked round. I'd actually overlooked the ancient sorcerer, sitting slumped and alone at a table in the corner. He looked very old and very tired, even for a fifteen-hundred-year-old corpse. His grey face was slack, the crimson flames barely stirring in his empty eye-sockets.

"Keeping Lilith out, holding her off, is taking everything I've got," Merlin said, not even looking at me. "It's draining me dry, Taylor. I need my heart. There's still time. Find my stolen heart for me, bring it here, and put it back in my chest, and I could be a Power again. I could bring myself back to life, wrap myself in glory, and go out to face Lilith head to head."

"I don't think so," I said. "You are Satan's only begotten son, born to be the Antichrist. I won't risk loosing that on the Nightside."

"That's right, blame me for my family background! You of all people should know that we aren't always our parent's children. Do you want me to beg, Taylor? Then I'll beg! Not for me, but for the Nightside. For all of us."

"I can't do it," I said. "I know where your heart is. And there's no way I can get it for you."

"Then we're all dead," said Merlin. "Dead and damned."

"Look, if he can't protect me, then I'm getting the hell out of here," said the Collector. "Come on, Henry, I only agreed to come here because you assured me this bar was safer than any of my bolt-holes. I only agreed to rescue Taylor because you said he was vital to our survival."

"Shut the hell up," I said, feeling the anger build within me. "You don't get to complain, Collector. Not when all of this is your fault anyway! You made possible the Babalon Working that brought Lilith back out of

Limbo! You put my father together with my mother and made me possible!"

The Collector wouldn't meet my eyes. "I was misled," he said finally. "I thought I was doing the right thing."

"Leave Mark alone," said Walker, moving forward to stand beside the Collector. "We all thought we were doing the right thing, back then. Including your father. We never meant for any of this to happen . . . . You're looking at me strangely, John. What is it?"

"I've just had an idea," I said. I could feel my smile spreading into a broad grin, and suddenly I didn't feel tired any more. "I'm John Taylor, remember? I always have one more trick up my sleeve. And this one's a beauty! There is a way to stop Lilith that doesn't involve fighting. All we have to do is put together the three men who originally summoned Lilith through the Babalon Working, have them restart the spell, then reverse it, sending Lilith back into Limbo! The door you created with the Working is still open, isn't it?"

"Well, yes," said Walker. "We never got the chance to close it. By the time we realised the door hadn't shut itself, the three of us had separated, determined never to work together again. It wasn't as if the door mattered; it was only slightly ajar, undetectable except to the three of us. No-one else could use it. Lilith's entrance had attuned it to her, and her only."

"But the three of you working together could restart the magic," I said. "Push the door all the way open, force Lilith through it, into Limbo, then close the door after her! It would work! Wouldn't it?"

"Technically, yes," said the Collector, frowning. "Though one of us would have to go through the door with Lilith, to make sure she couldn't open it again from the other side, until we closed the doorway. And whoever went through . . . would be trapped with Lilith in Limbo, for all eternity. So you needn't look at me. I have far too much to live for. And I never got on with her anyway, even when she was only Charles's wife."

"You never did understand about duty," said Walker. "I'll do it."

"No," I said. "I'll go. You know it has to be me."

"No it doesn't!" said Suzie, almost savagely. "Why does it always have to be you, John? Haven't you done enough?"

"This is all, unfortunately, quite irrelevant," said Walker. "It's a good plan, John, but there's no way we can make it work. It took the three of us to establish the Babalon Working, and only the three of us could hope to restart it. And your father is dead, John."

"Not any more," I said. "Lilith raised the dead in the Necropolis graveyard, remember? Brought them all back to life and sent them out into the Nightside." I could see the light of understanding dawning in everyone's eyes. "He's out there, somewhere. My father. Charles Taylor. And who's better suited to find him than me?"

I forced my gift awake, and it showed me a vision of my returned father. He was doing research in the Prospero and Michael Scott Memorial Library, rooting through the ruins and collecting books from overturned stacks. He piled the books up on a desk, and searched desperately through each volume, looking for . . . something. I studied him for a while. He didn't look much older than I was. In fact, he looked a lot like me. I took hold of Walker's and the Collector's hands, so they could see him, too.

"Typical Charles," said the Collector, almost wistfully. "He never could abide taking orders from anyone. Including, it would seem, an ex-wife who brought him back from the dead. She should have known he'd go his own way."

"I don't think she knows about him," said Walker. "She's got other things on her mind, just now."

"What's he doing, burying himself in books when the world's coming to and end?" said the Collector.

"Doing what he always does," said Walker. "Research. He's looking for answers."

I looked back at Merlin. "Open a door for me, between here and there. I need to talk to my father."

The dead sorcerer scowled at me. "If I remove my concentration from the bar's defences, even for a moment, Lilith will know what's happening here."

"Let her," I said. "All that matters now is getting these three old friends back together. So they can put right their old wrong."

"God, you sound like your father sometimes," said the Collector. "He could be a right pain in the arse on occasion, too."

Merlin gestured angrily with an unsteady hand, and the Library vision became real as an opening appeared in space, linking the bar with the Library. My father was so immersed in his books he didn't even notice. I stepped carefully through the opening into the Library and coughed meaningfully. My father scrambled up out of his chair and backed away from me, holding a heavy paperweight like a weapon. I slowly raised my hands, to show they were empty.

"Take it easy," I said. "I'm not here to hurt you. I need your help."

Charles Taylor studied me suspiciously, then put the paperweight down on the desk. "You look familiar. Do I know you?"

It hit me harder than I'd expected, to hear my father's voice again after so many years. It made him real again, in a way just the sight of him hadn't. I lowered my hands, and suddenly I didn't know what to say. Too many things I wanted to tell him, needed to tell him, but I couldn't find the words.

"How did you find me here?" he said. "You don't have the look of one of Lilith's creatures. Though I'm sure I've seen you somewhere before . . . but it doesn't matter. I can't help you. You'll have to leave. I'm very busy."

"You know me," I said. "Though it's been a long time. I'm John. I'm your son, John."

"My God," he said, and he sat down suddenly on his

chair, as though all the strength had gone out of his legs. "John . . . Look at you . . . All grown-up. You look . . . a lot like my father. Your grandfather. Of course, you never knew him . . ."

"You went away," I said. I tried to keep the anger out of my voice, but that only made it sound even colder. "Abandoned me to my Enemies, when I was just a child. You left me alone when I needed you the most. You drank yourself to death rather than raise me. Why?"

Charles sighed heavily. He looked at his books, as though for answers, and then he made himself look back at me. "You have to understand . . . I'd been betrayed so many times: by friends I thought I could trust, by the woman I believed loved me. Your mother . . . was my last chance. To be a man again, to be sane again. To do good work, work that mattered. She was my life, my hope, my dreams. I never loved anyone like I loved her. When Pew told me the truth, showed me the hard evidence . . . I almost killed him. I went looking for her, but she was already gone. Just as well. I don't know what I would have done . . . And you, John, you'd meant so much to me, and now I was afraid you were a lie, too. Because if I couldn't depend on my wife to be my wife, if she wasn't even human . . . how could I depend on you to be my son? I was afraid you'd turn out to be a monster, like your mother."

"No," I said. "I'm nothing like my mother."

He smiled, and it was like a hand crushing my heart. I remembered that smile, from long ago, though I'd forgotten it till that moment.

"I've been reading about you, son. Reports of your old cases, in the *Night Times*. Quite the adventures, I gather. Helping people who couldn't help themselves, solving mysteries, bringing down the bad guys . . . I also read some of the editorial pieces, by Julien Advent. The great Victorian Adventurer. He doesn't seem too sure whether he approves of you, but he approves of what you achieved, and that's good enough for me. You've made yourself the hero I always meant to be, but life got in the way . . ."

"It's not too late," I said. "There is a way you can stop Lilith. Come with me. Two old friends are waiting to greet you."

He got up from his chair and stood before me. We were exactly the same height. Two men of roughly the same age, but with far more than our share of experience.

"There is a way?" he said. "Really?"

"I believe so."

"Then let's do it." He put a hesitant hand on my shoulder. "I'm sorry I let you down, son. Sorry . . . I wasn't strong enough."

"Everyone else let you down," I said. "They all lied to you. Betrayed you. That stops now."

"I read everything they had on you here," said Charles Taylor. "You've done well, in my absence. I'm proud of you, son."

"That's all I ever wanted," I said.

I think he would have hugged me then, but I wasn't ready for that. I still had to be strong. I led the way back through the opening, into the bar, and he came through after me. Merlin immediately shut the opening down. My father looked around him.

"My God, it's Strangefellows! Is this dump still going? Damn, I had some times here . . ."

"Yes, you did," Walker said dryly. "Though I seem to recall I always ended up having to foot the bill. You were famous in those days for never having your wallet on you."

My father turned round and looked at Walker, then at the Collector. He frowned, clearly uncertain, and then his face broke into a broad grin, and all three of them laughed. It was an open, happy laugh, blowing away all the old hurts and quarrels, and the three men fell on each other, clapping shoulders and backs with loud happy words. It was odd to see Charles Taylor looking so much younger than his contemporaries, but there was no deny-

ing how naturally they fit together. As though they belonged together, and always had. Eventually they stood
back and studied each other.

"It's good to have you back, Charles," said Walker.
"You're looking good. Being dead clearly agreed with
you."

"I've missed you, Charles," said the Collector. "I
really have. No-one could hold their own in an argument
like you. So; what was it like, being dead?"

"I really don't remember," said Charles. "Probably
just as well. But look at you . . . both of you! Henry . . .
what happened? You look so distinguished! And you always swore you'd rather die than be trapped in a suit and
tie, like all the other city drones. Are you really part of
the Establishment these days?"

"Hell," said the Collector. "He is the Establishment."

"And Mark . . . Ten out of ten for style, but when did
you get so fat?"

"Now don't you start," said the Collector. "Do you like
the blazer? I got it from this retired secret agent. I got his
weird car, too, while he was looking for his blazer. You
have got to see my collection, when all this is over. I've
acquired more fabulous junk and kitsch than any man
living!"

"I always knew you had it in you, Mark," my father
said solemnly, and all three of them laughed.

"This is a new thing," Merlin said quietly to me. "Un-
foreseen and unexpected. Who knows what might come
of this?"

"You never foresaw what's happening here?" I said.

"I don't think anyone ever foresaw this, boy! So many
disparate elements needed, so many unlikely happen-
stances, to bring these three together again, after so many
years. And all because of you, John Taylor."

"So," I said. "We have a chance now?"

"Oh no," said Merlin, turning away. "We're all still
going to die, or be destroyed, along with the rest of the
Nightside."

"The Babalon Working," said Charles Taylor, and I immediately paid attention again. My father was frowning thoughtfully. "Our greatest achievement, and our greatest crime. Do we really dare start it up again?"

"Do we have time?" said Walker. "Back then, it took us days to get the ritual up and working properly, nearly destroying ourselves in the process. And we were a lot younger and stronger and better prepared, back then."

"We don't need to go through the whole ritual again," the Collector said confidently. "You never did listen when I explained the theory of it, Henry. The magic is still operating in infraspace, because we never shut it down. It's hanging there, suspended at the moment we were interrupted. That's why the door we opened is still ajar. All we have to do is make contact with the magic again."

"And that should be easy enough," said Charles. "We're the only three keys that fit that lock."

"On the other hand," said the Collector, "a lot could go wrong. It's always dangerous, picking up an interrupted magic. We could all be killed."

"Dying would be vastly more pleasant than what Lilith has in store for us," said Walker.

"True," said the Collector. "And I think . . . I'd like a chance to be the man I used to be, one last time. Let's do it."

In the end, there was no need for any chalk circles, no chanting or invoking of spirits; the three old friends simply closed their eyes and concentrated, and a powerful presence filled the whole bar, beating on the air. There was a feeling of something caught on the edge, struggling to be free, to be finished. And after more than thirty years the three old friends stepped effortlessly back into their old roles, meshing like the parts of a powerful engine that had forgotten just how much it could do. Raw magic sparked and flared on the air around them, and the Babalon Working was up and running again, as though they'd never been away.

But almost immediately another presence forced its way into the bar, slamming through Merlin's defences. A door appeared in a wall where there had never been a door before, a ragged hole in the brickwork like a mouth or a wound, and stretched out beyond it was a narrow corridor, impossibly long. It led off in a direction I couldn't identify, which had nothing to do with left and right, up and down, that my mind couldn't deal with or accept, except simply as Outside. And down that awful corridor, slowly but inexorably, a single figure came walking. It was too far off in that unacceptable distance to see clearly, but I knew who it was, who it had to be. Lilith knew what we were up to, and she was coming to stop us.

Merlin came forward to stand before the corridor, staring down it and blocking the way. He looked . . . smaller, diminished. He raised his dead grey hands, already spotted with decay, and traced vivid shapes on the air, living sigils that spat and shimmered with discharging energies. He forced old and potent Words out of his ruined mouth, summoning up ancient forces and terrible creatures with the authority of his terrible name, but nothing happened. The Princes of Hell were more afraid of Lilith than they were of him. Merlin tried to open up interspatial trapdoors under Lilith's feet, to drop her into some other, dangerous dimension, that she'd have to fight her way back from . . . but Lilith just walked right over them, as though they weren't there. And perhaps for her, they weren't. She was Lilith, imprinted on the material world by an effort of her own will, and he was only a dead sorcerer. Step by step she drew nearer, smiling her awful smile, despite everything Merlin could do to stop her, or even slow her down. And, finally, she stepped out into the bar, and the corridor disappeared behind her, the wall just a wall again.

"Hello, Merlin," she said. "What a fuss you made. Anyone would think you weren't glad to see me. And after I went out of my way to find a nice present to bring you." She held up her left hand, and showed him a dark necrotic mass of muscle tissue. He knew what it was immediately, and made a sound as though he'd been hit. Lilith laughed prettily. "Yes, it's your long-lost heart, little sorcerer. That's what I've been doing all these years, since I had to give up being a wife and a mother. I knew I had to find your heart before you did, because you were the only one who might have stood a chance against me. If only you'd been whole. Merlin Satanspawn, born to be the Antichrist, but you didn't have the nerve. By the way, I spoke with your father recently, and he's still really mad at you."

"Give me my heart," said Merlin.

"It was very well hidden," said Lilith. "You wouldn't believe when and where I finally found it."

"What do you want from me?" said Merlin.

"That's more like it," said Lilith, smiling on Merlin like a teacher with a slow pupil. "You can have your heart back, Merlin. All you have to do is bow down to me, kneel at my feet, and vow on your unholy name to worship me all your days."

Merlin laughed abruptly, a flat ugly sound, and Lilith reacted as though he'd spat in her face. "Kneel to you?" said Merlin, and his voice was full of amused contempt. "I only ever knelt to one person. And you're not fit to polish his armour."

Lilith's left hand convulsed, crushing the decaying heart into crimson-and-purple pulp. Merlin cried out once and collapsed, the magic that had sustained him for centuries torn away in a moment. He curled up in a ball on the floor, withering and falling in on himself as the flesh fell away from his old bones. The fires in his eyes went out. Lilith took a bite out of the crushed heart and chewed thoughtfully.

"Tasty," she said. "Now die, fool, and go to the place appointed for you. Your daddy's waiting."

Merlin twitched and shuddered for a few moments

more, but finally lay still, little more than a desiccated mummy. But I would swear that just before the end, I heard him say *Arthur?* So maybe he escaped his fate, after all. I'd like to think so.

Lilith looked unhurriedly about the bar. While I was still thinking what to do to distract her, and keep her from realising what three old acquaintances of hers were up to, Alex produced a pump-action shotgun from behind the bar, and handed it over to Suzie.

"Do something with this, Suzie. Avenge my ancestor. He might have been a pain in the arse, but he was family. The magazine holds silver bullets rubbed with garlic, napalm incendiaries spiked with holy water, and buckshot made from the ground-up bones of saints. Something in that mix ought to upset her. I find it works very well for crowd control on nights when the trivia quiz gets out of hand."

"Why, Alex," said Suzie, training the shotgun on Lilith, "I'm seeing you in a whole new light."

She fired the shotgun at Lilith again and again, working the pump action incredibly fast, emptying the whole magazine. And Lilith just stood there and took it, entirely unaffected. Suzie lowered the gun, and Lilith shook a finger at her admonishingly. She turned away to look at the three men working their magic, so wrapped up in what they were doing they hadn't even noticed her arrival. Lilith studied them for a moment, her head cocked on one side.

"What are you doing, you naughty boys? Some last desperate spell, to wish me away? It feels . . . familiar." She broke off, her face suddenly blank. "Henry? And Mark, and . . . Charles. Well, well . . . Dear husband. I'd forgotten they buried you in the Necropolis graveyard. Stop this nonsense and look at me, Charles. And let me tell you what I have in mind for our special, gifted, ungrateful son."

"Tell me," I said. "If you dare."

I strode right up to her, radiating poise and confidence

and arrogance. I had to hold her attention, buy some time for the three to get their Working under control again. I glared right into Lilith's face, and she smiled back at me.

"You shouldn't have come here," I said. "This is my ground, my territory, and I am so much more, here. You think you can compel me to do your will and find you the Nightside you want? Let's see you try. Mommie Dearest."

"How sharper than a serpent's tooth it is, to bear a stupid child," said Lilith. "You will do whatever I want you to do, John. You don't have a choice. I saw to that long ago. So let's start with something simple. Make your mother happy, John. Kill your father."

Her words went right to the geas she'd planted deep in my mind. And braced though I was, all my mental shields in place, I still shuddered and almost collapsed. Because her little time bomb was set *inside* my shields . . . But still I stood my ground, refusing to move, refusing even to look at my father. I could feel her will taking hold of my body, my mind, pressing down on me like an unbearable weight. My hands knotted into fists so tight they ached, and I wouldn't, wouldn't move. Except I already was, my head turning slowly to look at my father despite everything I could do to stop it, the geas burning in my thoughts like a gleeful traitor. And then, suddenly, I wasn't alone in my head any more. Suzie was there, and Alex, adding the strength of their will to mine, holding me where I was.

Well, said Suzie. *This is different. Stand your ground, John, the cavalry's just arrived.*

How? I said.

I do know a little magic, Alex said smugly. *I am Merlin's descendant, after all. How do you think I've been able to run this bloody place, all these years?*

Shut up and concentrate, said Suzie.

So the three of us stood together, and we fought Lilith with all the strength of wills hardened by long lives of loss and hardship and adversity, honed by a refusal to give in to forces that should have broken us. Three old friends, closer now than ever, who cared more for each other than they'd ever been able to say. We stamped down the geas in my mind, breaking its hold over me through a concentrated effort of will, and it died screaming. Lilith's will slammed against us openly, like an ocean storm battering a single rock, but we would not yield.

Even though it was killing us, by inches. We had to tap into our life energies to power the magic that held us together, and even our combined energies were nothing compared to the resources Lilith had to draw on. We felt our lives draining away, felt the darkness closing in around us, but not one of us wavered. Suzie and Alex could have withdrawn, saved themselves, but it never even occurred to them. I was so proud of them.

We couldn't hope to hold Lilith off for long. We knew that. We were buying time, for three old friends to work their magic and open the door into Limbo. We were holding Lilith's attention, so she wouldn't understand what was happening until it was too late. She could have stopped them easily if she hadn't been so determined to break my spirit. But still we three were dying, and we knew it, and we didn't care. We were friends together, doing something that mattered, something we believed in. Perhaps for the first time in our lives we had no doubt we were doing the right thing, and that was worth dying for.

And then, finally, the Babalon Working manifested, and it was glorious indeed. Its presence saturated the whole bar, soaking into everything, making us all unbearably vivid and significant. Strange energies sleeted in from unfamiliar dimensions, as a door left ajar for so long finally swung wide open. I couldn't see it, but its presence filled my mind, as though someone had pushed back the curtains to give me a glimpse of what lay behind the scenes of the world. Lilith howled with rage and horror as she finally realised what was happening, and tried to attack the three men responsible, but Suzie and Alex and I held her where she was with the last of our strength. Dying as we were, we held her there.

A great wind blew out of Limbo, through the open door, redolent of other realms, other places, then reversed itself, surging back in. It tugged at Lilith, and we let her go. Step by step, fighting it all the way, she was pulled towards the door. She stopped, right on the edge, and would go no further. Someone had to force her back through that door, and go with her into Limbo, to hold the door shut from the other side until the Babalon Working had been properly dismantled and shut down. And that had to be me. Because that was the only way I could be sure that never again would I ever threaten the safety of the Nightside. I swore an oath, to a dying future Razor Eddie, that I would rather die than see the Nightside destroyed because of me; and I meant every word.

But I never got the chance. My father broke away from his friends, grabbed his ex-wife by the shoulders, and sent the two of them hurtling through the open door into Limbo. The door swung shut; and, in the very last moment, my father looked back at me, and smiled.

"For you, John! For my son!"

Lilith's final scream was cut short as the door to Limbo slammed shut. Without the three to maintain it, the Babalon Working collapsed, and Walker and the Collector quickly shut it down, forever. And that was that. All was still and quiet in Strangefellows. Walker and the Collector stood together exhausted, leaning on each other for support, looking older than their years. Suzie and Alex, no longer in my mind, came unsteadily forward to stand with me. I looked at the place where the door had been, and thought of my father and my mother, together again, for all eternity.

And the things we sacrifice, for love.

EPILOGUE

With Lilith gone, her army of followers soon broke up and turned on each other. They were quickly defeated and dispersed by Walker's people, commanded by Julien Advent. Lilith's surviving offspring, seeing which way the wind was blowing, quietly slunk back to the Street of the Gods. And as quickly and easily as that, the War for the Nightside was over.

With the Authorities dead and gone, Walker is in charge of the Nightside now. Inasmuch as anyone ever is. No-one's seen the Collector since that night in the bar. He disappeared when no-one was looking, along with what was left of Merlin's heart. Alex is back behind his bar. Suzie and I are talking about becoming partners in a detective agency. And about other things, too. One step at a time.

Many old friends and enemies are still missing, presumed dead.

The Nightside goes on. The terrible future I first saw in the Timeslip is now only another timetrack, no more likely or inevitable than any other glimpsed future. For the first time in a long time, the Nightside is free to make its own destiny.

And so am I.

AVAILABLE NOW IN HARDCOVER FROM
NEW YORK TIMES BESTSELLING AUTHOR
Simon R. Green

JUST ANOTHER JUDGEMENT DAY
A NOVEL OF THE NIGHTSIDE

*Come to the Nightside, where the clocks
always read three A.M., where terrible things
happen with predictable regularity, and where
the always-dark streets are full of people
partying like Judgement Day will never come.*

Judgement Day has arrived and the Walking Man,
God's own enforcer whose sole purpose in life is to
eliminate the wicked and the guilty, has come to
the Nightside. Given the nature of the Nightside,
there's a good chance that once he gets started,
he'll just keep on going until there's no-one left. Private investigator John Taylor has been hired by the
Authorities to stop him. But legend has it that he
can't be killed...

"A macabre and thoroughly entertaining world."
—Jim Butcher,
author of the Dresden Files series

penguin.com